THE GREEN SAMURAI

BRIAN SHEA

TY HUTCHINSON

SEVERN RIVER PUBLISHING

THE GREEN SAMURAI

Severn River Publishing
www.SevernRiverBooks.com

ISBN: 978-1-64875-386-2 (Paperback)

ALSO BY THE AUTHORS

Pressure

Remote

Flashpoint

To find out more, visit

severnriverbooks.com/series/sterling-gray-fbi-profiler

PROLOGUE

The night was still young in Tokyo's Shibuya district. Diners were out enjoying the numerous eateries, boutique shops had their fair share of shoppers, and bars were seeing the first of their nightly revelers.

Keiji had made arrangements to take his girlfriend, Yui, out for a dinner to celebrate their six-month anniversary of seeing each other. She was beyond excited and had been reminding him all week long about the special date. "Don't forget about Thursday," she'd say.

Both were young and didn't make much money at their jobs. The couple had agreed to a set amount they would spend on a gift for each other: five thousand yen. But Keiji had been saving up for this day and wanted to get Yui something extra special. Along with a bottle of perfume, Keiji had decided to purchase matching necklaces with small cat pendants. Yui loved cats and would think it romantic that they wore the same necklace.

The plan was to meet outside the Shibuya Metro Station. Keiji had made reservations at a nearby teppanyaki restaurant that friends of his had recommended as a fun place to eat. He got there early and waited patiently for Yui to arrive. He held a bag in one hand with the presents he was sure she'd love. In his other hand, he scrolled through his social media on his phone. Every few seconds, he'd look around for Yui.

He eventually spotted her walking among a crowd of shoppers. She looked stunning in a pink and white outfit. But Keiji thought she looked stunning in every outfit. She hadn't seen him yet and for a few moments, Keiji watched her. It reminded him of the first time he saw her eating with a group of friends. She stood out like a sparkling star, much like she did that evening. He raised his arm and waved, grabbing her attention. A smile formed on Yui's face when she locked eyes with him.

"Keiji, happy six-month anniversary," she said.

"Happy six-month anniversary, Yui. You look beautiful tonight."

"Thank you."

No sooner had those words left Yui's mouth than a piercing scream grabbed their attention. They looked in the direction it had come from. Running straight toward them was a man with his arms out front, waving them around like a crazed zombie. It took a moment or two for Keiji to make sense of what was happening. But he finally zeroed in on why the man was running like a blind fool down the street. Two knives were stuck in each of his eyes.

1

Kazz Chano was a kyodai in the Yamaguchi syndicate of the Yakuza and led a group of fifty men. They had gathered in the last car of a train in Tokyo's underground metro; civilians had been chased out earlier. Chano was a stout and muscular man with an intense stare. Most of the young recruits in the organization feared him, the stronger ones respected him. He didn't say much, but when he did, his words carried strength. He stood at the front of the car, facing his men.

"Tonight, we'll take what is rightfully ours," he said. As a big brother to the younger recruits, he was tasked with leading his men into the Shibuya district. They were just one of the groups of men converging in that area.

"We must not fear what is coming. This is our opportunity to make the boss proud and bring glory to the Yamaguchi. We must not let him down."

Five hundred men dressed in black suits and armed with various knives, tanto swords, and handguns had traveled to Tokyo by vehicle, underground metro, or train. Like ants appearing from the cracks in a home, the Yamaguchi syndicate wanted to infiltrate the city. As far as the Yamaguchi knew, the Sumiyoshi, their rival syndicate that controlled most of Tokyo, had no idea war was coming to their doorstep.

The Yamaguchi had been planning this attack for weeks. They'd intended to strike where the Sumiyoshi least expected it: in Shibuya, one of their strongholds. The Yamaguchi believed if they could strike fast, chaos would ensue, and the Yamaguchi could move in. The Sumiyoshi would fall quickly, leaving the capital for the Yamaguchi to rule. They had split themselves up into ten groups of fifty men, which would then converge on various locations.

One such destination was Shibuya Crossing, the world's busiest pedestrian crossing outside Shibuya Station. Nearby was a statue of an Akita dog named Hachikō. It was a popular meeting spot for people. As a gesture of goodwill, the Sumiyoshi were planning to pass out miniature statues of the dog to passersby on the sidewalk. It was a way to ensure their continued positive standing in the community.

Chano's men waited patiently, quietly as the train barreled toward Shibuya Station. He watched them carefully, searching for anyone who looked unsure. He couldn't afford to have anyone who wasn't one hundred percent committed. He'd rather cast them out right there than carry on with them.

The train came to a stop at the station, and the men exited the car, making their way to the surface. Two other groups of Yamaguchi were set to attack from other directions. Chano had already received word from them that they were closing in on the crossing.

"There aren't that many," one of the Yamaguchi men said as they filed out of the station.

The Sumiyoshi had advertised the event that night, and the Yamaguchi had expected at least one hundred Sumiyoshi to be in attendance. But from the looks of it, maybe twenty-five men at the most were scattered around the crossing. Chano's men alone clearly outnumbered the Sumiyoshi. He called the operation's leader and reported what he saw.

"It's just a small gathering," he said. "Hitting them now won't send the right message and won't do anything to their ranks."

"Our order is to attack the Sumiyoshi at Shibuya Crossing," the leader said. "We will continue as planned and be home sooner than we'd thought."

With their weapons ready, Chano led his men toward the crossing, sending crowds of people in the area running for safety.

Chano swung his tanto sword, striking down the nearest Sumiyoshi.

Another Sumiyoshi rushed him with a machete, slashing at his head. Still, Chano was faster and dropped down, swinging his sword. The blade cut deep into his attacker's thigh, sending him stumbling away.

Chano popped back to his feet and spotted a brother fending off two Sumiyoshi. He and another Yamaguchi came to their brother's defense, quickly striking down the two Sumiyoshi. By then, the other groups of Yamaguchi had arrived and quickly surrounded the remaining Sumiyoshi.

"They're falling," Chano yelled out. "Don't stop until every single one of them is dead on the streets."

No sooner had those words left his mouth than rapid gunfire grabbed his attention. Chano spun around and spotted a swarm of Sumiyoshi filing out of the shadows and toward the crossing. These men weren't armed with the typical Yakuza weapons. They were wielding assault rifles.

One by one, Chano watched as bullets punched holes in his men, stopping them in their tracks. Others cried out as their limbs were ripped off by the powerful rounds. Chano knew their numbers meant nothing compared to the Sumiyoshi's firepower. They were open targets with no way to defend against, or even escape, the Sumiyoshi.

Chano ducked behind a bench. Never before had he witnessed such immense firepower during a turf war. Short of arming themselves with the same guns, no amount of preparation could have readied them for this.

The Sumiyoshi had to have known they were coming and allowed the five-hundred-strong Yamaguchi contingent to believe they had passed into Tokyo undetected. Chano had led his men into their trap, and now they were paying the price. Were the other locations that the Yamaguchi targeted also traps? Were the Sumiyoshi waiting in the shadows with their guns, ready to eliminate every single Yamaguchi?

Chano looked down at the short sword he held in his hand. A single stream of blood snaked from under his jacket sleeve onto the sword's handle. Only then did he realize he'd been shot in the arm. He looked back up and caught the eye of a determined Sumiyoshi running toward him as he shouted a rallying cry. Chano watched as the man raised his rifle and took aim. It was time for him to join his brave brothers.

2

The United Kingdom's Interpol National Central Bureau was located in Manchester, England, but Special Agent Sterling Gray and a few others worked out of a small satellite office in London. Once a week, they'd make a trip back to the home office, but other than that, they spent their time in the same building that housed the Metropolitan Police Service, or the Met, as the Londoners referred to it.

It had been a quiet day for Gray, and even though he was currently in between assignments, he'd been anxious all day. He was scheduled to have a call at two o'clock with his supervisor, Phillip Cooper, back at Quantico. Cooper was the unit chief for the Behavior Analysis Unit. He was why Gray had been living in London and on loan to Interpol. Gray was a rising star at the BAU. The best profiler the unit had seen in ages. So when Interpol reached out needing help profiling a killer in London, Cooper was only too eager to show off what his unit was capable of. Before Gray knew it, he was on a plane to England. What should have been a one-time assignment had since morphed into a semipermanent posting with no end in sight.

It wasn't all doom and gloom. Working with Interpol meant Gray could be assigned to cases worldwide. Anyone needing his specialized skill set could request him. Not everyone was granted full access to Gray. A lot of the time, he'd consult on an investigation from his office. It could be something as simple as giving a profile created by another person a second look. But for the significant cases, the exceptional ones, Gray was sent to work directly with the local law enforcement.

But when he wasn't gallivanting around the world, he rode a desk like the rest of his colleagues.

"Did you have your call yet?"

Lillie Pratt, a criminal intelligence analyst with Interpol, stood in the office doorway. She was the analyst who'd initially reached out to the bureau for help and the reason Gray had first come to London. They'd since developed a close friendship.

"Any minute," Gray said. "I'll let you know how the call goes after."

Gray glanced at the clock on the wall. It was two minutes to two o'clock. In the email sent to Gray, Cooper's administrative assistant would be the one to initiate the call. His phone rang right on time.

"Special Agent Gray speaking."

"Sterling, it's good to hear your voice."

Marilyn Parks had been Cooper's assistant since Gray started in the BAU. She was less than a year away from retirement and made it no secret how much she was looking forward to it.

"Hello, Marilyn. How are you?"

"I'm healthy and counting the days."

"Where are we at?"

"167 days left."

"I'm really happy for you."

"Thank you. Are you ready for him?"

"Ready as I'll ever be."

There was a brief moment of silence while Parks transferred the call.

"Gray, how are you holding up?" Cooper said loud enough that Gray had to pull the phone away from his ear.

"I'm doing well, thank you."

"Look, I'm tight on time this morning, so let's just get to the meat of this call. I know you've been with our friends in the UK for nearly a year. And I can imagine you're eager to get back stateside. But ..."

There was always a "but" with this guy. Gray knew Cooper all too well. It was why he had been anxious all morning. He'd been trying to pin Cooper down for three weeks on the decision to bring him home. And now that he'd finally locked down a call with the guy, he had a "but."

"As you know, you're one of the best profilers I've come across. We miss you and could use your magic touch on a dozen or so cases, but the reality is you've done such an incredible job with the investigations given to you by Interpol. I'm not sure we can pull you out just yet."

"What does that mean?"

"It means a lot of people with much higher pay grades than myself feel the world needs your expertise. It's complicated, Gray."

Complicated? Gray hated when Cooper said that. All it meant was he was avoiding the truth. It was no secret Cooper was angling for a promotion. There were rumors that the current director of the FBI had talked about stepping down. Cooper had been spending time in DC and at the White House, probably angling for votes of confidence to grab the president's attention so his name made the short list.

"There's nothing complicated about buying a one-way plane ticket."

"Look, Gray, I know you want to come back. I promise you, when the time is right, I'll book that damn ticket myself. But until then, I need you to keep doing what you're doing. No one else has done what you have. I hope you understand what this is doing for your career. You could very well replace me one day. This is good for you."

It might be, but nothing you do is in the interest of others.

"What are you working on at the moment?"

"I'm currently in between assignments."

"Is that so? I'll tell you what, if I have to lose my best guy to Interpol, I certainly don't want to hear that you're twiddling your thumbs at the office all day. I'll make some calls and see if I can get you on a juicy assignment. Gray, keep toeing the line. You'll thank me later."

The line went dead and Gray put his phone down. A beat later, it rang. Gray thought it was Cooper calling him back, but the caller ID said it was his sister.

Fleur was his younger sister. She was married with two kids and lived in upstate New York.

"Fleur, is everything okay? How are the kids?" Gray asked.

"Yes, Sterling, everything is fine. The kids are alive. No one is in the hospital. Why do I always sense panic with you when I call?" she asked in a quiet, comforting voice.

"I, uh, I don't know."

"I'll tell you why. It's because we don't talk much anymore. So when we do, it feels like an emergency call."

"I'm sorry. I know I've been bad about keeping in touch."

"I miss my big brother. It's been two years since we've seen each other in person. When are you moving back? I thought that assignment in Warsaw was the last."

"It's funny that you ask, I just got off a call with my supervisor."

"Let me guess, he wants you to stay in London longer."

"I'm not happy about it. He knows I want to come back, but . . ."

"Politics, right?"

"Yes."

"You must have vacation time. Can't you come back for a visit? Surely a week is doable. You can stay at the house. The kids would love having their uncle around."

"That sounds great. I'll see what I can do about a visit."

"I'm holding you to it this time. Make an effort, Sterling. I'm serious."

"I know you are. I promise I will."

"Are you dating anyone?" Fleur asked. She always asked.

"Not at the moment."

"I worry about you, Sterling. You need someone to take care of you, someone you can spend time with. And your friends at the pub don't count."

"I wish you could meet them. You'd like them."

"I'm sure I would, but I'd much rather meet your girlfriend. Oh, Sterling, I have to go. The renovators are here. Let's talk soon."

Before Gray could say goodbye, Fleur had disconnected the call. But she was right. He needed to make more of an effort. As it stood, he felt like Cooper's puppet, doing whatever the master directed. Gray wasn't interested in Cooper's job, not if it meant shoving his head up someone else's butt or politicking his way through the day. But he also wanted a say in his career. Sure he was doing a fantastic job, and it seemed like every country wanted Gray's help with an investigation. But that right there was the problem. How would this assignment ever end if Gray continued to do a good job?

3

Mariko Tamura was an inspector with the Tokyo Metropolitan Police Department's Organized Crime Control Bureau. She'd driven herself to the first of three Yakuza crime scenes located at Shibuya Crossing as soon as she'd gotten word. An officer stopped her about a block away.

"We can't let you drive in. There are too many—ah—casualties. You'll have to park here and walk in."

Tamura knew a gang war between two Yakuza syndicates had broken out. Most of Tokyo was controlled by the Sumiyoshi Yakuza, who had a tight grasp on the country's capital. The largest syndicate was the Yamaguchi, headquartered in Kobe. The two had been fierce enemies ever since Tamura could remember. She'd witnessed the aftermath of a dozen battles between them during her time with the TMPD. But nothing could have prepared her for what she would see that night. She stepped out of her car and was led forward by one of the officers guarding the perimeter.

"How many bodies are there?" she asked.

"I believe the count is over one hundred and fifty at this location, but I'm not sure."

"One hundred and fifty!" Tamura said. "Were civilians killed?"

"One civilian was injured, but they have already been taken to the hospital. The dead men are . . ."

Tamura had already picked up the pace and left the officer in her wake. She needed to see with her own eyes. She'd expected to hear the numbers "four or five" come out of the officer's mouth.

As she closed in on the crossing, bodies spread across the road became visible, all dressed in the standard uniform of the Yakuza: a dark-colored suit. From afar, they looked like piles of clothing that had been dropped on the ground. As expected in these encounters, the fallen weapons on the road ranged from short knives to machetes to long samurai swords. But she also spotted a couple of pistols.

The metallic smell of blood in the air was strong as she approached the first few bodies. She knelt next to one in a large pool of blood. His body looked like he'd been shot at close range multiple times. Bullet casings littered the area around the body. The body a few feet away had the same shot-up appearance.

As Tamura moved closer to the crossing, it became increasingly difficult not to step in puddles of blood. She took a moment to take in the scene. The dead practically covered the entire intersection. It would be impossible to walk through them without stepping on them. Some of the men had fallen on others and were piled three high. Tamura understood then why the officer wasn't sure about the count. They'd only fully know once they'd carted off the bodies.

Tamura recognized a face. The dead man had been a member of the Yamaguchi syndicate, the most prominent Yakuza clan in Japan, and worldwide. Even though their numbers had diminished over the years, it was still estimated that they had 8,500 members inside the country.

The slaughter had taken place in Sumiyoshi territory. The Sumiyoshi syndicate was the second-largest in the country, with 4,000 members. While smaller than the Yamaguchi, they could still boast that Tokyo was their territory. It was no secret that this did not sit well with the Yamaguchi leadership. It appeared they had plans to rectify that.

Tamura walked around the bodies the best she could. She stopped at another that she recognized, a young recruit for the Sumiyoshi. He wasn't shot up like the Yamaguchi men. He had died from a neck wound most likely caused by a sword strike.

"Inspector Tamura, there's a witness," an approaching officer called. "He says he saw everything."

The young man stood back on the sidewalk while smoking a cigarette.

"Hello. I'm Inspector Tamura. I'm told you witnessed what happened here?"

"Yes, I saw it all."

"I'm surprised you didn't run off when the shooting started."

"I hid behind that vending machine." He pointed.

"Tell me what happened," Tamura said, even though she knew she could pull footage from the CCTV in the area.

"I'd come here to get a free statue of Hachikō. These ninkyō dantai were passing them out."

Tamura knew that ninkyō dantai was how the Yakuza liked to refer to themselves. It meant chivalrous organizations. The police and the government call them bōryokudan, violent groups.

"What happened next?"

"A large fight broke out. I was afraid, so I ran and hid behind the vending machine. Then more men appeared, surrounding the ninkyō . . . I mean the bōryokudan. I didn't know who was who at that point. There were so many men fighting. And then I heard a machine gun shooting. That's when another group of men appeared from over there. They were hiding in that alley. They are the ones who had the big guns. And they started shooting." The man pretended to hold a gun and shoot. "Brrrraaatttt! That's what it sounded like when they shot it. It was madness. I thought I was going to die."

"The men with the big guns, what did they do when they stopped shooting?"

"Well, they checked all the men to make sure they were dead. Some weren't and they shot them again. I swear I heard some of them laugh. Then they ran away."

Tamura thanked the man for his statement and started walking back to her car. She'd seen enough already to know what had taken place. The Yamaguchi had attempted to make a move on the Sumiyoshi. With the number of dead bodies lying in the street, they should have been victorious. But it seems they underestimated the Sumiyoshi's firepower. This wasn't the first gang fight involving guns but it was definitely the deadliest. If this level of violence wasn't enough to sound the alarm on the rising gun violence in Japan, Tamura wasn't sure what would.

Over the past two years, Tamura had done her best to convince her bosses that gun violence was on the rise. But not a single one believed her. They had always claimed the incidents that Tamura had brought forth were isolated cases. Tamura thought they were either out of touch with reality or in serious denial.

Her bosses were all men in their late fifties and early sixties who had spent their entire lives in law enforcement. All were around when the current gun control laws were introduced in 1958, but policy on gun control dated back way before that. These men had policed a country that was considered to be safe and peaceful. To suddenly make comparisons to the gun violence that took place elsewhere, such as in the United States, was incomprehensible to them, and insinuated that they weren't in control.

It was no surprise to Tamura that these men couldn't accept that gun ownership and violence were rising on their watch. Japan had always been a country that deterred its citizens from gun ownership. In fact, it was tough to own a gun, and if one did obtain a license, it was only for shotguns, air rifles, or handguns. The thinking was that responding to violence with violence would never work. Rarely had the Japanese police ever had to use guns to apprehend a criminal. They relied on martial arts to subdue a person. Even Tamura had yet to have a real need to fire her weapon.

But by the end of the night, Tamura would discover that five hundred members of the Yamaguchi syndicate, and a handful of Sumiyoshi, had the streets of Tokyo running red. It would be difficult for her superiors to come up with an excuse or even turn a blind eye to that. These men might all be gangsters, but one couldn't ignore that illegal weapons, possibly assault rifles, were somehow entering the country on a large scale.

4

In a room on the second floor above a small electronics shop, a handful of men were sitting around a large round table. They were tossing back shots of whisky while retelling highlights of the night. They were members of the Sumiyoshi syndicate.

The group leader was Sora Iwata, who had roughly fifty men under his command. Many men in the Sumiyoshi organization wanted to work under Iwata, but he was picky about the men he commanded. They needed to be able to think like Iwata. He loved to break down traditions. He believed following the old ways was a sure way to die early. Innovation and change, those were the two words Iwata loved to throw around. In fact, it was because of his advice that the Sumiyoshi was victorious that night.

"Tonight, we showed those Yamaguchi scumbags who the real power in Japan is," Iwata said with a raised glass. "Sumiyoshi-kai!"

"Sumiyoshi-kai!" the men repeated.

Iwata had petitioned their leadership to attack the Yamaguchi in packs rather than gather and face them as one army as they had always done. Had they not followed Iwata's recommendation, the Yamaguchi would have surrounded them, and perhaps they would not have had such an outstanding victory.

That night the Yamaguchi had also tried something different. They'd split up into smaller groups rather than attack as one. They assumed the Sumiyoshi would group into a pack and believed they could surround them if they broke up into smaller groups. They had the men necessary to overpower the Sumiyoshi. There was no questioning that. But they did not consider the might of the Sumiyoshi's firepower.

"The Sumiyoshi is stronger than ever," Iwata said. "Not even the government will be able to contain us."

The men cheered with raised glasses and weapons.

Sitting next to Iwata was Jun Mizuno. He was Iwata's best friend and second-in-command. The two had met in primary school and had been crime partners ever since. They both had their eyes set on joining the Yakuza from a young age. The only question in their minds was which syndicate they would call their brothers.

Iwata had taken an interest in the Sumiyoshi because of how the organization structured itself. It didn't have a rigid hierarchy like the other syndicates had. Sure they had a godfather, but the organization was made up of smaller groups headed by chiefs. They still reported to the leadership but had the freedom to govern themselves. This is what eventually sold Iwata on the Sumiyoshi.

"We did well tonight," Mizuno said. "The leadership will notice us."

"I don't care what they notice. They have outdated thinking. We are the new Sumiyoshi. We have the progressive minds needed to take this organization to the next level, with or without them."

"You're right about that, brother. You were always an out-of-the-box thinker." Mizuno raised his rifle. "This is proof of it. Before you joined the Sumiyoshi, these guns never existed. Now every member in the organization has one."

"We're not stopping here. It's time the Yamaguchi realize they are no longer feared. They may have the numbers, but they don't have the firepower. We are changing history right now," Iwata lowered his voice and leaned in toward Mizuno. "One day, people will say, Iwata and Mizuno, not Sumiyoshi."

Mizuno clinked his glass against Iwata's before finishing his drink. He turned to the flat screen hanging on the wall. The news media had begun to report on the gang war.

"Look at the police," Mizuno said. "They look lost, like idiots in uniforms. What will they do, beat us down with their batons?" Mizuno laughed before turning back to Iwata. He poured them each a fresh glass of whisky.

Iwata pushed back from the table and stood to face his men. "Take a look at the television. See that? This is what we're capable of. This is a new Sumiyoshi and a new Japan."

5

After visiting all the crime scenes, Tamura spent the rest of the night working on a presentation she intended to make the following day. The heads of law enforcement were meeting to discuss what had happened, especially at Shibuya Crossing. It was time to wake them up to the new reality. And she had over five hundred reasons why they needed to listen to her.

Tamura arrived at the National Police Agency headquarters a little before seven in the morning. The NPA coordinated all of Japan's law enforcement and oversaw the police departments of many of the country's forty-seven prefectures. She wanted to ensure she made it into the room where the meeting was taking place. Once the doors were closed, no one was allowed to enter or leave until the meeting was adjourned.

Tamura had made a point to be friendly with all of the administrative staff. They always knew when the high-profile meetings would start and in what conference room they would be held. Tamura had picked up a box of daifuku, a Japanese pastry made with mochi and a sweet filling. This particular daifuku was stuffed with fresh strawberries and sweet red beans.

"Inspector Tamura, I know why you're here so early." The woman sitting behind a desk gave Tamura a playful wink.

Tamura placed the box on the woman's desk. "You know me so well."

The woman smiled as she gave the box a cursory glance.

"The meeting you want to be a part of will start at eight a.m. sharp in conference room F. Come back here ten minutes before, and I'll walk you inside before everyone else arrives."

"Thank you so much."

Tamura headed to her department on another floor shared with Interpol. She dropped her belongings off at her desk and then headed to a break room to grab a coffee from the vending machine. Tamura slipped a few yen into the machine and a chilled can rolled out. She opened it and downed it quickly for that rush of energy. She would need that extra bounce later as she would not be a welcome party in the meeting. But she knew once she was inside no one would ask her to leave or prevent her from speaking.

Tamura printed out enough copies of the presentation for all in attendance. Usually, she would have just made a passionate oral argument, but this time she decided to make a PowerPoint. She wanted her words to stick in their heads.

Tamura was escorted into the empty meeting room at ten minutes to eight. She placed a deck in front of each chair and the remaining in the center of the table. Afterward, she chose a seat right in the middle of the long side of the table so she could look everyone in the eyes.

A few minutes later, people began to arrive. No one paid her any attention, not even a good morning—a reminder that she was a woman working in a man's world. Most of her colleagues felt she should be at home caring for children. But Tamura was single and childless. While she needed a job to support herself, most men didn't think she needed to be an inspector with the TMPD. Working as a shopgirl should have suited her just fine in their opinion. Instead of caving to the whispering behind her back, she'd become the first woman inspector in the TMPD.

That morning Tamura had a plan. One that would have everyone listening whether they wanted to or not. As soon as the last person arrived and took his seat, Tamura stood and proceeded to speak as if she had called the meeting.

"I want to thank everyone for attending this early meeting, but in light of what took place last night, I feel it's necessary. Please open the presentation deck in front of you."

On the very first page were photographs of the more than five hundred bodies lying in the streets of Tokyo.

"Last night, the Yamaguchi launched an all-out attack on the Sumiyoshi, but most of those bodies do not belong to the Sumiyoshi. They are Yamaguchi. Almost every single one of them was shot multiple times. Some of the bodies were so badly mangled that the remains had to be scooped up with shovels. The Sumiyoshi did not come to this fight with knives and swords. They came with high-caliber assault rifles. And not just one or two. They were all armed with these guns. If you turn to the next page, you'll see screenshots from CCTV footage of the Sumiyoshi gunning down the Yamaguchi."

Tamura went on to talk about how the media covered the incident. She inserted a flash drive into the control panel for the large flat-screen TV that hung on the wall and played footage from the newscasts. Their playful headlines didn't denounce the Yakuza. Instead, they celebrated them.

"Yakuza Are Back!"

"Land of the Rising Bōryokudan!"

"Go! Go! Gokudo!"

"For the better part of a year, the media has done nothing but romanticize the gangster life, comparing them to the Italian Mafia," Tamura said. "This year alone, numerous Yakuza-themed movies have flooded the cinemas, and even more have popped up on streaming sites. A dozen or so manga come out weekly with Yakuza characters. Young people can't get enough. Rappers are rapping about them. Young men are dressing like them. Women are flocking to these bad boys hoping to become their girl-friends. Make no mistake, the bōryokudan is on the rise, and they are well armed."

A throat cleared. "Inspector Tamura, if I might say something. First, I think everyone here appreciates your efforts to bring us up to speed on the situation, but I like to think we are already aware of what took place."

The speaker was Ren Miyajima, the director of the TMPD. He and Tamura never saw eye to eye. He was part of the old guard that Tamura felt was responsible for allowing the Yakuza to continue gaining power.

"As devastating as the events of last night were, fearmongering doesn't help."

"With all due respect, director, I am stating facts. Gun violence is up. Last month alone, there were ten murders in Tokyo that were committed by citizens. That's more than we've had in the last decade."

"And that makes my point," Miyajima said. "This is nothing more than a one-time occurrence."

"I'm sorry, but if you think this an anomaly, then I must disagree with you," Tamura said. "These gangsters have managed to make guns fashionable. And it's not just them who are interested in these weapons. The public's appetite for gun ownership has exploded. The application for licenses is backed up for over a year. People will stop waiting and find another way to own a gun."

"Is this really what you think?"

"It's what I see with my own eyes. The Sumiyoshi weren't firing pistols last night. They fired fully automatic machine guns. Our country is somehow being flooded with weapons . . . weapons that have been reserved for law enforcement or our defense forces. What is happening is unprecedented—"

Miyajima held up his hand, stopping Tamura. "What are you suggesting? That we go to war with the Sumiyoshi? To what extreme will you go?"

"I believe we must do whatever is necessary. But I want to make one thing clear right now. I do not believe this is a Yakuza problem. This is a trafficking problem. If we can stop the flow of weapons into the country, we might have a chance at restoring order."

6

Gray exited the restroom and returned to the table where Pratt was sitting. It was a Sunday afternoon, so the pub was packed, but they had managed to get a table near the window.

"Any news?" he asked as he took a seat.

"You mean about your assignment?" She didn't bother to look up from her phone. "No, not yet." After a few seconds, she shut it off and cleared her blond hair from her eyes. "Are you eager to get out of here?"

Gray shrugged. "Just wondering." He took a sip of his beer.

"You never told me how your call with your boss went."

"There's not much to tell. He was pretty clear that he wanted me to remain here. You know he actually put the blame on me."

She frowned. "Oh, do tell."

"He said my performance was beyond what anyone expected. How could he pull me out now? Plus, he added that his superiors were happy with the arrangement, which made it seem like it was out of his control. But he orchestrated this whole thing. I swear he's using this as the angle for a promotion."

"I don't doubt it. But I will agree with him about your performance, there is no shortage of inquiries for your service. Word has spread, Sterling. You're the 'it' person right now." Pratt gave Gray a playful punch in the arm.

Gray waved her off. "I'm not special. I'm just doing my job."

"That's true, but you are extremely good at what you do. Most of the requests that come through you never hear about. If it makes you feel any better, look at it this way. You are in a unique position to cherry-pick the best assignments around the world."

"But you filter them."

"Trust me, some of these aren't even worth you looking at. If you want, I'm more than willing to share every request. There was one that came through the other day. Law enforcement in Johannesburg had requested your help with a murder."

"What type of murder?"

"Just your average everyday murder. I think sometimes they want an easy solution by bringing a guy like you in to do their job. But like I said, if you want to field all these requests, I'm happy to share the workload."

"No, that's quite alright. I can't be the only one working around here."

Pratt lifted her pint but stopped short of taking a sip. "Are you unhappy here?"

"It's not that I'm unhappy. It's the limbo that bothers me."

"You feel like you're not in control of your life."

"Yes, that's exactly it."

"It's understandable. Even I'm surprised you've been here this long. Don't get me wrong, I love having you around as a colleague and close friend."

"Hey, if it wasn't for you and Chi, I'd be miserable."

"Speaking of Chi, shouldn't he be here already?"

"He's on the way. He sent a text a few minutes ago. There he is." Gray pointed out the window.

Standing on the other side of the road was Chi Gaston, a detective inspector with the London Metropolitan Police. Gray had initially come over to help Gaston with an investigation.

"What is he holding in his hands?" Pratt asked with a crinkled brow.

"You don't know? Chi was bragging about this cheese his family makes. It's called Époisses cheese, supposedly one of the world's stinkiest. I told him I had never met a cheese I couldn't eat. So now we have a bet for ten pounds. He made the cheese especially for me."

"Good afternoon," Gaston said as he arrived at the table with a smile. His hair was messy, and his five o'clock shadow appeared darker than usual.

He placed an object wrapped in a small towel on the table. Both Gray and Pratt immediately pulled their heads back.

"That smell, is it the cheese?" Pratt asked.

"You guess correctly." He unwrapped the towel, revealing a plastic container. "Banned from the French public transportation system, and illegal to carry on your person because of the bacteria from the listeria family. I present Gaston's Stank You but No Thank You Cheese."

Gaston peeled back the plastic cover, revealing a single triangle wedge. The reddish-orange rind was firm and slightly wrinkled. It actually resembled the crust of a baked pie. The gooey center looked very much like most smear-ripened cheese.

"The rind is washed in brine and brandy. A delicacy."

"Hey mate, what's causing that wicked smell?" a man from a nearby table asked.

"An easy ten pounds," Gaston answered.

Gray took a closer look at the slice. "It's creamy. I like that. Lillie, would you like to try it?"

"If it tastes anything like it smells, I'll pass."

Gaston placed his hand on Gray's shoulder and squeezed. "If I had to describe it, the taste is garlicky, meaty, and earthy."

"Doesn't that paint an appetizing image," Pratt said with a chuckle.

Gray clasped his hands together and gave them a vigorous rub. "Okay, Chi. How am I eating it? Do you have crackers?"

Gaston grabbed one of the clean forks sitting on the table and handed it to Gray. "You're eating it as is. You can wash it down with the rest of your pint."

Gray used the fork to scoop up the soft center of the cheese and brought it up to his nose. "Now that's ripe." He popped the cheese into his mouth and chewed. A beat later, his eyebrows popped. "Hey, that's not bad. In fact, it's pretty darn good."

"The smell gets everyone, but the taste is incredible, especially my family's version."

Gray scooped up another chunk. "Lillie, are you sure?"

"I don't want to ruin the bet. You must finish it all to save yourself a tenner."

Gray ate the remaining bits of cheese. "It actually pairs well with my pint. Chi, you're an excellent cheese maker. Hats off to you. Now hand over the winnings."

While Gaston fished his wallet out of his back pocket, Pratt's phone chimed.

"Sterling, I have an answer to that assignment."

"And?"

"You're heading to Tokyo."

7

Gray touched down at Narita International Airport in the early afternoon. According to his itinerary, an Interpol contact would meet him and take him to his hotel. Since this was Gray's first visit to Japan, he'd studied a map of Tokyo on the flight over, as he always liked to familiarize himself with the general directions of a city. Gray planned to stay in Tokyo for seven to ten days. As usual, he packed light, just a roller carry-on, figuring he could purchase anything else he needed. He also expected to be holed up in Interpol's office the entire time.

After passing through the customs inspection, Gray made his way to the arrivals lobby. He spotted a sign with his name and walked over to the gentleman holding it.

"Hi, I'm Sterling Gray."

"Ah, Agent Gray. I'm pleased to meet you. I am Katsu Kita, an analyst with Interpol." He bowed slightly. "I am pleased to welcome you to Japan. I'm told you come highly recommended."

"I'm happy to be here to help."

Kita held out his business card. "May I give you my business card?"

"Yes, of course. Dozo yoroshiku onegai itashimasu."

Gray had studied some Japanese phrases during his flight, including the polite way to say he was looking forward to working together.

"Your Japanese is quite good."

Gray promptly retrieved one of his cards and handed it over.

"Kochira koso, yoroshiku onegaishimasu," Kita said. He looked down at Gray's luggage. "Is it just the one piece?"

"Yes."

"Please, come with me. Have you visited Japan before?"

"No, this is my first time in the country, but I've heard nothing but good things. Will I be working with you during my stay here?"

"No."

Gray expected Kita to expand, but he didn't. He just kept quiet. He was on the shorter side, which was amplified when walking next to Gray. Kita didn't make much eye contact and kept his gaze downward. Gray chalked it up to shyness.

Outside there was a car with a driver waiting for them. They both climbed into the back seat of the vehicle.

"Do you know anything about the case I've been assigned to?" Gray asked, hoping to keep the conversation alive and avoid an awkward silence.

"Not very much. Did you get the packet of information?"

"I did."

"I'm not sure why your expertise was requested. You might be overqualified for the task ahead."

"Well, I know Interpol is careful where they send me. Someone evidently thought it was important that I be here."

"You're probably right."

Conversation with Kita felt like talking to a distracted child, so Gray gave up and settled on staring out the window at the passing scenery. The drive into Tokyo took about an hour. Since it was nearing five o'clock, Gray looked forward to checking into his hotel and grabbing a hot shower. But the car stopped in front of a large office building.

"I'm guessing this is where the Interpol offices are located?" Gray said as he climbed out of the car.

"Yes, where did you think we were going?"

"To be honest, my hotel, only because it's the end of the workday, and I thought I saw it mentioned in the itinerary."

"I apologize, but we have paperwork to fill out. I understand that the proper paperwork was never filed while you were on assignment in Poland. We are not like the Interpol offices in Warsaw."

"This is a big building for Interpol," Gray said as they headed inside.

"This is the CGB2, short for Central Government Building Two."

"How many central government buildings are there?"

"Many. This building also houses the NPA, the National Police Agency, which governs all twenty-seven police prefectures, including Tokyo Metropolitan Police, also in the building."

"So everything law enforcement in one area."

"Yes. We prefer efficiency."

After exiting the elevator, Kita led Gray down a hall with offices. Many were empty, and some had a few individuals working. It was clear to him that most workers were heading home for the day.

"Please have a seat while I work on the paperwork," Kita said as they entered his office. Kita handed Gray a small bag. "This is your welcome package. While here, we insist that you use the agency-issued cell phone that's been provided. Also, your security key card to enter the building is in there. Please do not misplace it."

Gray took a seat and waited quietly with his luggage while Kita worked on his computer.

"You mentioned the TMPD is in the building. Are they on this floor?"

"Yes, they share the same floor as us. Once we're finished, I'll introduce you to Inspector Mariko Tamura. She works in the Organized Crime Department of the Criminal Affairs Bureau."

Gray waited patiently for Kita to finish but soon felt the need to relieve himself.

"Sorry to disrupt you, but where is the men's restroom?" Gray asked.

"Left down the hall," Kita said without looking up.

Gray made his way to the restroom. While there, he fired off a text message to Pratt.

Gray: I met my handler here at Interpol: Katsu Kita. Have you heard of him?
Pratt: No, why?

Gray: He's a bit standoffish. They're also by the book here. Nothing like Warsaw.

Pratt: That's a good thing, right?

Gray: I guess.

Pratt: Just do what you're there to do and come back. Chi is in cheese-making mode, and I can't be his guinea pig.

Gray finished up his business and headed back to Kita's office. When he got there, he found it empty with the light turned off. Gray's luggage and the welcome packet were still where he'd left them. Gray stepped back out of the office and listened before walking down the hall toward the elevator. There he caught sight of a woman just getting into a car.

"Excuse me," Gray said, grabbing the door and stopping it from closing. "Do you know Katsu Kita?"

"Yes."

"I was with him in his office but stepped out to the restroom. When I came back, he was gone. Have you seen him?"

"I haven't, but I assume he left for his holiday."

"Holiday?"

"Yes, starting tomorrow, Katsu Kita has a two-week holiday in Hawaii."

8

You have got to be kidding me! I can't believe I just got ditched.

Gray stood outside the elevator for a moment before returning to Kita's office. He looked for a note from Kita, but there wasn't any. He had simply jetted out of there like a man ready for a vacation.

This explains the ride to the office. The guy had already checked out.

Gray walked through the hall to where Kita had mentioned Inspector Tamura's office would be. But all he saw until he reached the end of the hall were empty desks and offices.

I could have sworn the Japanese were known for working late. Maybe I was wrong.

Gray wasn't about to overthink the situation. The way he saw it, the TMPD needed his help, not the other way around. Plus, he knew the name of the investigator he was assigned to work with and where the department's offices were. He could just return the following morning. Gray collected his luggage from Kita's office and made his way out of the building in search of a taxi.

I'll get a room, some dinner, and then call it a night.

But hailing an empty taxi proved impossible during the evening rush. There wasn't much passing by the CGB2 to begin with. Gray figured he'd just walk a little bit. There had to be a hotel nearby. A quick check on his phone showed the area was restricted, so every building was a government building: no hotels.

Dammit, Kita! I hope it rains while you're in Hawaii.

According to Google Maps, the Roppongi district was a thirty-minute walk away. Gray knew the US embassy was there, so there had to be hotels.

Don't get worked up, Sterling. Look at the positive side. The weather's nice, and you'll see a little of Tokyo along the way.

Rolling his suitcase behind him, Gray set off toward Roppongi. There wasn't that much to look at, mainly office buildings. The upside was that he reached Roppongi quicker than anticipated. He headed into the first big hotel he saw and booked a room. Once in his room, he unpacked and then took a hot shower. It felt good to wash away the travel grime. He was dressed and ready to walk out the door when the cell phone that had been provided for him rang.

"Special Agent Gray speaking."

"Agent, this is Inspector Mariko Tamura. Are you free to talk?"

"I'm glad you called. I was at the CGB2 earlier, but your offices were empty."

"We're not in the office much. Where are you right now?"

"I'm at the Mitsui Garden Hotel in the Roppongi district."

"I know that hotel. If it's okay with you, I thought we could meet tonight, and I would go over the investigation with you. Have you had dinner yet?"

"I haven't, and yes, I'd love to meet."

"Great, I'll be at your hotel in twenty minutes. Oh, and don't wear a suit. I'm not."

––––––––

Gray took a seat while he waited for Tamura in the hotel lobby. He took Tamura's advice and wore jeans and a button-down shirt. He had no idea what she looked like but kept an eye out for a casually dressed woman by herself.

While he waited, Gray checked his email on his personal phone. He must have lost track of time because a woman clearing her throat interrupted him.

"Agent Gray?"

Gray looked up and found a short woman standing in front of him. She looked nothing like he had imagined. She wore a leather jacket, faded blue jeans, and boots, and had a face that belonged to a model.

"Inspector Tamura." Gray stood up and extended his hand. "Pleasure to meet you."

"Likewise. Do you like ramen?"

"I love it."

"Great. There's an amazing ramen shop within walking distance of here."

Tamura led the way down a narrow walkway between two buildings. It was filled with tiny restaurants specializing in sushi, ramen, or even tonkatsu. They entered a ramen shop that was so tiny Gray had to turn sideways to fit through the entrance. The place had two small tables and seating at the counter.

"Konnichiwa! Welcome to my shop!" The proprietor shouted out. He was a short, stout man with a crooked grin. "Please sit down," he said in accented English.

"The menu here is simple," Tamura said. "The chef specializes in chashu ramen in a shoyu- or tonkotsu-based broth. The shoyu is flavorful, but I prefer the creaminess of the tonkotsu broth."

"I'll take your advice and have the tonkotsu," Gray said.

Tamura placed their orders with the owner and shortly after, two large bowls of ramen were delivered to their table. They both dug in without saying a word. After a few slurps of the noodles and broth, Gray came up for air.

"This is amazing. The pork chashu is so tender, and the broth, you weren't kidding when you said creamy."

"This place is a hidden gem. I come here all the time when I'm in the area."

"I'm assuming your jurisdiction is strictly Tokyo."

"Officially, yes, but the Yakuza is all over the country."

"Inspector Tamura, if—"

"Please, call me Mariko."

"All right, and you call me Sterling. If I understand correctly, the recent turf war was between the Sumiyoshi and Yamaguchi."

"That's correct. The Sumiyoshi is the largest syndicate in Tokyo."

"So the Yamaguchi is an up-and-coming gang trying to muscle in on new territory?"

"Quite the opposite. The Yamaguchi is the largest in Japan and around the world. They control most of Japan, headquartered out of Kobe. But Tokyo is the one place they have no rule over. The Sumiyoshi control most of the city."

"Ah, okay. It makes sense. They wanted to take it over?"

"That's what we believe happened. I've worked organized crime for most of my law enforcement career, and I've never seen a fight like this."

"You mean with the guns?"

She wiped her mouth with a napkin. "Gun ownership is rare in Japan and has been for decades. The same goes for gun violence. When Yakuza fought each other in the past, they used swords, knives, and bats. Sure they possessed handguns, but those were mostly used for assassinations. Accessing guns in this country is difficult."

"That is until now."

Tamura nodded as she sipped a spoonful of broth. "For the past year and a half, gun violence has risen quicker than I could ever have fathomed. Even civilians are getting their hands on these weapons."

"So let me make sure I understand this correctly. Are you asking me to profile someone within the Sumiyoshi organization?"

"Yes and no. My bosses would have you believe the problem is the Yakuza, and they just need to be put back in their place. I believe the real problem is weapons trafficking. If we can stop the flow of guns into the country, then we can turn our attention to the Yakuza."

"So the Sumiyoshi is responsible for trafficking the weapons."

"That's what I think. They're the only ones armed with high-caliber assault weapons."

"I apologize if I'm being blunt, but it seems as though you already know who to go after. I'm not sure how I can add to that."

"You're right. It doesn't make sense to bring someone like you in on the investigation. We've already picked up and questioned every known trafficker inside and outside the Sumiyoshi organization. It didn't matter what they trafficked: drugs, women, or counterfeit goods. If they were involved in moving illegal goods in or out of the country, we took them off the street."

"But the guns are still coming in?"

"Yes, unless they brought in an enormous amount previously and had them stashed away someplace, but those assault rifles are new. Before, it was mostly handguns."

"I see what you mean."

"What makes it even more difficult is how the Sumiyoshi is organized. They are not set up with a singular chain of command. Instead, they're made up of small gangs. Each one has a leader that runs that group. A godfather oversees the organization, but even he shares power with others. Each group is empowered to do their own thing."

"So it could be anyone in the organization bringing the weapons into the country. Taking out the leadership won't do anything."

"That's right. There are close to four thousand members. We need to narrow the field. The leadership might not even be involved and could be simply reaping the rewards. We've really run into a dead end here. I have no idea who in that organization is bringing in the weapons or how they're doing it. I hope your fresh thinking will steer us in the right direction."

"As a profiler, I paint a picture of the person you should be looking for. At the very least, I can help you figure out the motive, but I'll do my best to narrow it down."

"Anything will be helpful."

"I'm eager to dive into all the previous casework connected to the Sumiyoshi and the gun violence. I want to get up to speed on the organization and what they've been up to. How soon can you provide that for me?"

Tamura lowered her chopsticks. "I actually have something else I'd like to try. If you want a basic understanding of the Yakuza, you can read the reports, listen to the interviews we conducted, and so forth. Or you can embed yourself within the organization."

Gray cocked his head. "Embed? I'm not following."

"I'm suggesting you go undercover and pose as a real estate developer in town for business. If I can create a situation where you can actually mingle with the Yakuza, you'll learn far more from that firsthand experience than you could by reading old reports. How does that sound, Agent Gray?"

9

The following morning Gray sipped coffee while waiting in the hotel lobby. While initially on the fence regarding Tamura's plan, he eventually came to agree with it. What Gray had known about the Yakuza was surface level and tainted by the depiction given them by Hollywood. Interpol kept official documentation on criminal organizations worldwide, and before his flight, Gray had read what they had on the Yakuza. Surprisingly, it wasn't that far off from Hollywood's take. As a profiler, he was intrigued about meeting a real Yakuza but figured it was a long shot. It wasn't like Tamura had plans for him to infiltrate the organization like a mole. It was more like being in the same room as them and observing.

As he finished the last of his coffee, Tamura walked through the entrance. She had her hair up in a French braid, wore a navy blue skirt suit, and had a black leather briefcase in her hand. She certainly looked the part.

"You clean up well," Gray said as he stood.

"Thank you. You don't look bad yourself."

Earlier that morning, Tamura had asked Gray to wear a suit, use the agency-issued cell phone, and leave his personal phone and any identification in the hotel safe.

"I present to you your new identity," she said as she handed over a handful of business cards.

"My name is Jimmy? Just Jimmy?"

"I didn't want you to come across as stuffy and old-fashion. You're a new breed of real estate development consultant. The phone number is real. It's attached to an answering service."

"Do you think I'll hand out cards to the Yakuza?"

"I hope so. Business card culture here is taken seriously, so you'll want to hand them out like they're free candy. I'll be honest with you, I don't know if this plan will work. But I know that I need fresh thinking, and I want to give you the best shot at giving me that."

"Where are we heading?"

"I thought I'd take you to the districts where the Sumiyoshi has strongholds. We'll start right here in Roppongi."

A surprised look appeared on Gray's face. "I didn't realize they were here. It seems so, ah . . ."

"Upscale and filled with foreigners?"

"Yeah, you could say that."

"Like any other people, the Yakuza like the modern and luxurious aesthetics of the area. Also, Roppongi has a pretty energetic nightlife. I wouldn't say it's as rowdy as Shinjuku, but it can get crazy in its own way."

Tamura and Gray walked along a busy street filled with shops and restaurants. Most of the high-rises they passed were office buildings.

"It's my understanding that there are many embassies in this area," Gray said.

"That's true, but one thing you need to know about the Yakuza is that this is their home turf. They are comfortable everywhere."

"Do they have offices here?"

"They do. They have made inroads into owning legitimate businesses in the last two decades."

"Let me guess: construction, real estate, and entertainment."

"Yes."

"Will we visit those places?"

"Not just yet, but I'm taking you to a place that's business related: the

Okura Hotel. This is where businessmen like to have their power breakfast meetings."

At the small but posh hotel, Tamura and Gray were seated at a table near a window that overlooked a garden. Men in suits having polite discussions filled most of the tables at the restaurant.

"That table over there," Tamura motioned with a tilt of her head. "Those men are from the Inagawa syndicate, based in Yokohama."

Gray glanced at the table and saw a bunch of older men dressed in black suits. "I imagine they all have full-body tattoos."

"You'd be correct."

"Do they still chop their pinky fingers off?"

"That's still a thing, though it's becoming less common. You'll find those body modifications in the older generation but not so much in the younger ones, especially with the Sumiyoshi. The same holds true for full-body tattoos. The younger generation will still get tattoos, but they don't follow the traditional design and put them in places where clothing covers them; they put them on their necks. To them, it's a fashion statement."

While they ate breakfast, Tamura pointed out another table of Inagawa men. They looked exactly like the other group. Gray couldn't gain any sort of insight without hearing what was being discussed, except that they appeared and acted civil.

After breakfast, Tamura took Gray to an area known for luxury and boutique shops. There, he observed the wives and girlfriends of the Yakuza. They looked like your average rich women shopping as if money was no concern. They also visited a few of the office buildings owned by the Yakuza. But as far as Gray was concerned, none of it added value.

"Mariko, I hate to tell you this, but this excursion isn't all that helpful for what I need to do. I'm not gleaning anything insightful."

"You're right. But this is exactly how I wanted you to come away from this. Everything I've shown you so far is 'Yakuza,' and now I want you to forget everything. Throw it out of your mind. Because the Yakuza we need to focus on is nothing like the old guard. I believe the new generation is responsible for the trafficking and the rise in gun violence. They're young, adventurous, and don't believe in following tradition. They're better at forging their own way and breaking new ground."

"With guns?"

"Exactly. Japan's culture has always been anti-gun. To bring them back and make them fashionable can only come from out-of-the-box thinking. You won't find their bodies covered with traditional tattoos or missing fingers. They definitely don't dress in traditional black suits. I've seen this new breed infiltrate all the syndicates, but the one with the largest contingent of these brash, young gangsters is the Sumiyoshi."

"So where do we find the young ones?" Gray asked.

Tamura glanced at her wristwatch. "It's too early to hit the bars in Shinjuku, Tokyo's red light district, but we can visit Akihabara, where the otaku live."

10

Tamura had turned on her heel quickly, leaving Gray to catch up.

"Hold up, what is otaku?" Gray asked.

"Otaku are people obsessed with pop culture, particularly gaming and anime. I don't mean just a fondness but an obsession. To many otakus, it's a lifestyle."

"So people who cosplay are otaku?"

"If they cosplay on days not labeled as Halloween, then yes. The otaku hang out in the Akihabara district, where everything gaming, electronics, and anime live. It's quite a sight to see if you've never been."

Gray crinkled his brow. "Are you telling me some of the Sumiyoshi are otaku?"

"The entire Akihabara area is a stronghold for the Sumiyoshi. They own and manage many businesses there, though it wouldn't surprise me if some of them were Otaku."

Tamura and Gray headed for the entrance to the metro. They were making their way back up to the surface a short ride later. When Gray exited the metro, he saw what Tamura had been talking about.

His first impression was that he was looking at a page torn out of a comic book. Every building was covered in electronic signage flashing bright reds, blues, and yellows alongside playful Japanese language character fonts. Large billboards featured the familiar doe-eyed girl characters in school uniforms or the macho, sword-wielding boyish men with gravity-defying hair to promote the latest manga or video games.

The sidewalks were packed with young people, many dressed in cosplay ranging from a simple red wig with an elf-like costume to highly realistic and expensive outfits. Gray watched three men in robot costumes transform into a semitruck, a car, and a fighter jet.

"Sheesh, you weren't kidding," Gray said. "This is amazing. This is what you get if you combine Willy Wonka's factory and the Las Vegas strip, with a healthy dose of Japanese flair."

Tamura laughed. "That's the first time I've heard someone describe it that way. But it works."

"And the Sumiyoshi hang out here?"

"They do because there's a lot of money to be made. This is the epicenter of electronics. They have a piece of everything here. They also own and manage a lot of the maid cafés."

"I hate to ask because it's suspiciously self-describing, but what is a maid café?"

"It'll be much more fun to show you."

Gray followed Tamura, and, after a series of lefts and rights, they arrived on a street with numerous cafés with names like Maidreamin, Cure Maid, and Pinafore Maid. Each of them was staffed with young women dressed in sexy maid costumes.

"It's exactly what the name suggests," Gray said. "Should we visit any particular one?"

"Look at this one," Tamura pointed at the café. "What do you see?"

"I see people having coffees with fancy desserts. And the maids are serving them."

"That's right. Nothing special. They're probably all tourists."

Tamura led Gray to the next café and asked the same question. Gray gave her the same answer because that's what he saw. But at the next café, Gray was about to give the same response when he paused.

First, it wasn't super crowded like the others. Second, three men were sitting at a table at the rear. Two were dressed in fashionable long-sleeve shirts and loose jeans. One wore Adidas sweatpants with a matching top and looked like he'd just filmed a music video for an 80s rap group.

"That's not cosplay," Gray said.

"No, it's not. Those are Sumiyoshi."

A bubbly server greeted Gray and Tamura at the entrance and escorted them to one of the pink and white tables. The vibe of the cafe was Hello Kitty without the kitty. The maid placed two anime-styled menus on the table and a piece of paper on which she wrote a few Japanese words before leaving.

"What's this say?" Gray asked as he picked up the paper.

"That's the bill for the entrance fee."

"There's an entrance fee for this place?"

"I know it sounds strange to pay to visit what is essentially a coffee shop, but you have to look at it as an entertainment venue."

The menu was in Japanese, so Tamura ordered for both of them.

"They definitely look nothing like the men we saw this morning," Gray said quietly after the server left. "They're hip and fashionable."

"I know what you're thinking," Tamura said. "I could have given you surveillance photos and videos back at the office."

"The thought crossed my mind because that's what most people would have done, but I'll be honest, being directly in their presence is a different vibe. The contrast from this morning is night and day. This is much better than a bunch of photos taken from afar."

Tamura smiled. "And that's why I did what I did. I'm glad you get my motivations. Most people, especially my superiors, don't understand my way of doing things. I've been referred to as idealistic, childish, and unrealistic, but I think that's exactly what my department needs. Fresh thinking to attack new problems."

"I agree. So are those Sumiyoshi the owners of this place or the help? It's not like this is a casino; they don't need to guard the money. This café seems pretty tame, and the customers are a mix of tourists and locals."

"They're just hanging out, making sure things run smoothly. The later it gets, the older the crowd gets, and more alcoholic drinks are ordered."

"Are the locals even aware of who those men are?"

"They are now. Young people visit these maid cafés to catch a glimpse of the Sumiyoshi. They've become popular, much like how Hollywood glorifies the Italian Mafia."

Just then, Gray watched two young women approach the Sumiyoshi and ask permission to take a selfie with them. The Sumiyoshi didn't push them away or give them a threatening look. They posed for the photo like it was a daily occurrence.

When their food arrived, the server made a show of presenting it. She placed a plate in front of Gray with food that looked like a cartoon bear. The face was a hamburger patty with two smaller half-patties made to resemble the ears. The eyes were made of two halved black olives, two dollops of ketchup made up the rosy cheeks, and the mouth was a potato slice with black sauce filling in the details.

"Kumatan," the girl said in a high-pitched voice before giving Gray a playful pinch on his cheek.

She then placed a dish in front of Tamura. It had two cute bears made out of brown rice snuggled under an egg omelet blanket.

"Kumatan," the server said before pinching Tamura's cheek.

They were both served a carbonated beverage. Gray had a blue one. Tamura a pink.

"What's Kumatan?" Gray asked after the maid left.

"Kumatan is a popular bear character."

While they ate, Gray kept an eye on the Sumiyoshi. They were either talking to each other or playing with their phones. One would call a maid over to refresh their drinks every now and then. None of them had an intimidating look, nor did they grunt their words. They laughed and smiled. This new breed of Yakuza fascinated Gray.

"Do you know these men?" Gray asked.

"No. To do my job, I try to remain undercover around the Yakuza. I haven't seen these three before, but we probably have a file. My department has been trying to catalog as many Sumiyoshi in Tokyo as possible. Why do you ask?"

Gray shook his head. "Just wondering. I still can't get over how skewed my thinking was before coming here. Traditionally the Yakuza have looked and acted the same for decades. The ones we saw this morning fit that stereotype to a T."

"That's right, but the Sumiyoshi is breaking new ground. That's why I did what I did today. I needed to ensure you understood that, or any profile you deliver would be off."

"You're right. But I'm also not sure you need a profile. I mean, you know who's responsible for the weapons. Good old-fashion police work should be enough to figure out who in the Sumiyoshi organization is trafficking the weapons into the country."

"It should be as simple as good police work, but it's not. Something is happening here that doesn't fit the mold, and I can't get my head around it. Honestly, I don't care about a profile. I said whatever needed to be said to get my superiors on board and for Interpol to send you here. What I want from you is your thinking. I'm hoping you see something that I don't. I hope my honesty doesn't ruin the assignment for you."

"It doesn't. If anything, it's more exciting. We have a similar way of approaching things."

"And what's that?"

"Whatever way works."

Gray and Tamura paid the bill and made their way outside. The sun had nearly set, and the buildings were lit up like neon Christmas trees.

"You mentioned that the other syndicates were also being infiltrated by similar men," Gray said after drawing a deep breath.

"That's correct, but the Sumiyoshi seems to be the ideal organization for these young men."

"But the other organizations must keep a close eye on what's happening."

"They do, but they are stifled by tradition. It's like they're deer frozen in the headlights. The Sumiyoshi is far ahead of the others even in how they operate."

"You're referring to their flat organizational structure, right?"

Tamura nodded. "By empowering the people on the front line to make decisions, they can take advantage of opportunities quickly. The leaders of those federations simply don't need to run everything they do up the chain of command. There's a lot of freedom to try new things. Of course, they'll feel the repercussions if they make a stupid decision." She looked up at Gray. "Are you ready to learn more?"

"I had a feeling there was more up your sleeve."

"You haven't even seen the good stuff yet."

"Are you thinking we head to Shinjuku now?" Gray asked.

She shook her head. "I have one other thing I want to show you while we're still here."

"What's that?"

"Are you familiar with Mario Kart?"

"I am if you're talking about the Mario Brothers video game?"

"Good. I thought we could play the game in real life."

11

A little while later, Gray stared at a gas-powered go-kart. About fifteen were painted bright yellow, red, or blue, along with characters from the Mario Bros. video game. And Gray and Tamura weren't the only ones eyeing the karts. A bunch of locals and tourists were quickly selecting their karts. Some were busy changing into Mario costumes.

"You're kidding, right?"

"I'm not. Have you driven a go-kart before?" Tamura asked.

"It was a while ago, but I can still swing it. Is this another strange tactic you're using to teach me something?"

"Nah, this is just for fun. It's a fun way to tour the Akihabara district. Do you want to put on a costume?"

"I think I'm good."

"Okay then, strap into your kart."

After a quick safety spiel by the tour guide, the group took off racing down the street. Gray and Tamura were in the middle of the pack zooming past cars and spectators snapping photos. To Gray's surprise, the kart had a quick pickup and responsive steering wheel.

"Keep up, you slowpoke," Tamura said as she zipped by.

Gray tried to catch up with Tamura, but she had found an outside lane with a clear path to the front of the pack. Gray tried his best to move around the other karters to catch up but was stuck.

The pack zipped through an intersection, making a left across traffic. The light changed as Gray approached the intersection, forcing him and a few others to stop and wait. Gray looked around at the others next to him and realized that they were Japanese men dressed in costumes. Otaku, Gray figured.

The group continued through the intersection when the light changed, hanging a left. Gray thought the tour guide would be ahead waiting, but that wasn't the case. So he followed the kart in front of him. The buildings on either side were covered with bright, flashing neon signage. Gray could see inside as every building had street-facing windows showing rows of people sitting at what looked like slot machines. The two karts in front of him came to a stop next to the curb, and Gray also brought his kart to a halt, thinking this was the end of the tour.

The man in the kart climbed out and disappeared into one of the buildings. Gray stood and searched for Tamura, expecting to find her waiting, but he didn't see her anywhere. A man parked his kart behind Gray and motioned for him to follow.

The cigarette smoke was the first thing to hit Gray when he entered the building. It was so thick that it caused Gray to cough. But once past that, Gray got a good look at the place. A mix of bells, whistles, and cartoon voices echoed from rows of standing pachinko machines. They all had LCD screens with flashing lights to keep score. Almost every machine had a person sitting in front of it, watching the silver balls bounce off the metal pins to the target below. The place reminded him of the slot machines in a Vegas casino, except these were themed after anime characters and well-known video games.

Gray stood behind an older woman playing on a mermaid-themed machine. The silver metal balls bounced around the pins, like a pinball, as the score was tallied.

An attendant approached Gray and instructed him to sit before handing him a bucket of balls. Before Gray could say anything, the attendant walked away. Gray still hadn't seen any sign of Tamura. In fact, he'd also lost sight of the men he'd walked into the parlor with. He took out his phone and sent a text message to Tamura.

Gray: Where are you? I'm in a pachinko parlor.

    Tamura: Sorry, work. I need to take care of something. Enjoy yourself. I'll find you when I'm done.

The old woman sitting next to Gray poked his arm and motioned him to feed his balls to the machine. Gray poured the silver balls into the metal tray and took hold of the dial that controlled the direction in which the balls were shot.

One by one, the balls shot up toward the top of the machine. He watched as they bounced off the pins and headed to the bottom. Gray got lucky quickly and hit the jackpot, winning himself more balls to play with. The old woman laughed as she encouraged Gray to continue.

The attendant returned and placed a drink next to Gray. The old woman smiled as she pointed at his glass and then at herself.

"You bought this for me?"

She smiled and raised her glass to cheers. Gray cheered the woman and took a sip of his drink: whisky with soda.

Gray decided to just enjoy himself while he waited for Tamura. Gray hit more jackpots and had more drinks with the woman next to him. Before he knew it he had filled up three buckets with his winning balls. The woman held up a blue token and then pointed to his buckets of balls.

"Exchange?" Gray pointed at his balls, then at her token.

The woman nodded as she stopped a passing attendant, instructing him to help Gray. The attendant asked Gray to follow him to the counter, where prizes on display could be traded for the balls. The attendant took Gray's balls and handed back a bunch of black tokens along with a flyer written in English and Japanese. It was a small map directing him to another shop.

Unsure of what to do next, Gray returned to the old woman and showed her the flyer. She held up her token and then pointed to the shop high-lighted on the map.

"Okane," the woman said.

Gray knew that word meant money in Japanese. He thanked the woman and left the parlor, following the map.

As he stood outside the parlor, a young woman dressed in a sexy sailor outfit approached Gray. "Can I help you?"

"Uh, I'm trying to find this shop," Gray said as he showed her the flyer.

"I know this place. Follow me."

Gray followed the woman as she skipped to a narrow entranceway. She knocked on the metal door, and a window slid open, revealing the eyes of a stranger. The two exchanged a few words before the door opened.

"This man can help you exchange your tokens for yen," the woman said.

Everything made sense at that point. Rather than trade in his winnings for cheap prizes, the old woman had instructed him to trade them in for cash. Gambling was illegal in Japan, so Gray figured this was a loophole and the tall skinny man waiting for Gray to enter was Sumiyoshi.

Gray followed the man down a narrow hall to a counter. Two more men were sitting behind the counter, staring at their phones. One of the men stood and came over to the countertop.

"Tokens," he said.

Gray put fifteen tokens down on the counter. The man looked up at Gray. "This is all yours?"

Gray nodded. "I was told I could exchange them for money. Is it a problem?"

The man held up one of the black tokens. "Each black token is worth 10,000 yen," the man said. "You want to trade for 150,000 yen?"

"I had no idea it was that much. It's fine if it's too much. I'll just leave."

As Gray moved to collect his token, the man stopped him. He then spoke Japanese to another man who quickly disappeared behind a curtained doorway. A few moments later, another young man appeared. He was dressed fashionably, his shirt unbuttoned, showing off his gold chains.

"You want to exchange tokens for 150,000 yen?" the man asked.

"This was my first time playing pachinko. Dumb luck, I guess."

Gray couldn't help but think these men were discussing whether he had somehow cheated. More huddled conversations between them took place. Eventually, one of the men made a call on his cell phone.

"We just need to confirm which machine you won on," the man with the gold chains said.

An awkward silence came over the room as they waited for a callback. Gray began to think it wasn't worth the trouble. He hadn't come to Japan to strike it rich in a pachinko parlor. He was about to tell the men to forget about his winnings when they received a call.

The man wearing the gold chains turned to Gray and flashed a smile.

"Is everything okay?" Gray asked.

"Everything is fine. We will give you your money, but our boss wants to meet you first."

The front door to the shop opened, and two confident-looking men dressed in fashionable suits walked in.

"Congratulations," one said as he stuck his hand out. "My name is Sora Iwata. This is my associate, Jun Mizuno. We heard you got lucky today."

12

"Go ahead, count the money," Iwata said as he handed over a white envelope.

Iwata was tall for a Japanese man, only an inch shorter than Gray. He had a pleasant smile and a tiny scar across his left eyebrow, and he styled his hair with gel. Mizuno, on the other hand, was stocky, muscular, and kept his head shaved.

"I'm sure it is correct," Gray said. "I trust you."

Iwata and Mizuno locked their gazes on Gray, prompting him to check the envelope.

"Seems to be all here."

All Gray wanted at that moment was to get the hell out of there. Being confined to a small area surrounded by Sumiyoshi, unarmed and without backup, wasn't exactly how he expected his day to turn out.

"I'm sure you guys are busy. I've already taken up a lot of your time." Gray moved toward the door, but a hand on his shoulder stopped him.

"You never told me your name," Iwata said, smiling pleasantly.

"It's Jimmy."

"Jimmy? Are you here on holiday?"

"Business. I'm in real estate development."

Gray turned and started to head toward the door.

"Business or residential?" Iwata asked as he followed Gray.

"Both. I represent multiple investors back in the UK."

"You sound American."

"I am, but I have clients in the US and the UK."

Gray exited the building and was reminded of how bright the neon lights were on the buildings. "It reminds me of Las Vegas."

"Jimmy, please have a drink with me," Iwata said.

"You know, I'm actually here with a business associate . . . we got separated."

Iwata looked around. "It'll be easier to find you if you stay in one location. There's a lounge on the second floor . . . over there." Iwata pointed across the street.

Gray looked at the men surrounding Iwata. He didn't get the impression it was an invitation he could turn down.

"Okay, one drink." Gray took out his phone. "What's the name of the lounge?"

"It doesn't have one. But tell your associate it's across the street from Supreme Pachinko."

Gray quickly typed out a text message informing Tamura about his situation and to get there soon.

"Don't worry, Jimmy. You're in good hands," Iwata said as he and Mizuno sandwiched Gray between them and ushered him across the road.

"I'll be honest," Gray said. "Part of me thinks you're not convinced I hit the jackpots fair and square."

"We've already confirmed nothing was wrong with the machine. You deserve your winnings," Iwata said.

"That's good to hear."

Mizuno led the way up the stairs and through a tinted glass door. The lounge was dark, with mood lighting. Playing on flat-screen monitors were videos of women in bikinis set against J-pop. Sitting at various tables were men dressed in suits. One or two beautiful young women accompanied each one.

Mizuno led them to a large booth with a round table. Iwata and Mizuno sat on either side of Gray. Within seconds three hostesses appeared with bottles of whisky, mixers, glasses, and a container of ice. They proceeded to fix everyone at the table a highball.

Iwata raised his glass. "To our new friend, Jimmy. I hope his luck runs out."

"Kanpai!" the table said with raised glasses.

Gray lifted his glass and acknowledged the toast, unsure if Iwata was being tongue-in-cheek.

"Jimmy, how long are you in town?" Iwata asked.

"Just a week."

"Is this your first time in Japan?"

"No. I visited a year ago," Gray said, not wanting to come off as a complete newbie.

One of the pretty hostesses refreshed Gray's drink.

"Is pachinko the only business you're involved in?" Gray asked.

"I have many interests. It's good to keep an open mind."

"That's where the opportunity lies."

Gray checked his phone to see if Tamura had answered his text.

"You have to be somewhere, Jimmy?" Iwata asked.

"Just making sure I don't leave my associate wondering what happened."

"Your clients in the UK are looking to develop property here in Japan?"

"They're interested in finding deals they can be a part of rather than spearhead."

"Real estate is tough in Japan. There is only so much land." Iwata took a sip from his drink. "Did you know homes in Japan lose their value annually for thirty years until they are deemed worthless?"

"I think I heard something about that."

"It's true. It's too easy for a home to be destroyed by an earthquake, typhoon, or tsunami. Unlike in America, where you buy a house as an investment."

"What happens to the home after thirty years?" Gray asked.

"Usually, it's demolished. The land has value."

"I take it you're not involved in real estate development."

"That's an old man's way of doing business."

"So NFTs? Crypto? Are those areas that you dabble in?"

Iwata smiled. "I dabble in quick money with low overhead."

"Pachinko?"

"I have a lot of different businesses in the Akihabara district. I don't have to do anything to bring the customers. The otaku bring themselves and empty their wallets."

"There must be a lot of competition for those low-hanging fruit."

"We're not worried about the competition here. Our businesses have a good reputation." Iwata tilted his glass at Gray before taking a sip.

The hostesses refreshed Gray's drink for the third time. By then, he'd grown more comfortable in the Sumiyoshi's presence. This meet and greet was not about whether he cheated in the pachinko parlor or about them wanting to get out of paying him. For some reason, Iwata had taken an interest. Gray wasn't exactly sure what the reason could be. He'd been cautious about choosing his words and not giving away his real identity.

He eventually chalked it up to everything Tamura had been saying about the younger generation; they're nothing like the Yakuza most people know. Perhaps this was normal. Maybe they could easily separate their day job from their social lives.

"What do you do for fun, Jimmy?" Iwata asked.

"When I have the time, I like fishing and hunting."

Iwata popped his eyebrows. "You hunt?"

"I grew up hunting deer and pheasant with my father. I'll admit, it's been a while since I've gone. Do you hunt?"

Iwata shook his head. "I haven't, but I want to. In Japan, we can hunt deer and boar, but a lot of regulation makes it difficult."

"Is that because of Japan's anti-gun culture?"

"Yes, but Jun owns a gun, right?" Iwata smiled at Mizuno.

"I have two rifles."

"Rifles? I would have thought a handgun would be easier to own."

Mizuno smiled.

"Do you hunt?" Gray asked him.

"I haven't been, but I like to shoot targets at the range."

"They have shooting ranges in Japan?" Gray looked back and forth at both men. "That's a surprise to me."

"Of course, you think only America is fascinated with guns," Mizuno said.

Iwata glanced at his wristwatch. "Your associate is either lost or not coming for you. Join us for some fun."

"Uh . . . what kind of fun?"

"America's favorite pastime."

13

Before Gray could refuse the offer, he was ushered down the stairs and into a car. Gray climbed into the back seat with Mizuno and Iwata. The other men got into another vehicle.

"Where are you taking me?" Gray asked as the car sped off.

"You worry too much, Jimmy."

"I'm worried I'm taking up too much of your time."

"We're just having fun."

Just then, Mizuno unzipped a black bag that he had with him and took out two compact assault rifles.

"Whoa!" Gray said. "When you said America's favorite pastime, I thought you were talking about baseball.

"Baseball?" Mizuno started laughing hard.

"America loves guns," Iwata said as he took one of the rifles from Mizuno. "This is a Kalashnikov MA. Easy to hide, but it has great stopping power."

"Yes, I can see that."

Both Iwata and Mizuno were admiring their guns with wide eyes.

"I'm guessing these rifles aren't sold in a gun shop."

"Special permission is needed to own a gun like this," Iwata said. "But we have connections."

"I imagine you do."

"As a hunter, I thought you would appreciate this."

"We use a different type of gun for hunting."

A short drive later, the car stopped, and Gray was hurried into a building. It looked neither residential nor commercial. Abandoned was the word that came to mind. They went up a flight of stairs and through numerous locked doors until they reached an unfinished open space. At the far end, Gray spied paper targets hanging on the wall. Mizuno locked and loaded a magazine into his rifle and took a stance. A beat later, he fired. Gray jumped back and quickly covered his ears. The echo in the space multiplied the gunfire. Iwata laughed as he handed a pair of earmuffs to Gray.

Iwata slipped a pair on and then began firing at the targets. If there was ever an opportunity for something to go wrong, that was the time. The wall wasn't designed to prevent the bullets from ricocheting off and back toward them. Gray didn't see the thick armor steel common in ranges where high-caliber rifles were used. Not even a simple granulated rubber trap. Instead, there were just large bags of rice leaning up against the wall—a makeshift space that Iwata and the others used to shoot their guns.

Better than nothing.

Mizuno turned to Gray. "Jimmy, can you handle a gun like this? Or are you one of those soft Americans?"

"You mean soft like that stomach of yours?" Gray shot back.

Mizuno chuckled as he walked over to Gray. A second later, Mizuno grabbed Gray by his suit jacket and threw him to the ground. Gray landed hard on his back, and the air shot out of his lungs.

"Jun here was a judo champion when he was a teenager," Iwata said.

Gray got to his feet and quickly moved behind Mizuno, slipping an arm under Mizuno's jaw so that it was tight against his neck while he pushed Mizuno's head forward. Mizuno fought back with foot stomps, but Gray avoided them. A few seconds later, Mizuno collapsed to the ground, unconscious.

"He'll be pissed off when he comes to," Iwata said.

"I thought we were showing off," Gray said.

Iwata put a fresh magazine into his rifle and held it out to Gray. "Have you shot this rifle before?"

"I haven't," Gray said as he took the rifle. "Feels lighter than it looks."

"It's made from hardened plastic," Iwata said. "Only the barrel and a few other parts are metal. It's only two and a half kilograms."

Gray unfolded the stock, shouldered the rifle, and peered through the sights.

"Pull the trigger," Iwata said.

Gray checked the fire mode, switched it to single fire, and let go of a few rounds. "It's solid, considering it's made from plastic."

Iwata switched the fire mode to full auto. "Try it now."

Gray gripped the gun tighter and took aim at a rice bag. The bullets tore through the pack, sending grains of rice exploding. Within seconds he'd emptied the clip.

Iwata clapped. "You're a good shot. Something tells me this isn't the first time you've shot an assault rifle."

"I was in the air force when I was younger."

"That explains it. Are you still with the US military?"

Gray shook his head. "I did my time. I'm finished."

At this point, Mizuno regained consciousness and stood with his fists balled tightly.

Iwata placed a hand against Mizuno's chest, stopping him from approaching Gray. Iwata said something in Japanese, causing Mizuno to eye Gray for a moment.

"I'm sorry, Jun," Gray said with a slight bow to ease the embarrassment Mizuno had to be experiencing. "I thought we were having fun. Maybe later, you can show me more of your moves."

One of Iwata's men produced a bottle of Japanese whisky and poured shots into glasses. Gray couldn't help but think mixing liquor with automatic machine guns was one of the stupidest things they could do.

Iwata shoved a glass into Gray's hand and took the gun away. He then exchanged the spent magazine for a fresh one and joined his men on the firing line. They all had MAs, and there was a crate filled with ammo.

Clearly, Iwata and his men had access to weapons being trafficked into the country. Part of Gray kept expecting the other shoe to drop. This was too easy. How on earth did he end up hanging out with the Sumiyoshi? Gray was pretty sure Iwata was associated with the organization. Their style and vibe matched what Tamura had told him earlier. Still, Gray kept waiting for something to go wrong. Surely, he wasn't that lucky?

Was Iwata setting Gray up? Did he have an inclination that Gray might be in law enforcement? Gray had been careful, but he couldn't be sure if he'd let something slip. Iwata didn't come across as an idiot. If Iwata knew, why continue the charade? Surely the Sumiyoshi knew they were being investigated by the TMPD.

Gray checked his phone to see if Tamura had gotten back to him. She hadn't. Gray leaned back against the wall and watched as Iwata and his men continued to fire the weapons. Could Iwata have a connection to the weapons trafficking, or was he nothing more than a low-level recruit? Whatever the answer, it wasn't what Gray expected when he found himself in a pachinko parlor.

14

The ringing from the hotel phone finally broke through, waking Gray from a deep sleep. He rolled over onto his back and reached out with a hand, feeling around the bedside table for the phone.

"Gray speaking. . ." He cleared his throat.

"Always answer as Jimmy if you don't know who's calling."

"Mariko?"

"Good morning. How are you feeling?"

"I have a splitting headache." Gray propped himself up on an elbow. He was still dressed in his clothing from the day before. "What happened to you yesterday?"

"I'll explain everything when I get there."

"You better have a good explanation," Gray said.

"Meet me in the lobby in one hour."

Just who does she think she is? Gray fished out a few pain relievers from his travel bag and downed them with water. *I'm done being Mariko's pawn in this experiment. That's not why I'm here. I need to lay the rules down now and ensure she's clear on them.*

After a shower, Gray got dressed and headed down to the lobby. He grabbed a cup of black coffee from the café and settled into one of the comfy chairs. The pills he had taken earlier had kicked in, minimizing his headache. All Gray needed was the caffeine to do its job, and he'd be good to go.

Tamura arrived on time dressed in another sharp skirt suit with a big smile on her face, but Gray wasn't about to fall for it. What she did was unprofessional, and he wouldn't stand for it.

"You ditched me."

"Before you bite my head off, let me explain," she said as she sat in the chair next to him.

"I can't see how anything you have to say would justify your actions."

"I'm sorry. But this wasn't planned."

"Uh, you disappeared during the go-kart tour. You mean to tell me that was a coincidence?"

"Yes and no. I did receive a call I had to deal with."

"You could have easily communicated that."

"You're right, but I wanted to see if the Sumiyoshi would bite."

"Excuse me, I'm not a tool for you to use. Is that clear?"

"Technically, you are. You're here to assist me."

Gray's jaw tightened.

"But I know it's still bullshit. I'm sorry. I had every intention of showing up after you spent some time in the pachinko parlor. I know the manager there. But when I discovered you'd hit the jackpot, I knew there was a chance you could collect a cash prize. The Sumiyoshi own and operate those shops."

"Mariko, you could have told me what you were thinking. We're supposed to be working on this investigation together. You need to communicate and allow me to say yes or no to your ideas."

"You were never out of my sight."

"So you were watching me the entire time?"

"Most of it. I didn't tell you because I wanted a natural reaction. You had to come across as genuine, or the Sumiyoshi would sniff you out. I can't get close to the Sumiyoshi, not in the way you can as a gaijin. Plus, you don't fit the mold of a typical gaijin tourist in that area. I had a feeling you would stand out."

"Yeah, and?"

"Honestly, I didn't think it would work. I was seconds from showing up when you decided to cash in your tokens. One hundred and fifty thousand yen is a large jackpot. It would garner attention."

"Did I really win it, or did you orchestrate that?"

"I'm not that good. You got lucky. Look, I'm not proud of what I did. I would be pissed off if someone did that to me. But look at the flip side, you got to spend time with the Sumiyoshi. You gained access."

"How can you be sure they were Sumiyoshi? Did you recognize them?"

"I recognized Sora Iwata."

"Yes, that was his name. The other one was Jun Mizuno."

"Iwata is the leader of a federation within the Sumiyoshi. He commands about forty to fifty men, maybe more by now. He's a rising star. I haven't been able to get close to him, but I think he could very well be connected to the trafficking."

"You no longer need to wonder. I can just about confirm that."

Gray told Tamura about their visit to the makeshift shooting range. "They were firing compact assault rifles, a Kalashnikov MA. They all had one, and ammo wasn't an issue."

"You're kidding me."

"I'm not, but I thought you had eyes on me the entire time?"

"Most of the time. Once you left the Akihabara district I used the city's CCTV system to track you. I couldn't see what you were doing inside the building."

"My memory is foggy after that. Can you fill me in?"

"You went to a club in the Roppongi district after and stayed there until they dropped you back off at your hotel."

"Great. Now Iwata knows where I'm staying. This just keeps getting worse. I feel betrayed."

"I understand, and I'm sorry. But this is much better than some generic profile of a person you would have eventually handed over. We knew we were looking for someone in the Sumiyoshi."

Gray held up a hand, stopping Tamura. "This was your plan from the start, wasn't it?"

"What did you think I meant when I said I wanted to embed you in the Yakuza?" Tamura asked.

"I didn't think you would throw me at any group with no support and roll the dice."

"Come on, I'm not that irresponsible. I had control over the situation until you drove off to the shooting range."

"You were planning the pachinko thing from the get-go, weren't you?"

"Do you really think a standard profile would have been better?"

"Well, we won't know that now, will we?"

"Gray, you've delivered something way more valuable. Access."

"Wait a minute, are you saying you want me to continue meeting with these guys?"

"That's exactly what I'm saying. Look me in the eyes and tell me the idea of mingling with the Sumiyoshi doesn't get you excited. You're naturally fascinated by human nature. You love getting into the minds of people. Right now, you can see how this new breed of Yakuza thinks and behaves firsthand."

"Look, you got exactly what you needed. I delivered the best profile possible—an actual person. Focus your investigation on him. You should be able to make headway with good old-fashion police work."

"But your cover isn't blown. You could continue to mine him for information."

"You don't get it. Everything worked out okay, but it could have gone sideways."

"You're right. I need to respect your decision. You're expected to be here for a week. I can set you up in an office at TMPD headquarters. Just ride out the remaining time there in case I have questions or need to pick your head more. Or . . ."

"Or what?"

"Meet with Iwata once more. But this time, we'll plan it together."

15

Over lunch, Tamura and Gray discussed the best way to orchestrate a meeting with Iwata again. Tamura couldn't be sure if Iwata would bite or if he had already lost interest in Gray, but she believed it was worth a shot.

"So you really think they'll seek me out?" Gray asked. "Maybe I should go back to the pachinko parlor."

"It'll make you look desperate. Remember, you're here on business, not to make friends with the Yakuza. You need to put yourself out there but not look obvious."

"So, what do you suggest?"

"What would you normally do on a business trip when you found yourself with some downtime?"

Gray took a moment to think. "Well, I'd probably walk around, see the sights, get something to eat, and maybe do some shopping."

"Perfect."

"You really think this will work? I mean, what are the odds of me ending up in the same place as Iwata without it looking like I staged it?"

"Zero. This only works if he seeks you out. He knows where your hotel is. He might send some men to watch you."

"He could be watching us now?"

"He could be, but I highly doubt it. It's early. If he does approach you, it'll be in the evening."

"How can you assure me that I'll be safe? And don't tell me you'll put a wire on me because that's not happening."

"I have a tight group of men back at the TMPD loyal to me. If Iwata makes a move, we'll be close behind. I'll also tap into the city's CCTV network. You can always text me."

"Are you sure he doesn't know you?"

"That I'm positive of. Look, if you feel your life is in danger at any time, send me a text, and we'll come in with force and pull you out. Your cover will be blown, but it's better than taking the risk."

"The rational part of my brain tells me this is a bad idea," Gray said.

"What does the profiler side of your brain say?"

"To be honest, it's filled with intrigue. The opportunity to mingle with these men is invaluable. Even if Iwata is not connected to the trafficking, we'll have a better idea of who we're looking for. That's for sure. Based on what you know, do you think Iwata is your guy? He's the head of a federation. This could be his thing."

"He's a person of interest, but I need more to merit twenty-four-hour surveillance."

"Are your supervisors aware of what happened?" Gray asked.

"Would it bother you if I said no?"

"They would never have sanctioned it, would they?"

Tamura shook her head. "I'm also dealing with old thinking. They've been solving the same problems with the same solutions for decades. It no longer works. Have you mentioned what happened to anyone at Interpol?"

"Not yet."

"There's a good chance they'll put you on a plane if they find out."

"I don't doubt that. I'm scheduled to be here for a week. Let's see how it plays out."

Tamura had to head into the office. She and Gray agreed he would stay out of sight until after four o'clock. At that time, Gray would walk around the Roppongi district, sticking close to his hotel. If there was no contact from Iwata after sundown, Tamura had instructed Gray to take the metro to Shinjuku, Japan's red light district.

At four o'clock, Tamura sent Gray a text letting him know that she and her men were in position and he was free to roam around. Gray dressed in a suit and left his identification and personal cell phone in the room's safe. He had returned to being Jimmy, the real estate developer.

Gray had been craving a bowl of ramen all afternoon and set out to find a shop close by. It had to be small, the owner needed to be the chef, and he wanted to hear a cheerful welcome when he walked inside.

"Irasshaimase!" The owner shouted enthusiastically as soon as Gray poked his head inside.

Gray gave a wave and a smile before taking a seat—it was just him and another man in the place—the early dinner crowd. He placed an order for chashu ramen. A few minutes later and Gray had a bowl of ramen in front of him. Layered neatly on top of the noodles were three round slices of pork belly. And sticking up from the side of the bowl like a black shark fin was a crispy piece of dried seaweed. He dipped his spoon into the broth and slurped.

Perfect.

As Gray ate his ramen, he thought about ordering a second bowl but opted to keep his stomach on the light side in case a meetup with Iwata happened. While eating his noodles, his thoughts drifted to how the investigation had morphed into something completely different from what he had initially been pitched in London. Similar events had taken place during previous investigations, prompting Gray to wonder if this was how it would always be. He had the impression that law enforcement worldwide worked on a different beat than it did in the UK or even the US. But to be honest, he didn't expect it from the Japanese.

From the start, Kita had given him the impression that everything was buttoned up and done by the book. That is until Kita cut out on him for his vacation. Gray didn't think Tamura was the type to cut corners, but he'd quickly learned she was willing to do anything for the sake of her investigation. She was working against a system that didn't take her seriously—her radical thinking was way too progressive for the old guard. Asking for permission to do anything out of the ordinary was a sure way to get shut down. It had Gray appreciating his supervisor, Cooper, a bit more. He had always been open to new ideas. Gray never felt the need to go around him.

He couldn't imagine being able to do his job if every single decision he made had to be in secrecy.

Gray wondered briefly why he was even in Tokyo. Why did Tamura make the case with Interpol that he was needed? She knew the person she was looking for was in the Sumiyoshi organization. She knew and understood them better than anyone else at the TMPD. What was she hoping to get from him? Sure she told him she wanted fresh thinking. But was that the truth or was it an excuse to cover up another trick she had up her sleeve? Was Gray about to be set up once again? Or was this simply a matter of access?

That had to be it. Gray did what Tamura and her men couldn't. This was about access from the very start. Tamura could only learn so much from the outside. To progress, she needed someone on the inside. Tamura didn't bring Gray over to draw up a profile. She needed him to infiltrate the Sumiyoshi.

16

Once that thought started rattling around in Gray's head, he couldn't shake it loose. The thought made him feel like someone's puppet. He wanted to give Tamura the benefit of the doubt. Maybe he was overthinking the situation, but the plausibility of it all made sense.

Tamura was a Japanese woman; there would be no way for her to infiltrate the organization. Even her men would have trouble. But Gray was a gaijin, a shiny, new toy. Tamura knew how the younger Sumiyoshi would react to someone like him. No doubt she understood how they thought and what pushed their buttons. She just needed the right vehicle.

How could he not have sniffed this out sooner? How could Pratt not have seen through it when she got the request? There had to be some back and forth between the agency and the TMPD.

Gray paid for his meal and left the shop. He thought of calling Tamura right then and calling the operation off, even leaving Tokyo sooner than expected. But what would that gain? How would that help the investigation? Gray had done what Tamura had hoped for: he made contact.

It was tradition that the Yakuza operated under secrecy. Only its members were truly aware of what took place in the organization. Suggesting a gaijin go undercover to her bosses would probably have gotten Tamura laughed off the force. That's because her superiors knew and understood the Yakuza of the old ways. Tamura had been focused on the up-and-comers who would eventually take over and lead.

Gray drew a deep breath as he walked along the street. He felt conflicted. He had been used like a tool, but at the same time, he had gained access to Iwata. During what time and place would that have been possible except with this investigation and under Tamura's lead? Had the stars successfully aligned? Was Gray looking his very own gift horse in the mouth? He'd thought being able to have daily conversations with a notorious human trafficker was a coup. He now had the opportunity to mingle with an actual Yakuza member. And not under the guise of Iwata having been arrested. This wasn't questioning or an interview under duress. This was hanging out and getting to know one another. This was throwing back drinks with the boys.

Right then, Gray decided to use this opportunity to find out as much as he could about Iwata and his men. And if Iwata was the wrong person, Gray would have a pretty good idea of who they should be looking for. A profile is never set in stone.

While Gray window-shopped, he received a text from Tamura. She suggested he make his way to the Shinjuku district. She didn't mention where she was, but she told him she had eyes on him. Her men must be pretty good because Gray had been trying to spot his tails since he left the hotel and hadn't picked them up.

Gray headed toward the metro entrance and was about to purchase a ticket when someone called his name.

"Jimmy!"

Gray spun around and recognized Mizuno and a few other men from the night before. Iwata was MIA.

"Jun, this is a surprise."

"Going someplace alone?"

"Shinjuku. I heard it's a fun place at night."

Mizuno's men surrounded Gray. None of them had friendly smiles, not like how he remembered the night before. Or was it just Iwata who smiled? Gray couldn't be sure.

"How is business?" Mizuno asked as he looked Gray up and down.

"Uh, business is fine. I had a few meetings today."

"I have some friends in real estate. They never heard of you."

"Doesn't surprise me. I haven't done any projects in Japan, but it's a market my clients have recently shown interest in."

"Have you spent your winnings from last night?"

"I used some of it to buy ramen for dinner."

"Then you have a lot left over. I have an idea."

"And what's that?"

"We go to Shinjuku together. You can buy us a drink."

Gray took a moment to look around. This was exactly what he was hoping would happen. "Where's Sora? Is he around?"

"Don't worry about Sora."

Fifteen minutes later, the train they had all gotten on stopped at the Shinjuku station. They exited the car and made their way up to street level. The surrounding area was made up of narrow lanes lined with eateries. There was a good amount of street traffic as most people were still getting off of work.

Mizuno led the way with a brisk pace. He seemed to know exactly where he wanted to go. Gray kept his mouth shut and followed, hoping Iwata would appear soon. He was the buffer. There was absolutely zero connection between Mizuno and Gray. If anything, choking Mizuno out the night before did Gray no favors. Without Iwata around, there was uncomfortable friction between the two.

"This is the Golden Gai," Mizuno said. "Have you heard of it?"

"I have," Gray said as he followed Mizuno down a small lane lined with dozens of tiny bars. Some looked as if they'd only fit three people, while others were a little bigger and could fit maybe fifteen. Each bar also seemed to have a theme ranging from punk rock to Pokémon, biker gang, and even French bakery.

Mizuno grabbed Gray by his arm and yanked him into a narrow doorway. The way Gray would have described this bar was psychedelic Alice in Wonderland. Blacklight made neon-painted characters pop off the walls.

Every character was using a bong or taking a drag from a fat joint. Classic American rock played from the speakers.

Mizuno forced Gray down into a booth and sat, blocking his exit. A few moments later a young woman wearing a short dress resembling Alice's outfit placed a bottle of Japanese whisky down on the table with a selection of mixers. She started to fix the drinks.

"You like Japanese whisky?"

"I don't mind it."

"We'll start with a highball."

Gray watched the server mix Suntory Toki whisky with sparkling water over ice. Another server appeared and placed two plates of edamame on the table. Mizuno peeled one of the green pods open and slurped the soybeans into his mouth.

"Is Sora meeting us here?" Gray asked before glancing at his watch.

Mizuno shrugged as he motioned for Gray to drink his highball.

There was no toast before Mizuno downed half of his highball right away. The server immediately refreshed his drink. There was a reason Iwata ran the crew and not Mizuno: personality. Iwata had a way of making Gray feel comfortable. Mizuno made Gray think he had a target on his back. Mizuno had to be following an order from Iwata. There was no way Mizuno would want to hang out with Gray.

Gray studied the faces of the three men who were with Mizuno. Two he remembered from the night before. The other was a new face.

"Is this also one of your businesses?" Gray asked.

Mizuno didn't bother to answer. Gray figured it was Sumiyoshi-owned. He assumed every establishment they visited would be.

By the time Gray started his third highball, he'd run out of questions to ask Mizuno. And it didn't help that his answers sounded like a series of grunts. Gray briefly thought of excusing himself for some fresh air. He could use that time to call Tamura and get her take on what was happening.

"Did you bring your guns out tonight?" Gray asked.

Mizuno looked at Gray from the side of his eyes. "Why?"

"Those were excellent rifles. I mean, nothing like what we got in the states, but still very good."

"What do you mean?"

Gray had finally grabbed Mizuno's attention.

"You know. Americans have easy access to guns. Japan has always been anti-gun. That's all I'm saying. I can own a gun legally in a couple of hours. And I have a selection of inventory to choose from that you wouldn't believe."

"You think only Americans have guns?"

"We have easy access to a large inventory of weapons. I can buy and own as many guns as I want and even walk around in public with a rifle strapped across my back."

"We have as many guns as we want."

"Yes, I saw your guns last night. Decent weapons, but it must not have been easy to get—"

Just then, Iwata entered the bar.

"Jimmy! So good to see you again." Iwata slid into the booth so he could sit next to Gray. "I apologize for my tardiness."

"I didn't realize we agreed to meet today," Gray said.

"Sure, we made plans last night. Don't you remember?" Iwata gave Gray a playful punch in the arm. "Maybe you had too much to drink. Do you have somewhere else you need to be?"

"I don't." Gray picked up his glass. "Here's to another great night."

The plan had fallen into place. All Gray needed to do was steer the conversation back to weapons and see what Iwata had to say.

17

Iwata wanted to make the rounds at several bars in the Golden Gai. They settled into a lively bar, much bigger than the first one Mizuno had taken Gray to. There was no actual theme except loud music. It wasn't lost on Gray that he was the only gaijin in the bar. Gray bided his time, waiting for a moment that made sense to bring up guns in the conversation. Thanks to Mizuno, Gray didn't need to wait very long.

"Hey, soldier," Mizuno said as he eyed Gray. He waved a small pistol around before placing it on the table.

Gray snatched the pistol off the table and noticed the safety was off. He slid the hammer drop safety up so the gun could not be fired.

"This is a Makarov. Standard sidearm used by the Russian military and police force," Gray said as he admired it.

"You have one?" Mizuno asked.

Gray shook his head. "Nah, but I'm familiar with it."

He turned the safety off, dropped the magazine out of the gun, and placed it on the table. He then pulled back on the slide to ensure there wasn't a round in the chamber. He released the trigger guard, pulled the slide back, and lifted it up and off the body. Lastly, he slid the recoil spring off the barrel and placed it on the table.

Iwata let out a loud belly laugh. "Jun, do you know how to put it back together?" he asked as Mizuno stared at his disassembled pistol.

"I'll put it back," Gray said as he reached for the pieces.

Mizuno slapped Gray's hand away and picked up the pieces.

Gray backed off and turned his attention to Iwata. "Before you arrived, I told Jun how easy it is to buy a gun in America."

"How many guns do you own?"

"Fifteen."

"Fifteen?" Iwata smiled. "Why so many?"

"Why not? I know it can be difficult for people outside of the US to understand this thinking, especially here in Japan with your strict laws." Gray leaned into Iwata. "I think I made Jun a little jealous." They both looked at Mizuno, who was busy assembling the gun.

"Our country is different from America, but it's also catching up in many ways. The younger people don't have the same thinking as the older ones. They're the ones who put those gun laws in place. My generation has different thoughts. We're not afraid of guns."

Gray nodded. "Didn't Tokyo just have a mass shooting? I saw it on the news."

"You see, we're already on the way to being like America."

"When you can walk into a gun shop and walk out an hour later with a gun, call me. Wait, do you even have gun shops here?"

"You forget about the rifles we shot last night? Those AR-15s you Americans are so fond of can't compare to the Kalashnikov MA."

"I'll give you the edge on that. We only have access to semiautomatic rifles, but we can easily purchase an AK-47. It's not fully automatic or as compact as the MA . . . I guess what I'm talking about is access. Those rifles you have had to have been smuggled into the country. I'm talking about legal access, the freedom to walk into a store and spend an hour looking at all the handguns, rifles, and accessories. Trying them out, you know, getting a feel for which one you want without any pressure. That's the choice I have back in the states. I don't see that happening in Japan."

"Legal, illegal. All that matters is access, right?" Iwata said.

Mizuno grunted something to Iwata, and they had a brief back in forth in Japanese. Gray got the impression Mizuno was complaining. *He can't still be bitter about me taking his gun apart, can he?*

Iwata slipped out of the booth. "Jimmy, come with us. We want to show you something."

"What's that? Another bar?"

"Something better."

Like the night before, Gray was driven to an unknown location. He did his best to try and remember landmarks he passed and a general sense of direction. He also hoped Tamura still had eyes on him. As reasonable as Iwata seemed, Gray didn't take his even-keeled personality for granted. He was still a member of a criminal organization and most likely participated in the mass shooting of the Yamaguchi.

The car stopped in an area where none of the buildings appeared to be residential, the streets were dark, and foot traffic was nonexistent.

"What is this place?" Gray asked.

None of the men answered as one climbed out of the car and unlocked the gate so they could enter the property. Inside they drove slowly down a gravel road. From what Gray could tell, there were three large buildings on the property. Two of the buildings had colorful murals of different fish and crustaceans.

"You in the cannery business as well?" Gray asked as they drove past the buildings.

The third building wasn't as large as the others and looked more like a warehouse than anything else. The driver brought the car to a stop next to a couple of other vehicles. Were they meeting others?

Gray climbed out of the car and looked around. Even if Tamura had managed to follow him, they were now on private property. No CCTV coverage.

"Come on, Jimmy. I have something exciting to show you."

Define exciting.

Gray followed the group to a single steel door. One of Iwata's men unlocked it and pushed it open. The building was a well-lit, standard warehouse stocked with hundreds of wooden, sheathed crates. There were also about a dozen other men in the warehouse. More Sumiyoshi? One of the men, an older one, spoke up immediately as he pointed directly at Gray. Iwata answered the man in Japanese, but it was clear to Gray that he was annoyed. He kept repeating the word gaijin. Their conversation soon turned into a shouting match.

The next thing Gray knew, he was struck from behind and fell face-first to the pavement. He rolled over onto his back and found two men pointing guns at him.

"Whoa, easy there. I'm with Sora."

The men either didn't understand Gray or didn't care, probably the latter because one of the men kicked Gray in his side.

"Sora!" Gray called out through gritted teeth. "Call them off."

Iwata said something, and his men intervened, pushing the armed men back. That didn't stop the older man from shouting.

Iwata raised his voice, and whatever he said was enough to calm the older guy down. Iwata pointed at the crates and then at himself. Gray got back to his feet and brushed off his hands. Having been in the military, he had seen sheathed crates before. They were used to transport weapons. This had to be where the Sumiyoshi kept their stockpiles; from the looks of it, Iwata was claiming responsibility or ownership.

Gray needed to see inside one of the crates. He needed to see with his own eyes that they were stuffed with weapons. He moved over to where Mizuno stood.

"Kalashnikov?" he whispered to the man.

Mizuno didn't answer, but he did smile. Iwata threw his hands up before ordering his men to leave. Mizuno gave Gray a shove. As they walked to the exit. Gray did his best to take in as much as he could. If Tamura wanted a better lead, this had to be it.

18

Gray again found himself waking up in his hotel room, unable to recall how or what time he had returned. However, he did remember that warehouse. Gray grabbed his cell phone. There were a dozen missed calls and text messages from Tamura. He unscrewed the cap off a water bottle and chugged it while waiting for Tamura to answer her phone.

"Gray? Are you okay?" she asked as soon as she picked up. "I lost you for a bit last night."

"I'm fine. I'm at my hotel, but I have news for you. How soon can you get over here?"

"I'm on my way."

Gray showered and dressed before heading down to the lobby. Tamura arrived just as he stepped off the elevator.

"I need a coffee," he said as he made his way to the café. "Can I get you something?"

"Black coffee, hot."

A few minutes later, Gray joined Tamura.

"Here you go."

She took the coffee and immediately took a sip. "That's good. So tell me what happened."

"I'll skip to the good part. You said you lost eyes on me last night."

"Yes, briefly. We tracked you to an area known as the Keiyō Industrial Zone. It's located along the northeastern coast of Tokyo Bay, in the Chiba prefecture. It's a major base for shipping, petroleum refinery, steelmaking, and whatnot."

"Well, there's a property with a seafood cannery and a warehouse. That's where the Sumiyoshi is storing their weapons."

"Wait. You saw the weapons?"

"Not quite, but I saw hundreds of stacked wooden crates. They were unmarked, but those types of crates are typically used to ship and store weapons."

"You weren't able to look inside?"

Gray explained what happened as soon as he arrived at the warehouse.

"Did you get a name for this man arguing with Iwata?"

"I didn't, but it was clear that he and his men were tasked to guard the goods there. And they took their job seriously."

"But you said he backed down from Iwata."

"He did. I didn't get the impression he worked for Iwata or was a part of Iwata's federation, but when push came to shove, Iwata was definitely the alpha. I think Iwata took me there to show off the weaponry."

"Sounds like it."

"It would have been nice if I could have ID'd the weapons, but if you put eyes on that warehouse, you'll collect a trove of information."

"Do you think Iwata is the trafficker?" Tamura asked.

"All indications point to him."

"This is all too surreal. I can't believe Iwata took you to where they store the weapons. Is that stupid or incredibly trusting?"

"Both, but I'm convinced watching that place will reveal what is in those crates."

"He definitely took you there to show off their weapons. You managed to push a hot button for him when you bragged about the weapons in the US."

"It was easy to lead Iwata. He has a huge ego and craves recognition. If he could have attached a 'like' button to this trafficking operation, he would have."

"Gray, you did a great job. I hope you don't take this the wrong way, but

I need to pull you off this investigation. I'm concerned for your safety. Now that we know where the weapons are, any sort of slipup will come back to you. I'm not saying you need to leave the country. I'm happy to have you stick around and be part of the investigation, but I think you should limit yourself to our headquarters. I also think you should change hotels."

"Do you think Iwata will keep seeking me out, especially after last night?"

"Hard to tell, but you're not here to make friends. I think you should disappear from his life. You were in Tokyo on business, and now your business is finished. End of story."

"This is your town, and you know the Yakuza better than most. I'll defer to your judgment. What now?"

"I need to update my superiors and set up surveillance on the warehouse. Get yourself set up in a new hotel and then meet me at headquarters."

19

Ichiro Kitagawa had been with the Sumiyoshi since he was twenty-two years old—just last month, he turned forty-six. He knew Iwata referred to men like himself as wasted space and said that they only held the Sumiyoshi back from greatness. On the other hand, Kitagawa viewed the younger ones, like Iwata, as cocky know-it-alls. He felt they were poisoning the organization with disregard for tradition, even though the Sumiyoshi was the least traditional syndicate. Iwata often referred to Kitagawa as an old fool who'd been a soldier his whole life and nothing more. The two couldn't be further apart in thinking.

Kitagawa was still fuming from his spat with Iwata the night before. He and his crew were in charge of security at the warehouse. No small feat considering the value of what they were guarding.

"How stupid is Sora?" Kitagawa slammed his fist onto the desk. "Bringing an outsider here."

"And a gaijin."

The man sitting opposite Kitagawa was his number two. He was two years younger than Kitagawa and also couldn't stand Iwata. Both had joined the Sumiyoshi at the same time and had been partners ever since.

"Iwata is a perfect example of the young recruits who will ruin the Sumiyoshi," Kitagawa said. "They have no respect for tradition. They're reckless and don't think long-term. They only want to live in the moment."

"What can we do? He's connected."

"If it weren't for his connection, I would have dispatched him last night," Kitagawa said. "I'm not afraid of him, and neither are our men."

Technically, Kitagawa had higher esteem and respect in the organization than Iwata. But Iwata had fresh ideas that earned the organization a lot of money. It also didn't hurt that Iwata's uncle was Shingo Matsumura, the so-honbucho, or headquarters chief, in Tokyo. He was one rank below the oyabun, the organization's leader.

"Be careful of your words, Ichiro. It will do us no good if Matsumura hears them. Iwata is his nephew."

"We have been loyal, hardworking, and productive since joining. Why are we guarding this stuff?" Kitagawa asked.

"Because we can be trusted. The weapons make money, and the bosses like money."

"How is Iwata doing it anyway? What experience does he have in trafficking that he can pull something like this off?"

"I don't know, but Iwata is doing something no one has done before. We have access to more guns than we know what to do with. We can replace the Yamaguchi. Everyone sees this."

Kitagawa scratched his chin. "Yes, I never thought he would be able to do it, but that son of a bitch did."

"If we want to beat Iwata, we need bigger ideas or we need to find a problem connected to him."

Kitagawa's gaze fell to the floor as he got lost in his thoughts. A few moments later, he snapped his finger.

"I got it. This gaijin he brought here last night. Who is he? Is he working for Iwata? Is he the connection?"

"I've never seen him before. If he is helping Iwata, how can we mess with him without it affecting the weapons?"

"We don't know if he's helping Iwata bring in the weapons."

"So you want to dig around and find out who this gaijin is?"

"No, we'll make Iwata tell us. Even his uncle will see things our way if we tell him Iwata brought a gaijin here. Iwata will fall in line, but we need to understand the role of this gaijin, or this plan could backfire on us. Get a hold of Iwata and tell him to meet us here immediately. If he pushes back, tell him we'll have no choice but to report what he did last night."

A few hours later, Iwata and Mizuno showed up at the warehouse.

"Kitagawa!" Iwata shouted as he entered the building. "Where are you hiding?"

Kitagawa exited an office on the second level and stood on an elevated pathway.

"Iwata. I appreciate your speediness."

"My speediness? Do not mistake my coming here as me catering to your will. If you waste my time, I will leave as quickly as I came."

Kitagawa climbed down a ladder and walked over to Iwata as his second-in-command joined him.

"What do you want?" Iwata asked.

"Tell me about this gaijin?"

"This is why you asked me to come here? Because of someone I brought by?"

"Only Sumiyoshi are supposed to be in this building."

"Don't forget who is responsible for filling this building."

"That may be true, but I'm responsible for security. I can't allow you to step over protocol. If something were to go wrong, I would be held accountable."

"You worry too much."

"I'm doing my job. Tell me who this man is. Is he a part of the trafficking?"

"He's a real estate developer. I have new ideas for making money. Instead of worrying so much about what I'm doing, I would advise you to come up with your own money-making ideas."

"Real estate? What's his name?"

"Jimmy."

"Just Jimmy? I have a lot of connections in real estate. I've never heard of a gaijin who only goes by one name."

"Maybe it's because the people you know are old and outdated."

Kitagawa chuckled. "You have forty-eight hours to tell me everything about Jimmy. I want to know who he's working with, what deals he's involved in, and I also want names of trustworthy people who can vouch for him."

"If you're so connected to real estate, you can find this information yourself. I don't work for you."

"If you prefer, I can bring this up with the so-honbucho. He will ask the same questions I just asked. Shall we do it that way? Are we in agreement?" A devilish smile appeared on Kitagawa's face.

Iwata sneered. "Give me a day."

20

After checking out of his hotel and into a new one, Gray made his way to the TMPD headquarters. Before heading to Tamura's office, Gray peeked inside Kita's office. The lights were off, and he was still very much on vacation.

Tamura was at her desk talking on her phone when Gray spotted her. He quietly sat in the guest chair and placed a bag on her desk. On his way over, he had passed by a street vendor selling taiyaki, a pastry filled with a sweet filling.

"Is that taiyaki?" Tamura asked after she ended her call.

"It is. There's a mix of chocolate and red bean paste."

Tamura helped herself to one. "I love these. Are you all settled in a new hotel?"

"I am," he said after taking a bite. "I'm not far from the old place, but I think I'll be fine if I stay out of sight for the next few days. What's the latest with the warehouse?"

"Everyone is on board. We already have a surveillance team set up to watch the place. They're also working on getting a camera inside."

"If you can do that, you could end up on the fast track to solving the trafficking problem. Just keep watching and learning."

"I agree . . ."

"What's with that look?" Gray asked.

"You know there's so much internal politics here. I never know if someone's running a side operation."

"You think your bosses have a different plan?"

"Anything is possible."

"You think they might change their mind and move on the warehouse? It could be tempting if they think there's a load of weapons in there."

"That's what I'm worried about. They're willing to see what watching for a week will produce."

"A week? What if more time is needed?"

"I'm not sure. That gunfight made the government look bad. They need a win."

"And they'll get it if they can bust the real people responsible for the weapons. If they move in and confiscate a bunch of guns, it'll look good, but that doesn't solve the problem. Honestly, I think you need more than a week."

"I agree, but I need to take what I can get."

"How can I help?"

"Everything is hinging on what's in those crates. I know there's no chance they'll move on the place unless they're sure there are weapons. They can't afford to lose face."

"I wish I had been able to look inside a crate."

"Is there anything else you can remember from that night that Iwata might have let slip?"

"There might be, but once we left the warehouse, we went drinking again, and it all became a blur from that point on. I tried to keep my senses, but I felt like if I tried to bail right after, or if I turned down their drinks, it would have raised suspicions."

"It would have. You did the right thing. How confident are you that it's Iwata behind this operation?"

"I know you want me to say yes with absolute confidence, but I can't do that. What I do know is that Iwata is the person you need to be focused on right now because he's your best lead. Iwata is a walking profile."

"But in your gut, what do you think?"

Gray popped the last of his taiyaki into his mouth and thought about Tamura's question.

"I would be doing the same thing you're doing if I ran this investigation. If it's not Iwata, then it's someone who is like him. I know time isn't on your side, but you must let this play out."

"You're right."

"I get the impression you don't trust your bosses."

"I don't. They wanted to take down the warehouse when I told them about it. I had to fight for a week of surveillance detail."

"A photo op with a warehouse full of weapons won't solve the problem. It's shortsighted. If you think my getting in front of your bosses will help, I have no problem backing you. I was brought in to help you find the trafficker, not find the weapons."

"I appreciate that, but I think what you said earlier is right. Let this play out for a week and see what comes of it."

"If you change your mind, let me know. I'll back your argument."

"Thank you. Since you're in a holding pattern and need to lay low, would you be interested in coming with me to my hometown? My parents live just outside of Tokyo, and I'm due to visit them."

"That sounds like fun."

"And since you love the ramen here, I should also tell you that my father is a professional ramen maker. He's owned and operated his own shop for thirty-five years."

"Really? That's awesome."

"If you're up to learning the process, my father would be thrilled to teach you."

"One hundred percent I'm interested. Sign me up."

"Great. We'll leave in an hour."

21

Tamura's parents lived in the Chiba prefecture, near Narita International Airport. It was an hour-and-forty-minute train ride from the TMPD headquarters.

"You flew into Narita, right?" Tamura asked.

"I did. Kita met me at arrivals and drove me straight to TMPD. Why?"

"Well, there's a historical village near the train station. It's lively and the complete opposite of Tokyo. I thought we could walk through it while on the way to my parents' home. They live just off the village's main road, not far from the Shinshoji temple."

"Sounds great."

Gray and Tamura exited the train station a little after three thirty. Gone were the high-rise office buildings of Tokyo. This area looked more like a Japanese village from a historical TV show.

"This is Omotesando Road," Tamura said. "It winds its way through three neighborhoods. Almost all the flight crews from the international flights stay in this area near the station. There are a lot of charming restaurants and bars, and if you're a fan of street food, this is the place for it."

"This is neat. The traditional architecture makes me feel like we time traveled back to the days of the samurai lords."

"That's the attraction for—oh look, my favorite." Tamura hurried over to the food vendor who was grilling something.

"Smells good. What is it?"

"This is called shoyu senbei. It's essentially rice crackers dipped in soy sauce and then grilled. Don't let the rice cracker part fool you. This is far from being a healthy food option."

Gray took a cracker from Tamura and bit into it. "It's like potato chips but made from rice."

"It's a great beer snack."

Tamura introduced Gray to a few other traditional snack food as they strolled along. However, Gray let her know that he wanted to make sure he had room for her father's ramen.

"Are your parents aware that I'm coming?" Gray asked as they continued walking.

"Yeah, they know. My father can't wait to show you his ramen-making process. Normally he prepares the noodles earlier in the day, but he's willing to make a new batch just for you."

"I'm excited. Any word yet from your surveillance team?"

"They think they found a way to get a camera installed. I'll know in the next hour or so if they're successful. We were able to get a few men embedded in the cannery that's on the property."

"Do the Sumiyoshi own the cannery?"

"I'm sure they do. The business is legit, though. They might be cleaning money through it, but that's not my concern."

"You know, a thought popped into my head earlier," Gray said as he ate the rest of his cracker. "There were a lot of crates in that warehouse . . . assuming they're all filled with weapons, it seems like overload. Is it just the Sumiyoshi that's armed?"

"The other syndicates have always had access to small arms, mostly pistols. But assault rifles were a game changer. I'm not sure if I told you we were able to ID the assault rifles used in the gunfight. They were all armed with the Kalashnikov MA."

"Those are the exact same rifles Iwata and his men had."

"What are you getting at with the weapons overload?"

"It just seems like a lot of inventory to be sitting on. I thought they might be selling to the other syndicates."

"From what we can see, they aren't, at least not the assault rifles."

"So if this isn't a money maker for them, what is it then? That gunfight was the Sumiyoshi defending their turf from the Yamaguchi, right? You'd think they'd be on a major turf grab."

"Maybe that night was a test, and now they're planning it. But you do bring up a good point. I'd been so focused on figuring out how the weapons were coming into the country that I didn't stop to think why they needed so much beyond arming their own men. Maybe it is what it is: extra inventory."

"It looked like something else. Think about it, the Sumiyoshi is about four thousand strong. Let's assume they've already armed their men. The "extra inventory," as you put it, seems like overkill." Gray brushed his hands together. "When the team gets a camera inside the warehouse, and you can see the stash yourself, you'll understand why I'm thinking this. There's a lot of money tied up in those weapons."

"Maybe their plan is to team up with some of the smaller syndicates and take out the Yamaguchi. They could sell weapons to them."

"Do you really see them doing that?" Gray asked.

"There's no strong reasoning to do so that I'm aware of."

"Which brings us back to why the huge stockpile? If we could figure that out, it might help us determine how the shipments are coming in."

"You're right. They've already demonstrated that they can bring weapons into the country without us knowing. Why sit on so much inventory?"

Gray took a moment to think. "This can't be the initial shipment. You already said you've been tracking the rise in gun violence, especially with the Sumiyoshi."

"I have. Maybe they were initially selling smaller arms and keeping the heavy stuff for themselves."

"That makes more sense but still doesn't feel right. Also, another thing that bothers me is that building. I didn't think it was the most secure place to store a large supply of arms."

"Maybe it's temporary," Tamura said as she looked up at Gray.

"What? Like they keep moving their inventory around every few days? Nah, that would be too big of a job. Something else is at play here. It'll be interesting to see if the surveillance team notices a lot of traffic heading in and out of that place."

"We'll know soon enough, but I get your point. This setup doesn't make a whole lot of sense."

Gray shoved his hands into his pants pockets. "They might have another way to move the weapons. A tunnel comes to mind."

"All good points. I'll feed this information back to the team." Tamura pointed down a narrow lane. "My father's shop is over here."

"This might be a dumb question, but what's the proper way to address your father? He's a noodle master, so do I address him as sensei?"

"That won't be necessary. You can refer to him as Tamura-san. And he will call you Gray-san. But a little warning, his English isn't the best, but it's passable, thanks to the tourists that come for his ramen."

"We'll manage."

Tamura stopped. "This is it."

The small ramen shop resembled a home in a village with a thatched portico hanging over the entrance. Two lanterns with lettering hung on each side. A sign across the top featured the name of the shop: Tamura Rāmen. On both sides of the entranceway were circular wooden windows with bamboo accents.

The door opened, and a smiling elderly man appeared wearing a blue and white kimono. Tied around his waist was a black apron, and a red scarf covered his head.

"Otosan," Tamura said as she hugged him. She said a few words in Japanese before gesturing to Gray.

Tamura's father held out his hand, and Gray shook it while bowing. "Nice to meet you Tamura-san."

"Yōkoso Gray-san."

"He's welcomed you to his restaurant."

"Come, come," Tamura-san said as he motioned for Gray to follow him.

The inside of the shop was much bigger than Gray expected. It looked like it could sit about sixteen people at the tables and four at the counter.

The decor on the inside resembled a home from the village with a lot of dark wood accents.

"Sterling, I'll be back. I'm going to see my mother," Tamura said from the doorway.

"Don't worry about me. I'm good."

Tamura-san led Gray through a curtained doorway behind the open kitchen and into a storage area with a long countertop. There he had placed the ingredients for making the ramen. Tamura-san handed Gray the same blue and white kimono jacket that he wore.

"Wear."

Gray slipped the coat on and tied a black apron around his waist. Tamura-san then tied a scarf tightly around Gray's head before looking him over and giving a thumbs-up.

Tamura-san pointed at a small burlap bag. "Wheat flour." He continued pointing and naming the ingredients. "Water, salt, sodium carbonate. Make noodles chewy." Tamura-san pointed at his mouth while pretending to chew.

Tamura-san placed two metal bowls on the countertop—one for him and one for Gray. He then poured wheat flour into his bowl and weighed it on the scale, taking tiny scoops out of the bowl until he had exactly five hundred grams. He motioned for Gray to follow him. Then Tamura-san measured five grams of sodium carbonate, five grams of salt, and two hundred grams of water. Next, he mixed the salt and sodium carbonate into the water, stirring it with wooden chopsticks until it dissolved.

"This is kansui . . . alkaline water."

Tamura-san very slowly added the kansui into the bowl of flour. "Hydrate flour."

Gray followed Tamura-san's lead. As he mixed the flour with his chopsticks, it began to form small clumps.

Tamura-san then gently but firmly rubbed the clumps between his hands until the dough was equally hydrated. He transferred the dough to a plastic bag, squeezing out all the air before sealing it. He then placed the plastic bag on the floor and stepped on it, flattening the dough in the bag. He motioned for Gray to do the same. "Now, the dough sits for thirty minutes."

During this time, Tamura-san opened a small bottle of sake and poured two small shots.

"Kanpai!" he said as he held up his glass and took a sip.

Gray lost count of how often Tamura-san refilled their glasses while they waited for the dough to rest.

Tamura-san sprinkled starch on the countertop before placing his dough down. He then cut it into smaller pieces, took a rolling pin, and flattened the dough further. Next, he passed it through a hand-cranked, cast-iron roller until it was the right thickness.

Now that they both had large, flat sheets of dough, Tamura-san sharpened two knives before handing one to Gray. Tamura-san folded over the dough until it was in the shape of a burrito. Using his knife, he thinly sliced the dough. He was precise, and every cut was exactly the same size.

Gray did his best to follow Tamura, but when he finished, his noodles were uneven, while Tamura-san's noodles were all uniform in size, as if they had been passed through a pasta machine. Tamura-san chuckled but still gave Gray a thumbs-up. Mariko returned to the shop just in time to try Gray's ramen.

"Hey, these crooked noodles taste pretty good," she said.

"Your father is a master with that knife. I thought he would have used a pasta machine to cut the noodles."

"Nope. He's been hand-cutting the noodles since the first day he opened his shop."

"Now that's craftsmanship at its finest," Gray said before slurping a long noodle into his mouth. "Any news to report?"

"The team got two cameras into the warehouse, so they're watching. They haven't reported any unusual traffic going in and out, and, according to the city, there are no sewer lines under the property. If they're using a tunnel, they built it themselves."

"Is there a way to determine that?"

"They're working on it."

"I'm still bothered by the idea that A, they have such an excess of weapons, and they aren't selling it. And B, they're just keeping it in a warehouse. You'd think they'd find someplace outside of the city, someplace rural where they could store that stuff."

"I agree. Let's see if watching them gives us answers."

"I just hope your bosses don't backtrack if the right answers don't surface after a week."

"We'll cross that bridge when the time comes. For now, let's enjoy this ramen you made."

22

Iwata was in a sour mood when he and his men drove away from the warehouse. Whatever dislike he had for Kitagawa before that meeting had just been amplified.

"Who does that old man think he is? What has he done for this organization other than take orders? I don't even know why he's still a member."

"Men like Kitagawa should be pushed out," Mizuno said as he drove.

"Kitagawa cares more about rules than results. We deliver results. Who cares about how it's done as long as it gets done? But he had to cry to my uncle because I didn't follow the rules. You know, if it weren't for those weapons, he and his men wouldn't have a job. They'd be doing nothing, adding no value."

"We should teach Kitagawa a lesson."

"That's exactly what he wants us to do. Moving against him will put us in the wrong and give him an edge over us. The best way to deal with men like Kitagawa is to beat them at their own game. We'll keep making ourselves look good, and Kitagawa will look like dead weight. Let the bosses see that he doesn't add value."

"So, what do you want to do about Jimmy?" Mizuno asked. "We can't risk him complaining to your uncle. Want me to pick him up?"

"Let's go to his hotel. I want to talk to him now."

When they arrived at the Mitsui Garden Hotel, Iwata took a seat in the lobby while Mizuno inquired at the front desk.

"Sora, they don't have a guest named Jimmy," Mizuno said when he returned.

"Are you sure? Did he check out?"

Mizuno shrugged. "Can't say because they don't have anyone registered as Mr. Jimmy."

Iwata walked over to the registration counter to speak to the manager.

"Excuse me, but we're looking for our friend. He's gaijin. He's tall and has muscles."

"Do you have the guests name?" the man asked.

"I just described him to you." Iwata lifted his shirt to reveal the handle of his pistol tucked into his pants. "Are you deaf?"

It took a moment for the manager to compose himself after seeing the gun. "Just a moment."

The man stepped away to speak to a colleague. When he returned, he said, "Is your friend Mr. Gray?"

Iwata shrugged. "Show me the passport photo you have on file."

"I'm not allowed to do—"

Iwata reached across the countertop, grabbed the man by his tie, and yanked him forward. "I'm losing my patience."

The visibly shaken man quickly retrieved the photocopy of the passport. He still did his best to cover the information, only revealing the photo of Gray.

"Is this your friend?"

Iwata nodded. "Take me to his room, now."

"I'm afraid I can't do that. Mr. Gray checked out today."

"Where did he go?"

"I'm unaware of his destination."

"Did he leave alone or with someone?"

"I believe he left alone."

Iwata and Mizuno walked away from the registration counter.

"If he left the country already, we're screwed," Mizuno said. "Maybe we make up information."

Iwata walked back over to the manager. "What is Mr. Gray's first name?"

"Um, uh . . ."

"What is his name?" Iwata asked with a raised voice.

"Just a moment." The manager rechecked the information. "It's Sterling, sir."

"Sterling Gray? Not Jimmy?"

"Not Jimmy. Maybe it's a nickname."

Iwata snatched the photocopy from the manager's hand and walked away.

"Hey, you can't take that!"

"His name is Sterling Gray." Iwata handed the paper to Mizuno.

"A fake name? Who is this guy?"

"I don't know, but we need to find out quickly."

Mizuno took out his phone and did a search on Sterling Gray. "I don't see anything on him. But this name is from his passport, so it's real."

"Send this information to your hacker friend and tell him to find out everything he can on Gray."

"What will you tell Kitagawa? He won't wait long before he goes to your uncle."

"Don't worry about Kitagawa. Just tell your friend we need this information as fast as possible."

23

Yoshi Kuroda was the team leader in charge of all three Special Assault Teams assigned to the TMPD. He had previously served in the Riot Police unit and was no stranger to hostile missions. None of the men serving in his units were there for more than five years. This was to ensure only the best, mentally and physically, populated the SAT ranks. Kuroda was the one exception to the rule, proving himself to be the best the unit had ever had since its creation.

Fifty officers from the SAT had mobilized to an underground parking structure in Chiba, where they had been on standby, awaiting orders. They were fifteen minutes out from the target.

Kuroda and his men had been in a holding pattern all night as they awaited confirmation of weapons in the warehouse. His men were familiar with the drill and knew they could be ordered to move ahead or pull back. Mentally, this wasn't an issue, but this operation differed from the others. Their mission orders were to secure the warehouse and weapons at any cost. Command had made it clear that any Sumiyoshi encountered were to be eliminated. Standard protocol required nonlethal weapons to apprehend a person.

A little after four in the morning, SAT was given the go-ahead. Five armored SWAT vehicles drove single file under cover of night. Earlier, Kuroda had dispatched two sniper teams to monitor the warehouse from the rooftops of the nearby canneries. Their mission objectives had been updated to provide cover for the SAT team.

Kuroda and his team had trained for this scenario countless times, but nothing compared to the real thing, especially when the directive was to eliminate all targets encountered. Very few of Kuroda's men had experienced an all-out gunfight.

As they approached the entrance gate to the property, the snipers radioed Kuroda.

"We have you in our sights. The warehouse is quiet, and there are no visible threats."

Kuroda rode in the lead vehicle, and they picked up speed as they neared the gate. The armored vehicle smashed through the gate like it was made of plastic. All five vehicles drove unnoticed past the canneries and to the warehouse. The intelligence reports noted two entries into the warehouse. The main entrance was in the front of the building, and the smaller one was at the rear. Both doors were expected to be shut and locked, forcing them to breach.

The vehicles split. Three stopped at the front of the building while the other two continued to the rear. Kuroda climbed out of the front passenger seat while the rest of his men exited through the vehicle's rear door. Three teams of ten men each stacked up on both sides of the door. It had already been decided that a strip of C-4 would be used.

An explosive team moved toward the door and planted small strips of C-4 near the doorknob and hinges before backing away into position. Kuroda waited until he heard from the teams at the rear of the building that they were in position. On the count of three, the explosive went off, blowing the door entirely off its hinges.

Kuroda and his men filed inside the warehouse and were immediately met with gunfire. A man next to him was struck in the chest and went down. Kuroda grabbed him by the arm and dragged him behind a stack of crates.

"Are you okay?" Kuroda shouted.

"Yes, the vest caught the round."

Kuroda left his man and moved forward, firing back at the Sumiyoshi. He took down two targets right away before ducking down behind a couple of crates. Five Sumiyoshi used the crates for cover and kept his men pinned down. Kuroda crawled across the concrete floor on his belly. If he could stay out of sight, he had a strong chance of flanking the Sumiyoshi.

Inch by inch, Kuroda made his way into position. He peeked around the edge of a stack of crates and had a clear shot of the five Sumiyoshi firing at his men. They were all equipped with the same high-caliber assault rifles he had seen in the CCTV footage during the shoot-out between the Sumiyoshi and the Yamaguchi. But they were not wearing any type of body armor. Stupid.

Kuroda moved further into position and took aim. A beat later, he fired, and his bullets cut through all five men. Kuroda ordered a team to clear the second floor while he led a team down the left side of the warehouse. Over the comms system he wore, he knew the two teams had successfully breached the rear of the building but had come under fire. Kuroda split his team, one group to continue to the rear of the warehouse while he and a few other men headed upstairs to an elevated walkway.

At the top of the stairs, Kuroda encountered a Sumiyoshi firing from the doorway of a small office. He dropped back down the stairs as bullets skipped across the metal and pinged off the handrails. Kuroda removed a flash-bang from his chest rig, pulled the pin, and threw it. After the explosion, Kuroda shot the stunned Sumiyoshi, who was firing blindly. He was still alive when Kuroda approached him. He kicked the rifle away from the badly wounded man. Upon a closer look, Kuroda recognized him from the photographs provided by intel. This man had been identified as Ichiro Kitagawa, a known leader in the organization.

"How many men do you have here?" Kuroda asked.

Kitagawa tried to speak, but he'd been shot in the throat, which made it impossible. A few seconds later, he stopped breathing.

One by one, Kuroda heard the word "clear" over the comms system. All in all, the operation took twenty minutes from the time of breach to when the last Sumiyoshi had been killed. Two of Kuroda's men were injured, but their wounds weren't life-threatening.

Kuroda set up a security perimeter around the warehouse while the rest of his men documented the weapons. They were on the verge of confiscating the largest weapons cache Japan had ever seen.

24

Because the ramen shop had a busy dinner shift, Tamura-san had enlisted Gray and Mariko as help for the night. By the time the dinner crowd had subsided, they were beat. It also didn't help that Tamura-san poured sake shots all night for them. According to Tamura, sake was a nightly ritual. Since it was so late, she suggested they spend the night at her parents' home rather than head back into the city.

Gray woke the following day well rested without the headaches he had grown accustomed to after being out with Iwata. He'd spent the night in a guest room while Tamura had slept next door in her childhood bedroom. Gray bumped into her as she walked out of the bathroom.

"How did you sleep last night?" she asked.

"Like a baby. What time did you wake?"

"Early. I've been talking to my mother. Come on, breakfast should be about ready. I picked up some fresh eel this morning."

"Eel?"

"Yeah, this area is known for its freshwater eel shops. There must be a dozen of them a stone's throw away."

"I never tried it, but I'm looking forward to it."

Gray cleaned up before heading to the kitchen. There he found Tamura and her mother placing dishes on the table.

Gray bowed. "Good morning, Tamura-sama"

Tamura had told Gray to address her mother by that title. She would appreciate it.

She smiled and bowed back.

"Food looks great. Where's your father?"

"He's already back at the restaurant."

"No rest for the weary, huh?"

"That place is my father's second child."

Gray took a seat next to Mariko. Each place setting had a bunch of dishes with different offerings in each.

"This is a traditional Japanese breakfast. We have rice, miso soup, pickled vegetables, omelet, and the star . . . grilled eel or unagi."

"I've had unagi before, on sushi."

"Yes, that's the same thing, except I think the way we grill it is better." Tamura flashed a smile.

Just then, Tamura's mother tapped her on the shoulder and pointed to the small TV on the counter. There was breaking news. The TMPD had made a significant weapons bust. There was video footage of the officers who conducted the raid inside a warehouse posing next to open crates displaying weapons.

"Did you know anything about this raid?" Gray asked.

"No, I had absolutely no idea. I can't believe they went for the bust. It's a total PR move."

"And very shortsighted unless they came across information that told them more. We should probably find out the whole story before we jump to conclusions."

Tamura had already dialed a number on her cell phone and left the kitchen to have the call. Gray continued to watch the press event unfold. A spokesperson for the TMPD began answering questions from the press. The broadcast was in Japanese, but Gray got the gist of what was happening from the visuals. Tamura returned shortly after.

"So?" Gray asked.

"As far I know, once they had confirmation that there were weapons in those crates, they sent the Special Assault Team in. They had them on standby from the moment we fed them the information on the warehouse."

"They had no intention of finding out the identity of the trafficker. Are you sure they didn't kill him in the raid?"

"It's possible I don't have all the facts. Eighteen Sumiyoshi were shot dead during the raid. Is one of them the trafficker? Maybe. Is Iwata one of the dead? I need to head into the office and find answers to all these questions."

"Yeah, I'll come with."

"Sterling, until I get a handle on this situation, I think you should stay here. You were at the warehouse. If Iwata hasn't been killed, you will be suspect number one for tipping off the police. The Sumiyoshi might start looking for you."

"Yeah, you're right. It's a good thing I switched hotels. I bet Iwata is on his way there now unless he got caught up in the raid."

"Just hang out here for the day. You can help my father at the shop. I'm sure he'll be happy to have you there. We'll regroup this afternoon."

Iwata and Mizuno were in Iwata's apartment watching the news reports on the warehouse raid. They had only gotten word an hour ago, as they had both gotten drunk the night before and slept through multiple phone calls and text messages.

"I can't believe it," Mizuno said. "They took it all. Plus, they killed Kitagawa and all his men. What if Kitagawa already told the bosses about Jimmy? I mean Gray. Everyone will blame us."

"We don't know what Kitagawa said to anyone, if he did say anything. What we need to do is find Gray."

"And what then? We turn him over to the oyabun?"

"We can't do that. If they find out we brought a gaijin into the warehouse and two days later it's raided, everyone will think he tipped off the police and blame us. This will cause great trouble for the organization. We must find a way to make them believe they are shielded from this mess. Not even my uncle can save us in that situation. We have to hope Kitagawa or his men didn't say anything."

"How can we be sure of that?"

"We can't, but Kitagawa and his men are all dead, so there's no one to make the case to my uncle. We need to find Gray. He's the only one who can prove we took him to the warehouse. Call that hacker now and find out if he has news for us."

"And then what?"

"Gray is the loose end. The only way we can cover ourselves is to kill him."

25

Four men dressed in black and navy blue suits arrived at the teahouse in the Rikugi-in gardens. The garden dated back to the Edo Period in the seventeenth century and is located in Komagome, a peaceful and quiet district in north Tokyo. It had recently become a favorite meeting spot for the Sumiyoshi leadership because of the privacy the teahouse afforded them.

They had gathered quickly to discuss the raid that had taken place earlier that morning. The oyabun, the leader of the Sumiyoshi, would be expecting to hear answers soon. The men removed their shoes one by one before stepping onto the fragile tatami mats covering the floor. In the center of the room was a long table made from teak wood. The men sat around the table as a server quietly poured the tea. Once she had finished and left the room, one of the men cleared his throat: Shingo Matsumura, the so-honbucho.

"We all understand why we are here," he said. "First, allow me to apologize, as security and logistics fall under my responsibility."

The other three men in the room nodded. The saiko-komon, the assistant to the oyabun, shared equal power with Matsumura. The two other men were the wakagashira, second-in-command, and the shateigashira, the third-in-command.

"Shingo, we know what the news media is reporting, but will you tell us what you know?" the saiko-komon asked.

"What I've learned so far is no different than what is being reported. As you know, we lost all of our men at the warehouse, so there is no one to report otherwise. We must piece together information as we obtain it."

"I heard your nephew, Sora Iwata, was at the warehouse a few days ago," the shateigashira said.

"Yes, it's normal for him to be there as this is his operation. With my approval, he tasked Kitagawa and his men to provide security."

"I also heard he likes to party with gaijin."

"Gaijin? Who told you this?" the wakagashira asked.

"It's no secret. Sora loves to go to Shinjuku and spend the night drinking in the Golden Gai."

"I've heard the same news as you. But the Golden Gai is very popular with foreigners visiting Japan," Matsumura said. "Should he avoid all areas that the gaijin frequent?"

"Sora has been seen drinking with them, not among them."

Matsumura leaned forward. "Are you suggesting something?"

"The police had to have received a tip about that location. Iwata might have had too much to drink one night and opened his mouth when he shouldn't."

"Shingo, we shouldn't rule this out," the saiko-komon said. "We must look at everything before we meet with the oyabun."

"You are right. I will speak to Sora today. If he's involved, he will be dealt with."

"And if he's not, we still have a problem," the shateigashira said. "When Sora brought this idea to traffic weapons to us, one of my concerns was that it could cause problems for the organization."

"So far, it's been a positive thing," Matsumura said. "We are in a position to take on the Yamaguchi. They came to our turf, and we ended all of them. This problem at the warehouse is the first that we've had."

"But it's a big one. Even if Sora has nothing to do with the raid, he is still responsible for what happened there."

"I will speak to Sora and find out what he knows."

Iwata had been waiting all morning for the call from his uncle. As much as he had hoped that word about Gray visiting the warehouse had not gotten back to Matsumura and had died with Kitagawa and his men, he couldn't be absolutely sure. When his uncle called, his voice remained even-keeled like it always was. Iwata didn't detect any anger, nor did he hear any levity in it. But his uncle wasn't the type to be friendly on the phone, especially after what had happened that morning.

Still, he was shaken when he heard his uncle's voice on the other end of the line. He wanted to meet with Iwata right away.

"Do you want me to come with you?" Mizuno asked.

"No, he asked only to see me."

"We expected him to call. Those weapons are our doing; now, it's all been confiscated, and many Sumiyoshi men were killed. He has questions."

"You're right. If I were him, I would have also asked for a meeting."

"What time is your meeting?"

"Now, at his apartment in the city." Iwata looked himself over in a mirror.

"Change into a fresh shirt. That one has too many wrinkles," Mizuno said.

"I'll take a quick bath and put on a clean outfit," Iwata said.

"Do you want me to wait downstairs?" Mizuno asked when Iwata was ready to leave.

"No, I want you to keep working with this hacker. He's taking too long to find out any information about Gray."

"I'll see you when you return."

26

Iwata's uncle kept an apartment in the Aoyama neighborhood, the wealthiest place in Tokyo. However, it wasn't his permanent residence; he had a grand home in a discreet residential area called Denenchofu. Celebrities, diplomats, and top government officials all sought one of the highly coveted addresses there. Usually, when Iwata visited his uncle, it was always in Denenchofu because that place was reserved for family and close friends. His residence in Aoyama was where he hosted meetings. And being asked there gave Iwata reason to worry.

Iwata did his best not to overthink the situation. This was his uncle he was seeing, the brother of his mother, whom he was close with. If anything, his uncle would be looking out for Iwata. The weapons had been a huge coup for Iwata. No one believed Iwata knew how to bring the guns into the country or even had the capital to fuel such a plan. But Iwata told his uncle and the others that the cost was minimal.

But for the operation to work, Iwata insisted the way he brought the weapons into the country be proprietary information that only he would be privy to. He argued it was for everyone's protection. This would ensure that the Sumiyoshi could not be tied to the trafficking. They could deny any involvement and, if need be, point the finger at Iwata. At worst, all the government would be able to prove is that the Sumiyoshi were nothing more than customers buying illegal goods.

Many members of the organization dismissed Iwata, calling him cocky, but Iwata's uncle gave him the support and confidence to try. If he were successful with a test run, he could slowly gain the trust of the leadership and begin to move larger shipments into the country.

And that's what Iwata did.

He started small, with just a few weapons. Once he proved himself, he brought in larger shipments. He charged the organization a fraction of the costs to arm their members. No one could figure out how Iwata brought the weapons in or how he could sell them to the Sumiyoshi at a reduced rate. But he did, and not only that, but also he kicked up a portion of the proceeds to the bosses. No one complained about that.

After a year, whatever doubt there was about Iwata's operation had disappeared. Arming the Sumiyoshi with weapons that no other syndicate had access to slowly made them the strongest. They still couldn't match the membership numbers held by the Yamaguchi, but they had them outgunned. And they proved that when they decimated the men the Yamaguchi had sent to Tokyo.

But Iwata's silver bullet was leaving it up to leadership to determine how the Sumiyoshi wielded their newfound power. He knew they would believe they were in control by conceding that decision. Even though they weren't.

Iwata arrived at his uncle's place on time. Two Sumiyoshi men greeted him when he entered the building and promptly escorted him to the seventh floor. His uncle owned the entire top floor. No one in the building, not even the management, had access unless he gave the okay.

The men escorted Iwata into the apartment and told him his uncle was in his office. Just then, Iwata's phone buzzed. Jun had messaged him with an update. It was just three words: Gray is FBI.

"Sora!" Matsumura called out from his office. "Come inside."

Iwata swallowed as he erased the message and pocketed his phone.

"Ojisan," Iwata said, bowing in the doorway.

"Sora, welcome," Matsumura said. "Please sit down. Forgive me for moving straight to the point of our meeting."

"You are a busy man. How can I be of help?"

"We all know what happened this morning. A lot of good men were lost. Kitagawa being one of them."

"Yes," Iwata nodded. "Very unfortunate."

"How did the police find out about the warehouse?"

"This is a good question. I'm still looking for the answer. It's even harder since I cannot talk to Kitagawa or his men. Jun and I were there a few days ago. There were no problems from what we could see, so we were also surprised by the raid."

"The police had to have been watching the building for some time. Do you think they saw you and Jun there?"

"I can't answer that, but Jun and I have protocols in place for this very situation."

"Is that so? What are they?"

"We lay low, and all shipments are halted immediately."

"Do you have other inventory in the country right now?"

"I did. I've already moved it and," Iwata looked at his watch. "It should already be safely outside of the country."

This was, of course, all a lie. The police had taken everything Iwata had, but he did not want his uncle to know that.

"The police are reporting that they confiscated over two thousand weapons. How does that affect you? How does that affect your supplier?"

"My supplier is aware of the risks involved. Please do not worry about these details. The less you know, the better. I want to shield the organization. Worst-case scenario, I'll take the fall for everything. You know that."

"Do not tell me what to think," Matsumura said with a raised voice. "I want to know . . . the leadership wants to know who is responsible. This person could make more trouble for us."

"Yes, of course. I understand."

"I've been told you were partying with gaijins," Matsumura said as he eyed Iwata.

Shit! What does he know? "The bars and clubs I go to are open to the public, so of course, gaijin are there."

"Do you want to tell me about this gaijin you were seen with in the Golden Gai?"

Iwata felt like he'd just been punched in the stomach. Why would his uncle bring up a gaijin and then claim that Iwata was spending time with one in particular? *How can he know about Gray? It's impossible.*

There were many Sumiyoshi around Iwata those two nights he was out with Gray. Any one of them could have fed this information to his uncle. But how could they know Gray was an FBI agent? Even Iwata didn't know until just a few minutes ago.

Iwata had to be extremely careful and choose his words wisely. His uncle could know about Gray and who he is, or he could simply be fishing for information. This was typical Sumiyoshi behavior. To make someone believe you know everything when that isn't the case. Of course, the downside is they do know something. Iwata may be the son of his uncle's little sister, but Matsumura would not hesitate one bit to put a bullet in Iwata's head if he was the cause of this mess.

"I'm not sure I understand your question. Do you want to know about gaijin in the Golden Gai? They are mostly tourists out for a fun time. Sometimes I share a toast with them, but this is common behavior in a bar."

Matsumura leaned forward and rested his forearms on the desk. "If you know something, you would tell me, right? I can trust you to do that?"

"I have nothing to hide from you, ojisan. Is there anything else you want to ask me?"

Matsumura held Iwata's gaze for an eternity before shaking his head and leaning back in his chair.

"If that's all, Jun and I want to return to our search for the culprit. Let us show you and the others how loyal we are to the Sumiyoshi. We will find out who this person is and bring him to you."

Iwata's mind had become a mess on the elevator ride to the ground floor. He wasn't entirely convinced of what his uncle knew. But if he really knew of Gray and that he was an FBI agent, Iwata would not have left that apartment alive. Whatever his uncle had discovered, it wasn't enough for him to make a move against Iwata. He was safe for the time being. He just needed to find Gray first.

27

It was only a few hours after Tamura left when Gray heard back from her. And she didn't have good news.

"I sent a few officers over to your old hotel to pull the security footage," Tamura said over the phone. "Iwata and his men showed up. The staff at the reception desk confirmed that they were looking for you, and unfortunately, they gave up your information."

"They what? Why the hell did they do that?"

"Probably because they were threatened. Your cover's blown. Iwata knows your real name, and we have to assume he'll discover you're an FBI agent."

"That means I'm suspect number one for tipping off the police about the warehouse."

"That's right."

"So now what?"

"Well, that depends on you. Earlier, you said you felt the need to see this through. Do you still feel the same way, or do you feel like jumping on a plane and leaving the country?"

"What's your honest assessment of my safety if I stay?"

"Tokyo is a big city, but the Sumiyoshi has the advantage as this is their territory. But with that said, Iwata will want to keep this quiet."

"Why's that?"

"If the leadership finds out Iwata's responsible for bringing an FBI agent to the warehouse, Iwata only has one way out of that situation. And that's in a body bag. So it behooves Iwata to keep this quiet."

"There were other men at the warehouse. One, in particular, was not happy that I was there. In fact, he and Iwata got into a shouting match over it."

"Yeah, you mentioned it before."

"There's also a chance he might have dug into my background. He could blow this up if he found out anything."

"There were a lot of Sumiyoshi killed during the raid," Tamura said. "We have photos of them. I'll email them to you, and you can tell me if one of them is this man."

"If he's dead, then there's nobody to snitch to the bosses," Gray said. "Which is good because then it's Iwata and his men I need to be concerned about."

"The longer Iwata remains alive, the more likely the leadership doesn't know about you. I'll put some feelers out and see if my informants have heard anything."

"Mariko, if I'm a marked man, is it safe for me to remain at your parents' home? I don't want to endanger them."

"It won't hurt for the time being. I'm getting ready to walk into a meeting with my bosses. I'll bring up the idea of a safe house and security detail; that is, if you want to stay. Do you?"

"I do, at least for a little while longer."

"I'll call you when I have the next steps."

"Your father wants me to join him at the restaurant."

"That should be fine. Enjoy your apprenticeship."

"Thanks. I will."

Gray ended the call. Tamura's father had called right before she did, asking Gray to come there. He said goodbye to Tamura's mother and started the short fifteen-minute walk to the restaurant. Along the way, he poked his head into a few eel shops and bought a box of mochi and a few souvenirs for Pratt and Gaston. Gray wasn't especially worried about Iwata. This wasn't the first time he had been targeted. It was part of the job. He decided to stay instead of hopping on a plane that day just to see what the TMPD had planned. Plus, it was an opportunity to further consult with them and steer them back to catching the trafficker. But if taking weapons off the street was more important to the government than catching the man responsible for bringing them into the country, so be it.

Tamura walked into the conference room expecting to have a meeting with just her superior, Asuka Izumi, but found it wasn't just him. Other higher-ups were in attendance.

"Inspector Tamura. We appreciate you meeting with us," Izumi said. "I will get to the point. It has come to our attention that the intel you provided on the warehouse, while excellent police work, was obtained in an unusual manner."

"Yes, that's correct. I did not personally discover the warehouse. Special Agent Gray did that."

The men in the room looked at each other. Tamura had known this conversation would come sooner or later.

"Inspector Tamura, please explain to us how Special Agent Gray obtained this information."

Tamura came clean and told them all about Gray going undercover and meeting with members of the Sumiyoshi.

"Do you understand the risk you put Special Agent Gray in?" Izumi said. "This was irresponsible. Are you aware of the repercussions we would have faced should anything have happened to him? Not only was this operation unnecessary, but it was also unsanctioned."

"This unsanctioned operation allowed you to make the biggest weapons bust in Japan's history."

"That does not excuse your actions. The number of department protocols you broke is reasoning enough for dismissal from the force. Special Agent Gray should have been sitting in an office drafting a profile for you to work off of, not sitting in the bar having drinks with the Sumiyoshi."

"For us to tackle this problem, we needed a fresh approach. Continuing to police the same way we have always done no longer works. Gun violence continued to rise until I did what I did. My actions resulted in the confiscation of two thousand weapons. Had we not moved so quickly, we might also have obtained intel that could have led us to the trafficker. But you thought seeing your smiling faces on television was more important."

Izumi slammed his fist against the table. "Inspector Tamura, do not forget who you are speaking to!"

"I apologize, I am not trying to undermine your authority. I'm simply trying to do my job. You may disagree with my methods, but they have proven successful."

"Where is Special Agent Gray now?"

"He's in a safe location."

"Safe for how long? It won't take much for them to realize that Gray, or Jimmy, whatever his name is, is responsible for tipping off law enforcement."

"I realize that, and so does he. That's why I want the authority to move him to a department safe house and provide a security detail."

"Why would he need that? Special Agent Gray should be on the next flight out of the country. What reason does he have to remain here? We've confiscated the Sumiyoshi's weapons and curtailed any thoughts they might have to exert their force."

"I'm sorry, but that's a bold statement. The Sumiyoshi have been able to bring these weapons into Japan without us finding out. We still don't know how they are doing it. I'm sure they are working out the logistics for the next shipment. When the Americans confiscate a cocaine shipment from the Mexican cartels, it does not stop them. They continue to send other shipments. This is what will happen here, but with weapons. We must go after the trafficker and disrupt his routes."

"While you make a compelling case, we already have a plan. We will crush the Sumiyoshi with force. Their resources are limited at the moment. Now is the time to strike by raiding all their key strongholds. In fact, this operation is already being conducted as we speak."

"Your plan is to round them up and throw them in jail? All four thousand of them?"

"Inspector Tamura, we are both after the same information. We want the trafficker. There is no argument there, but we believe by interrogating key members of the Sumiyoshi, we will learn who is bringing in the weapons and how. This will also send a strong message to the Sumiyoshi and the other syndicates that the TMPD and the government will not allow them to do as they please. This decision is final. Please make arrangements for Special Agent Gray's return to the UK."

28

Within an hour of Tamura's meeting with her superior, the news media began reporting on the raids being conducted by the TMPD. Video footage of the Sumiyoshi being rounded up in handcuffs and hauled off to jail was a powerful image showing who was really in control. By the afternoon, more than two hundred members of the Sumiyoshi had been taken into custody. In addition, hundreds of assault rifles and ammunition were confiscated. Tamura sat in her office surrounded by other officers as they watched the events unfold on television.

"Do they really think this will work?" one of the officers loyal to Tamura asked. "What will they charge them with? Possession of illegal weapons? This won't harm them."

"They think they'll be able to find out who the trafficker is by interrogating these men," Tamura said. "Honestly, I hope it works because they totally screwed up my plan."

A breaking news alert appeared on the television. The TMPD had organized a press conference to address the raids. Tamura's boss, Izumi, was speaking on behalf of the department.

"Today, the Tokyo Metropolitan Police Department executed several raids on Sumiyoshi strongholds resulting in the arrest of over two hundred members and the confiscation of hundreds of weapons and thousands of rounds of ammunition. Fear not, Tokyo. We are here to protect and serve. We will not allow these bōryokudan to intimidate our people or our country."

"This is nothing but a PR stunt," an officer said. "All these old men care about is looking good until they retire. They don't care about the future of Japan. Mariko, tell us you have another plan in place. Tell us you haven't given in to their bullshit."

"I haven't, but I need to be careful. I've been warned. I can't do anything if I'm dismissed from the force. If they get rid of me, they'll also get rid of everyone working for me. Remember that."

"These are bold statements that Izumi is making," another officer said as he watched the press conference. "Does he really want to go to war with the Sumiyoshi? We already know they are heavily armed. Has he even thought about that?"

"I don't think they've thought it entirely through because they still believe in the old ways of policing," Tamura said. "But again, I hope it works because if this results in an all-out war, I fear Tokyo's streets will run red."

Tamura walked out of her office to make a phone call to Gray.

"Sterling, how goes the noodle making?"

"I'm getting better. My noodles are no longer crooked. What's the latest on your end?"

Tamura recapped the meeting with her bosses for Gray.

"Well, that went in a different direction. So the raids have already started?"

"Yeah, they arrested over two hundred Sumiyoshi."

"Any chance one of them was Iwata? If they have him in custody, now would be a great opportunity for you to question him."

"I have someone looking into it for me. If he has been picked up, I'll talk to him. But I need to keep this on the down low. If my superiors find out about Iwata and what we think his connection is, they'll want to take over."

"They'll screw it up if they do."

"I agree. That's not all. They also told me to start arrangements for you to leave the country. They feel as if your services are no longer needed. Though they thank you for the tip."

"I bet they did. So when am I leaving?"

"Well, they told me to start making arrangements, but I've been so busy that I haven't had time to start."

Gray chuckled. "Shall I just stay put until those arrangements are made?"

"Are you okay with staying with my parents?"

"They're great. I'm just worried because I'm still a target if Iwata is on the loose."

"I know, but there's no way the department can be involved with anything about you. Right now, Tokyo is hot. I'll bring you back into the city if it cools down tomorrow. I can put you in a location where I feel confident about your safety."

"Okay. Will you be coming back here later? Your father has already enlisted me as a server for tonight."

"Is that so? You might not be able to ever leave Chiba. You've been adopted."

"I'll let you break the news to him."

"When I have more to report, I'll let you know, but plan to come back tomorrow."

Tamura ended the call just as one of her men approached her.

"Bad news. Iwata and his men have not been arrested. That means they're still hunting for Gray."

Later that night, twenty armed men from the Sumiyoshi had mobilized in a quiet neighborhood in Tokyo where many government officials resided. They parked their vehicles a few blocks from their target location and made their way forward on foot. All of them were dressed in black from head to toe, with balaclavas hiding their identity. The Sumiyoshi leadership had had enough of the TMPD's bold rhetoric spewed across the airwaves. The TMPD had made it seem as though they were in the process of dismantling the organization, which was far from the truth. In addition, the press conferences portrayed the Sumiyoshi as a weak organization in the eyes of the other syndicates and the people of Japan. The Sumiyoshi had no choice but to strike back.

The men hurried down the road in single file toward their target: a large mansion behind a brick wall. Each man was armed with a Kalashnikov MA. Their goal wasn't to make this a quiet hit. The Sumiyoshi leadership wanted a response that would not only grab the attention of the Japanese public but also paralyze the country with fear. The target that night was the TMPD's director and his family.

29

By the time Gray and Tamura's father had closed the restaurant and returned home, news of the massacre at the director's home had spread. Every news media outlet had begun to make comparisons to the recent assassination of Japan's former prime minister, Shinzo Abe. He'd been attacked while speaking at a political event. The assailant had used a home-made gun to shoot Abe at close range.

But what had taken place at the director's home was far from a lone shooter with a homemade gun. Twenty men armed with high-caliber rifles had entered the director's home and shot him and his family while they were having dinner.

When it was later confirmed that the men were associated with the Sumiyoshi, the media was quick to illustrate how gun violence in the country escalated quickly. They posed the same question repeatedly: does the TMPD have the ability to keep Tokyo safe?

For the first time, Gray saw the violence's effect on Tamura's parents. He watched as they sat huddled in front of the television, eyes wide open and mouths agape. Gray wasn't sure if he should say something, not that they would understand him. It was probably best to let them take in the news and deal with it in their own way. What could Gray really say that would make the situation better? How could he relate to the emotions they had to be experiencing? They had lived their entire lives without facing something like this.

The media continued to hit the same talking points about how gun violence in Japan was out of control. Images of the director and the former prime minister were placed side by side, along with graphics illustrating the rise of illegal guns in the country. It painted a sobering account of Japan's current situation and presented a prelude to what was to come.

Since Japan surrendered to the Allies in 1945, it had focused on peace and prosperity. Most Japanese citizens knew only of this way, including Tamura's parents. They were born after the war and grew up in a country that had installed universal suffrage and guaranteed human rights. They stripped the emperor of any political or military power, making the role a state symbol. Japan had also adopted the idea of never leading a war again or maintaining an army. But the events unfolding on television over the last few days told a different story.

Gray had tried calling Tamura to find out what she knew, but she wasn't answering her phone. He figured she was busy and left a message that everything was fine and not to worry about her parents. The last thing Gray expected when he woke the following morning was an escalation. But that's precisely what happened.

Overnight, the TMPD declared war on the Sumiyoshi. To crack down on the violence and end it once and for all, they attacked the Sumiyoshi, raiding every known hangout or business owned or managed by the organization. They arrested anyone found on the premises. It was a comprehensive attempt to lock up as many Sumiyoshi as they could, as quickly as possible.

But the Sumiyoshi fought back.

The TMPD hadn't anticipated that and were caught off guard. They encountered massive firepower from the Sumiyoshi. Not only were they defending themselves, but also the Sumiyoshi had gone on the offensive and began attacking local precincts, wounding and even killing officers. Gray couldn't believe what he saw. He called Tamura again, but she didn't answer. He left a message that he was following the news and would stay at her parents' home until he heard back from her.

Iwata and his men had barely escaped the TMPD when they raided his shops in the Akihabara district. Never in a million years did Iwata think taking Gray to the warehouse would have resulted in an all-out war between the Sumiyoshi and the Japanese government. But it had.

"What the hell are we going to do?" Jun asked.

Iwata led the way up a narrow staircase to a tiny apartment he kept in the building. He, Jun, and the rest of his men filed inside, locking the door behind them.

"We'll be safe here for a while," Iwata said.

"It's a damn war out there," Jun said.

"I know, but we must remain calm and focus on finding Gray. Everyone, reach out to family, friends, contacts—everyone—and spread Gray's picture around. We might get lucky."

"Do you think he's even still in the country?"

"I think he is, and he's helping the TMPD. Why would he leave right after the tip-off?"

Iwata walked over to the closet and pulled out a crate. It was filled with rifles and ammunition.

"Everyone arm yourselves and take as much ammo as you can carry. If my uncle finds out about Gray before we find him, you know what will happen."

30

Tamura had been tied up in the command center at TMPD headquarters ever since the assassination of the director and his family. No one internally ever thought the Sumiyoshi was capable of such brash violence. It stunned the leadership. Even Tamura found herself taken by surprise, and she was considered an expert on the Yakuza. But this move only reinforced her thinking that the way the Yakuza were changing and how the TMPD policed them had to evolve.

The National Police Agency eventually stepped in and ordered the TMPD to retaliate. They wanted every available man on the streets. They even called in backup from the surrounding prefectures. Their strategy was to simply overwhelm the Sumiyoshi with massive manpower. Of course, Tamura argued that it was risky and could escalate the situation.

"The Yamaguchi sent a huge contingent of men to Tokyo for reasons unknown, but we can assume it was to grab territory," Tamura said as she made her case to her direct supervisor, Izumi. "The CCTV footage showed us that there were at least three Yamaguchi for every Sumiyoshi. And they still lost. The Sumiyoshi outgunned them."

"We are not the Yamaguchi, and we are well armed," Izumi countered. "These orders are coming from the commissioner general at the NPA. They have taken over and are coordinating all efforts."

"But all they need to do is look at the footage. Surely, they'll see that they are making the same mistake."

"What are you suggesting we do? We don't have time to sit around and plan an attack. We must respond now. Look, I understand what you're saying, and we were wrong to not have heeded your earlier warnings. But this is the situation, and there's no way to change it."

Tamura felt defeated. She knew Izumi was right. The situation was what it was. And their only real option at the moment was to squash the Sumiyoshi. But that didn't mean they had to give up on her original strategy: find the trafficker.

"The Sumiyoshi are fighting back," Tamura said. "They've gone on the offensive. We must assume they have the weapons and the ammo to continue the fight."

"You think that warehouse was just one of the locations where they kept their inventory?" Izumi asked.

"It's possible, but I'm saying the Sumiyoshi can continue to arm themselves because we still don't know how they are bringing the weapons into the country."

"What do you want from me?"

"Let me continue hunting the trafficker while the NPA hammers the Sumiyoshi. I was making great headway with Special Agent Gray."

"Gray? Is he still in the country?"

"He is. He wanted to take a day or two to sightsee before getting on a plane. But this war erupted. So he's still available for me to utilize. And he has no problem sticking around. If it makes it easier for you, we never had this conversation."

Izumi stood up and walked away. Tamura had her answer.

Iwata and his men remained holed up in the apartment while they reached out to people they knew all over Tokyo in hopes that someone might have seen Gray. Iwata had refrained from checking in with his uncle even though he knew it was good to keep up appearances. He figured with the war going on with the government, it bought him time to find Gray. Iwata felt it was only a matter of time before someone who knew something got in touch with his uncle. Even he and his men shuffling Gray's photo around could implicate them. But he had no choice.

Mizuno's phone rang, and he answered. From the conversation, Iwata could tell it was Mizuno's father on the other end.

"What did he want?" Iwata asked after Mizuno ended the call.

"My father's friend said he's seen Gray."

Iwata sat up. "What? Where?"

"Narita. He has a friend that owns a mochi shop on Omotesando Road. He's the one who saw Gray."

"Are you sure? He saw the photo?"

"There is a lot of gaijin in this area, but I'm sure he's used to seeing them and can tell them apart. It makes sense for Gray to stay near the airport, right?"

"When did he see Gray?"

"Yesterday. I think we should go. We're not doing anything but sitting in the apartment."

"You're right."

Iwata and his men left the apartment within ten minutes and were on their way to Narita.

31

Iwata and his men took the train to Narita even though they were carrying weapons. The staff at the station used handheld metal detectors, and Iwata knew them, so getting past with guns wasn't a problem. Most of the men carried handguns, including Iwata. Mizuno was the only stubborn one who wanted to bring a compact Kalashnikov. He kept it hidden under his jacket.

Omotesando Road cut through three separate neighborhoods. They were looking for the mochi shop in the second neighborhood from the train station. Iwata kept a brisk pace, as he was eager to find out if this lead was a dead end or not.

"That's it," Mizuno said as he pointed.

Up ahead was a typical mom-and-pop shop that was no bigger than 225 square feet. Inside was a display case with various types of mochi inside. Behind it stood an elderly couple.

Iwata and his men stayed outside while Mizuno headed inside. He bowed as he approached the display case. "Nakamura-san. I'm Jun Mizuno. You know my father."

"Yes, I know him. I was expecting you."

Mizuno smiled before pulling up the photo of Gray on his phone and showing it to the couple. "Is this the man you saw yesterday?"

"Yes, this is the man I saw. He bought mochi from me just before lunch."

"Did you talk to him about anything?"

"No, but I saw him later that day."

"So maybe he's staying in a hotel around here?"

"Yes, that might be true. I saw him enter a ramen shop." Nakamura-san pointed down a smaller side street.

"Thank you. You've been helpful."

Mizuno exited the shop. "He's positive it was Gray. He also saw him go into a ramen shop over there. He's probably staying at a nearby hotel."

"Let's talk to the ramen shop owner before checking the hotels," Iwata said.

Mizuno agreed and led the way down the small lane.

Since Gray was in a holding pattern, he continued to help Tamura's father at the ramen shop. He couldn't wait to return to London and invite Gaston and Pratt for homemade ramen.

While Tamura-san stepped out for supplies, Gray practiced cutting the dough into noodle strips. He'd gotten much better since that first attempt, good enough that Tamura-san served some of his noodles. Gray's goal was to hand over an entire batch that was useable.

Gray was in the back room when he heard the front door open. The familiar shuffling of shoes against the wooden floors caught his ear.

"Tamura-san," Gray called out.

Usually, Tamura-san would have answered Gray, but this time he didn't. Gray put his knife down and walked toward the doorway. Tamura-san was peeking out through the curtains that covered the windows.

"Tamura-san?" Gray said.

He turned around and motioned for Gray to come look outside. Gray took a peek. At first, he saw nothing, but then his eye caught sight of several men in the ramen shop directly across the way. One of the men had his finger in the owner's face. He then pushed the owner back against the wall.

Tamura-san gasped when he saw that. The shop owner looked as if he was pleading for his life. Then he started pointing outside. It was then one of the men turned and looked in their direction. Gray recognized Iwata right away.

"Come on, Tamura-san. We have to get out of here now!"

Gray locked the door before grabbing Tamura-san by the arm and hurrying him to the back door that led to a small alleyway. Once outside, Gray noticed Tamura-san was visibly shaken and starting to breathe hard. He could not continue to hurry Tamura-san at a fast pace.

Gray quickly typed a message into a translator instructing Tamura-san to go back home and call his daughter and tell her that Iwata was here. Tamura-san nodded and headed off.

Gray hurried in the opposite direction from Tamura-san and made his way around to the main road in front of Tamura's Ramen shop. There he saw Iwata and his men peering through the shop window. One of the men was jiggling the knob, and just as he was about to kick the door in, Gray called out.

"Hey, Iwata! Are you looking for me?"

32

Iwata squeezed off two rounds just as Gray stepped back behind the building. Over the last few days, he had walked the neighborhood extensively and gotten to know the maze of tiny lanes that made up most of the area. He slipped into a small lane to the right, one big enough for a bike and not much more. A few strides in, he turned left down another lane.

He could hear shouting behind him, though he didn't know what they were saying. Gray didn't have a plan except to try to lose Iwata and his men in the maze of lanes. He'd already decided he wouldn't head back to Tamura-san's home. The last thing he wanted to do was lead Iwata there. He'd have to wait it out until Tamura sent help. Hopefully, she would soon.

Gray cut to the right and then to the left again. The shouting had gotten softer, indicating that he was either creating distance or Iwata's men had split up. Gray cut left again down another lane and ran into one of Iwata's men. The collision sent both of them flying backward and onto their butts. The air had been knocked out of Gray, but he ignored it, rolled over to his side, and kicked the man in the face twice, dazing him further. Gray picked up the handgun the man had been carrying and continued moving. A sharp pain shot up his spine, causing him to stop and clench his jaw.

Sheesh, this isn't good.

He ignored the pain and pushed on, albeit at a slower pace. At least now he had a gun. Gray made his way down another lane, which ran along the backside of a building with many shops selling freshwater eels. There was a small delivery vehicle blocking the path, but the back door to the shop was wide open. Gray slipped inside and found himself in a kitchen, where the shop owner was paying for the delivery.

"Sorry." Gray smiled and bowed slightly. "I go out." He pointed to the front of the shop.

The owner frowned and started yelling. Gray waved the handgun, and the owner shut up immediately.

Gray stepped out of the shop and looked up and down the main road. He didn't see Iwata or any of his men, but the pain in his back was killing him. He slipped out of the doorway and joined a group of tourists walking down the road. He was taller than anyone in the group, so he didn't exactly blend in.

Bam!

Gray looked over his shoulder and saw Iwata and Mizuno running straight toward him with their guns pointed at him. He bolted from the group of cowering and confused tourists and crossed over to the other side of the road just as another shot was fired. This one scattered the crowds of people on the street. A deliveryman jumped on his electronic scooter and began navigating through the group. Gray quickly yanked him off the scooter.

"Sorry, pal. I need this more than you do," Gray said as he hopped on the man's scooter and drove off.

A bullet whizzed by Gray's head, striking a shop's plate glass window and shattering it. Gray looked over his shoulder as Iwata and Mizuno fired more shots. He drove in a zigzag motion, narrowly missing running people over in the process. A child darted out in front of Gray, forcing him to cut left quickly. The front wheel turned too much and sent him over the handlebars and into buckets of freshwater eels for sale. The slithering, slimy eels scurried across Gray as he forced himself to ignore the pain in his back and get back on the scooter.

The gun Gray had lifted from the other man was still tucked into his waistband. He thought about returning fire, but Iwata didn't care about collateral damage. There were still too many innocent people on the road, and he didn't want to add to the firefight.

Gray cranked the throttle on the scooter and made a right into the nearest lane. It wasn't as crowded, and he was able to create distance. He made a series of lefts and rights and felt good about his chance of escape.

When he drove past a capsule hotel, he stopped. He was familiar with these single-person rooms. Anyone could rent out the small space, which was large enough to sit and lie down inside and not much more. He ditched the scooter behind a row of vending machines.

The hotel had a sizeable plateglass window that ran the length of the space. Through it, Gray could see the other capsules facing the road. There were a row of stacked capsules—five on the bottom and five on the top and the place appeared to be self-service. Gray headed inside. He knew some capsule hotels had large chambers to hold a single bed, but these were outfitted with a narrow futon. Two of them had doors indicating they were in use. Gray chose the capsule at the far end on the bottom row. He crawled into the chamber and fed yen into the currency accepter, which allowed him to shut the door. He quickly realized he wasn't able to lock it.

Crap! What are the odds of Iwata or his men walking down this same lane and checking my capsule?

Gray removed the handgun from his waistband and lay down with his feet facing the door. The interior was well lit but made of plastic, as was the flimsy door. The capsule was equipped with a small television with a USB outlet and a map indicating where the communal baths, toilets, and vending machines were located. There were also two complimentary bottles of water and a few toiletries. Gray had a choice of turning the lights off or switching to soft, bluish ambient lighting. He did that.

He dug around in the toiletries and found what he'd been looking for: pain medication. He washed two tablets down with water before checking his phone for messages. That's when he realized the battery was dead.

That explains why I didn't hear from Mariko.

He found a USB cord in the capsule and plugged his phone in. The notifications lit up the front screen as soon as the phone had enough juice. There were a bunch of missed calls from Tamura. Gray quickly called her back.

"Sterling! What happened? I thought you were dead."

"Sorry. My phone died, and I had no idea. Iwata and his men are still in the area looking for me. They're armed and trigger-happy. Have you called your parents?"

"They're fine. I had them leave the house and check into a hotel in another neighborhood."

"Better safe than sorry."

"Where are you now?"

"I'm hiding in a capsule hotel. Let me send you a link to my location. Are you still at headquarters?"

"I am, but I have good news. You and I are back in action."

"Were we ever out of action? Those bullets fired at me earlier seemed pretty real."

"There's a lot to update you on. For now, stay put. I'm on the way."

"Got it."

Gray drew a deep breath after he disconnected the call. The pain in his back was still there but not throbbing like it had been earlier. A bit of rest would really help his back. Plus, Tamura should be there in a couple of hours. He just needed to lay low until then. Like he had thought earlier, what were the odds of Iwata and his men pinpointing his location to this capsule? No sooner had Gray relaxed a little than he heard shouting outside.

You have got to be freaking kidding me.

Gray pulled the door back a sliver, enough to see out through the front windows of the hotel. Sure enough, he spotted Mizuno giving an order to one of the other men. He was armed with one of the compact Kalashnikovs.

It's good he wasn't shooting at me with that thing.

Gray watched as more men showed up. They were checking the shops as they made their way down the street. And then Mizuno pointed at the capsule hotel. Gray heard the front door open and close.

He heard the door to a chamber open rapidly, followed by shouting from the person staying in it. The sound of another door being ripped open rang out, followed by shouting. Gray gripped the handle of his handgun tighter. He knew there were only three chambers with the doors closed. The rest were wide open, and one could easily see they were empty.

Gray heard the man's footsteps grow louder as he neared Gray's capsule.

Any second now.

The plastic door moved as he grabbed hold of the handle.

Don't do it.

The door got stuck in the rails at the first attempt at sliding the door back.

That's a sign, pal.

Gray took aim because he didn't know if the rails would save him a second time.

Just then, Gray heard a pounding on the glass window followed by shouting. The footsteps moved quickly away, and then Gray heard the front door open and close. He cracked the door and peeked out. He saw Iwata gathering his men and motioning them to follow him. A beat later, they all disappeared.

33

Gray awoke to his cell phone buzzing in his hand. It was Tamura calling.

"Sterling. I'm coming up to the hotel now," Tamura said.

"I'm in the last capsule, bottom row."

"I'll see you soon."

A few moments later, the door opened, revealing Tamura's face. "Mind if I join you?"

Gray scooted over, and Tamura crawled inside, shutting the door behind her.

"Very cozy," she said as she lay down beside Gray.

"And comfortable. I fell asleep. Your call woke me."

"Sorry I was late. I stopped by the hotel to check on my parents."

"And?"

"They're good. My father's worried about his shop. He thinks those men broke inside."

"I'm pretty sure I saved his shop by distracting Iwata."

"I'm sure it's fine. Are you hurt?"

"My back. I took a fall while running away from Iwata, but the rest and a couple of pain relievers helped."

Gray stretched an arm over his head. His and Tamura's faces were only inches apart. It was unavoidable, given the space of the capsule.

"Hey, don't look at me like that," Tamura said.

"Like what?"

"You know, like you want to kiss me."

"What makes you think I have that on my mind?"

"Um, because we're lying side-by-side on a small bed."

"You gotta give me more credit than that."

"How many investigations have you been shipped off to?"

"I think this is the fourth one."

"And while away on these investigations, have you ever had sex with anyone you were working with?"

"Define working?"

"I don't need to. You just gave me my answer. I mean, you're handsome, I'll give you that, but this isn't a James Bond movie, so don't expect me to fall into your arms."

Gray laughed. "I promise our relationship will remain professional."

He spent the next few minutes telling Tamura what happened after her father noticed the owner across the road being accosted until one of Iwata's men jiggled the door to his capsule.

"Now that's cutting it close. It'll be harder for you to move around with Iwata looking for you. Plus, he probably sent your photo to his contacts—extra eyes. It's definitely not safe for you."

"Are you suggesting I work out of this capsule?"

"I'm not suggesting anything at the moment. We just need to be extra careful."

"So tell me about this grand plan you have for us now that we're back in action."

Tamura shifted her body so she could lie on her back while she updated Gray on what the TMPD were doing.

"So your government is actually pushing this war with the Sumiyoshi?"

"I don't like it, but I'm afraid our options are limited. They shot and killed the director and his family. We needed a strong response. If we don't strike back hard and fast, that sends a message that we are weak and the Yakuza own Tokyo."

"Yeah, I see your point. It's not a great place to be in."

"The problem is the Sumiyoshi is attacking back. They're targeting kobans in small neighborhoods."

"What's a koban?"

"It's a small office used by officers to serve the community. It can be something the size of a UK phone booth manned by a single person up to a small cottage that supports five officers. They're gunning them down and even setting fire to them."

"Were any officers hurt?"

"A few of them have been wounded. I think one death so far."

"What about the Sumiyoshi? Have they lost men?"

"Yes, quite a few. I expect they'll increase their attacks."

"Boy, did this situation escalate fast. What do you think the Sumiyoshi's real intentions are? It can't be to keep this war going. It could weaken them and make them vulnerable to the other syndicates."

"I don't think they have a plan, and their moves are entirely reactionary."

"Kind of like your government."

"Exactly."

"What will break this feud?"

"I think we'll eventually win the game of brute force, but we must catch the real trafficker."

"So while the TMPD beefs it out with the Sumiyoshi, we hunt for the trafficker. Seems like it could work. Right now, the Sumiyoshi are distracted and prone to making mistakes. We can take advantage of that."

"That's what I'm hoping. I still think Iwata is our number one suspect for trafficking. I want to focus our efforts on finding him."

"Shouldn't be hard, because he's looking for me."

"I know. The trick is catching him, not the other way around. I have men loyal to me looking for Iwata right now in this neighborhood. We might get real lucky quick."

"Do you think the second hotel I moved into has been blown?"

"Probably not, but it's a hotel that many foreigners stay at. Iwata might have contacts there or eyes on the place. I have something else in mind."

"What's that?"

"A rabuho. A love hotel."

Gray thought Tamura was kidding when she mentioned a love hotel. But she wasn't laughing.

"Wait, you're serious?"

"I am. There are over ten thousand love hotels spread out across Japan, a thousand in Tokyo alone." Tamura peeked out of the capsule door. "It's dark outside. It's safe to move now. Come on."

34

The neighborhood that Tamura and Gray had gone to was in the Shibuya district, just next door to Roppongi, where Gray had initially stayed.

"You don't think this area is too close to home?" Gray asked as they made their way out of the metro station. "I feel like at any minute, we're going to run into Iwata."

"Trust me, the area we're heading to is low-key. Plus, he can't search every love hotel. He won't suspect you'll be staying in one. He'll focus on the hotels where gaijin tend to stay."

"Gaijin don't stay at the love hotels?"

"Some do, like backpackers, because it's affordable, but most guests are Japanese couples. And a lot of them are self-service. It's designed so you don't run into other guests."

"Ah, okay. I thought I might stand out as a single gaijin."

"You know, many of these hotels have separate front and back entrances so that a person isn't seen coming to the hotel with their partner."

"Is that coming from personal experience?"

"I have my own place, so I don't need a love hotel. I'm capable of hosting my own affairs."

Gray laughed.

"But really, the reason love hotels became so popular is that for most couples to be intimate, they need privacy. That's hard to come by in this city. Even older couples visit love hotels because their in-laws live with them. Japanese people see it as a completely normal thing to do. It's not considered sleazy, but some hotels can be flamboyant in their appearance."

"I'm assuming we'll avoid those hotels."

"Of course, unless you wanted photos for your Instagram account."

"I'll take a hard pass."

The walk to the love hotel took about fifteen minutes. Tamura stopped in front of a building on a narrow lane with little lighting. The only indication that it was a love hotel was a small sign with a heart and rose.

She pushed the door open and they entered the place. Straight ahead were two touch-screen menus on the wall. Tamura tapped at the screen until the available rooms appeared.

"Do you have a preference?" she asked Gray. "How about an underwater theme? It has a large whale swimming across the ceiling, and there are mermaids."

"Yeah, and the lighting is all blue light. I'd like something a bit more normal."

"They have the naughty maid theme. Ooh, la, la."

"I'm not in a feisty mood. What about that one?"

"A medieval theme? You can be someone's knight in shining armor."

"I like that it looks like I'm in the middle of a forest."

Tamura booked the room and was given the code to unlock the door. They made their way to the second floor.

"It's larger than I had anticipated," Gray said as he walked around the room. "I have a king-size bed, complimentary toiletries, condoms, and an array of packaged sex toys. I think I'm all set."

Tamura giggled. "You'll be comfortable here. There are vending machines on the first floor in case you get hungry. I need to stop by headquarters. There's a chance I might not make it back here tonight. I'll see you first thing tomorrow morning if that's the case. Are you okay with that?"

"Yeah, I'll be fine."

After Tamura left, Gray took a much-needed hot shower. He felt refreshed after; even his back wasn't bothering him anymore. With his stomach grumbling, he headed downstairs to the vending machines. They were loaded with prepackaged foods ranging from curry dishes to noodles. But Gray had a craving for ramen. He decided to poke around outside and see if there was a ramen shop nearby.

He got lucky and found one just around the corner. Only one other couple was inside the shop, probably from a nearby love hotel. Gray kept his head down, sat at the table farthest from them, and placed an order for shoyu ramen.

As he ate, Gray's mind turned to Iwata and how reckless it was for Iwata to take him to the warehouse. If he was the trafficker, he wasn't a complete idiot, but bringing him to that warehouse was an idiot move.

One thing stood out based on what Tamura had said about the younger Yakuza and what he had witnessed while spending time with them. They were very social. On their phones, he saw all of them, even Iwata, visiting all the social media sites. They weren't afraid to post photos and videos, even comment, and like other photos and videos. They had to know the internet was forever. But there they were, being social butterflies, craving attention just as much as anyone else from their generation. It was like that craving overrode common sense.

Was that Iwata's downfall? Did he seek fame? Did he want to be famous, even if it was infamously?

Until the recent events, the Sumiyoshi had managed to put a positive spin on their organization and the Yakuza. They were admired by the younger generation, who weren't old enough to have seen how the Yakuza ruled at their height. They just saw remarkable gangsters.

These actions weren't typical for the Yakuza. In fact, it was the complete opposite. And that was Tamura's whole argument. The new generation was nothing like the old guard. But her bosses wanted to treat them as if they were.

To make matters worse, Tamura didn't have a strong enough voice, or position, to override their thinking. Those men were so steeped in tradition and the old ways they couldn't see the forest for the trees. Gray figured he could make the same case as Tamura, which would also fall on deaf ears.

With that said, the Japanese government had its back against the wall. Even they could see that their options were quickly becoming limited. They would have no choice but to expand their thinking. There was proof, with Tamura's boss turning a blind eye to what she wanted to do.

The way Gray saw things, Iwata might have figured out a genius way to sneak weapons into the country, but he'd also become his own worst enemy. There had to be a way to exploit that and use it against him.

It was clear that Iwata had narcissistic tendencies. He sought attention, even if it was for something illegal. He wanted to shout out to the world, "I did this." Of course he was proud of it. No one had done what he had been able to achieve, and he wanted the credit and the admiration that would come with that.

Gray slurped the noodles into his mouth. They were tasty but chewier than Tamura-san's, which he'd come to regard as the best he'd had in Japan.

If I wanted to exploit Iwata's recklessness, where would I start? That's easy. His social media accounts.

While he continued to eat, Gray perused Iwata's Instagram account. He'd spied Iwata's page the last time they were out. His username was Tokyo Boy, with two pistol emojis.

"Alright, Tokyo Boy. What sort of tea are you spilling?"

35

Gray's escape in Narita still had Iwata fuming on the way back to Tokyo. They were armed, had the manpower, and still, he managed to escape. After searching for a couple of hours, Iwata and his men called it quits.

"You know these FBI agents, they're trained to evade," Mizuno said.

They were hiding out in an apartment belonging to Mizuno's aunt. She was currently in New York visiting friends.

"He must have help. How did he know we were outside that ramen shop or even in Narita? He appeared out of nowhere."

"You're right," Mizuno said. "Maybe he's been watching us. If he's working with the police, they might be following us, or maybe he has access to the CCTV system in the city."

"That's what I'm worried about," Iwata said as he poured himself a whisky. "Maybe the real reason he's here is not the shoot-outs and the weapons, but the trafficking."

"That's a good reason for the TMPD to involve the FBI. You think they sent more than one agent?"

"One, four, or ten agents. It doesn't matter. Gray is the target. He's the one that can be tied to the warehouse and to us. My uncle will have no choice but to put bullets in our heads if he finds out we're responsible for this war with the government."

"What are we going to do? We got lucky on that Narita tip, plus with the chaos outside, your uncle will ask why we aren't fighting against the police. We need to show effort."

"Take some men and find a koban nearby to destroy. Don't forget to take pictures after. That should keep him happy and distracted for now."

At the moment, the only thing Iwata had going in his favor was the fighting. It had the leadership distracted, but it wouldn't last forever. Eventually, they'd turn their attention to the weapons and the warehouse. No one would forget that the warehouse raid started it all.

But his uncle wasn't the only problem Iwata had to deal with. He still had the issue with his supplier. A lot of weapons were lost. Sooner or later, he'd have to answer for that.

Gray had spent the rest of the evening in the love hotel looking at Iwata's social media and his second-in-command, Mizuno's. He also found the social media accounts of the men that worked under those two.

Iwata's posts gave Gray a window into how he thought and acted. It was fascinating from a profiler's perspective. Gray wasn't the first gaijin that Iwata seemed to have taken a liking to. Over the last two years, he had posted numerous photos and videos of himself partying with gaijin, both men and women. It even looked like he dated gaijin. Of course, Mizuno was right by his side.

To Gray, it looked like they didn't have any social barriers between them and others. It didn't matter that they were Yakuza and the gaijin they were partying with were sometimes backpackers. Gray figured if Iwata liked you, he partied with you. He didn't worry about occupations or backgrounds. It helped Gray to understand why Iwata befriended him so quickly. He'd been meeting gaijin for a while. In fact, Iwata's Facebook page showed that he attended an international school as a teenager. He was comfortable around foreigners.

It doesn't seem like Iwata defines himself as just a Yakuza. He probably views it more like a job than a lifestyle, even though it very much is.

That explanation could be the reason Iwata took Gray to the warehouse. It was akin to taking him to the office to prove what he did for a living. In fact, Gray figured Iwata viewed the Yakuza as a way to attain fame and even celebrity status.

Gray better understood why Iwata and Kitagawa got into a beef so quickly at the warehouse. They both worked for the same company but had different perspectives of what that meant—boomers versus millennials.

This wasn't a Yakuza problem but a generational problem. If it happened in corporate work environments, why wouldn't it happen in criminal organizations? Each generation had common personality traits among its age group. It didn't matter much about their ethnicity, the country they lived in, or their jobs.

Iwata was a millennial forging his path and probably believed the generations before him had screwed things up. If he wanted the same successes the older generations had enjoyed, he'd have to obtain it differently.

Now he was a Sumiyoshi forging his way forward with his weapons trafficking. That was his path to success. Kitagawa, on the other hand, was old school. He did exactly what he was asked and was expected of him because he was told that was the path to success.

But what did all this mean to the investigation? Gray knew most millennials shared certain personality traits:

- They are open to change and can quickly adapt when needed.
- They are more imaginative in their thinking.
- They value teamwork and the social interaction it fosters.

It was clear to Gray that Iwata was capable of thinking outside of the box and shying away from tradition. Gray also wondered if Iwata came up with the idea himself. Someone might have brought the idea to him. And if that were the case, then Iwata's role was to recognize the brilliance in the concept.

A picture emerged as Gray continued to contemplate, though it was far from perfect. It resembled Picasso's cubism work. The face had two eyes, a nose, and a mouth. They just weren't in the right places.

36

The following morning Tamura arrived at Gray's love hotel, made her way up to his room, and knocked on the door. Gray answered, wearing a towel around his waist and wet hair.

"Did I catch you at a bad time?" she asked as she glanced quickly at his chest and abs before looking behind him. "Should I have brought three cups of coffee?"

"Funny. Come in." He pulled the door open. "I woke up late." Gray made his way back into the bathroom to dress.

"Did you sleep well?" Tamura called out as she placed the coffee she'd brought on a table.

"I slept fine. Give me a sec. I'll be right out."

A few moments later, Gray walked out dressed.

"I was up late last night looking at Iwata's and Mizuno's social media. It's crazy how much those two post, given who they are."

"Anything good come out of your stalking?" She handed Gray his cup of coffee.

"Their posts confirm a lot of things. First of all, they're typical millennials. Technology and social media are second nature to them. They have a cocky confidence, which you're already aware of, and they're open to new ideas, hence the weapons trafficking."

"They probably only needed a hot minute to consider that idea," Tamura said before she took a sip of her coffee.

"Yup. Goes against the grain. Really out-of-the-box thinking. Another interesting thing I discovered is that I'm not their first gaijin. Iwata and his men have partied with many foreigners: men, women, professionals, and backpackers. Iwata even attended international school as a teen."

"Really?"

"I believe Iwata, Mizuno, and the others can separate themselves from their Yakuza identity. It doesn't define who they are."

"It just a job to them?"

"That's right."

"Plus, he's comfortable around foreigners."

"His guard was down, so I was taken to the warehouse. Iwata craves attention. He knows the weapon trafficking is a huge win and wants credit. I don't think it matters where it comes from."

"He also wanted to prove to you that he could access weapons."

"That's right. That need to show that he was on equal footing led to his bad decision-making. Everything that is happening right now can be tied back to that night. And he knows it."

"What else did you glean?"

"Those were the notable things. But let's pair that up with the weapons in the warehouse. We both found it strange that they had a huge stockpile sitting there."

"It was like they were daring someone to raid them."

"Right. I could justify it if they were selling the weapons, but from what we can tell, they're not doing that."

"Nope, but everything we're learning continues to paint Iwata as the trafficker. I can make the case to my boss to put manpower toward hunting Iwata down and bringing him in."

"Good idea, but there's more. And you won't like hearing it."

"What?"

"My gut—and this is just my gut—but it's telling me Iwata's not the trafficker."

"Wait, what? You just laid out a compelling case that he is."

"I know, but that's the danger. It would be easy to go after him, and we probably should, but I think someone else is running the show, and Iwata is reporting to this person. He wants everyone to think he's the brains of the operation, but I'm not completely sold."

"Slow down, Sterling. Do you understand what you're saying?"

"I do. And that's why I said you wouldn't like it."

"You're right, I don't. It's like you're derailing my investigation."

"I'm not trying to do that. I know we were always on the same page, but sometimes things change. That's the nature of profiling. As I learn, the profile can change. I know it's difficult to hear this. It's difficult for me to put it into words right now."

"Well, you need to start convincing me why Iwata isn't our guy because saying it's a gut instinct doesn't cut it."

"You've always told me that the Sumiyoshi doesn't operate the same way the other syndicates do. And I can clearly see that. I feel that the leadership allowed Iwata to run with his idea because if it worked, they all benefited. If it didn't, Iwata would be punished. There's not much to lose."

"Okay, but I'm still not seeing a point here."

"Stay with me for a while longer. Iwata somehow brings in a small number of weapons. Everyone is happy. He continues with bigger loads each time until they can arm all their members. The Sumiyoshi has slowly moved into a position that will allow them to take over additional turf and the businesses that come with it. But now they have this huge problem of war with your government."

"But the warehouse raid caused that."

"What if the warehouse raid was the final straw that broke the camel's back?"

"You're saying there were already problems."

"I'm saying there's some dynamic internally that's happening because this operation is near perfect. If bringing in weapons was easy, why make a big deal over the loss? Just eat it and move on. The Colombian cartels always do it when they have a shipment of cocaine seized. Their next move isn't to go to war with the US government. But that's exactly what happened here. The Sumiyoshi moved from DEFCON 5 to DEFCON 1 overnight. This can't be tied to Iwata."

"I still don't understand why you think Iwata's not our guy."

"Because the dynamics within the organization are off. I don't know what it is or how it was done, but I believe there were problems within the leadership that had already been brewing. Secondly, if Iwata was the mastermind, he should have been able to calm the leadership down. But he couldn't do that because the operation wasn't his thing. He's going along for the ride just like the leadership had chosen to do with him."

Tamura drew a deep breath as she pondered what Gray had just said. "This is a lot to take in."

"I know. I'm not asking you to get on board right now, but I want you to consider this."

"But the trafficker has to be with the Sumiyoshi. They're the only ones who have access to the weapons. They would be selling the arms to every syndicate if it were someone else. And we've already arrested all the known traffickers. Iwata was the only hard lead I had."

"I know. That's why I'm saying there's some underlying problem within the Sumiyoshi. I can't put my finger on it because I don't know enough about their inner workings or the Yakuza to do that."

"Well, I can answer any questions you have."

"I know, but I don't think it will lead me to where I need to be. Iwata and the warehouse didn't come out of police work. We got there because I was able to assimilate with them."

"So what are you saying?"

"If I'm not mistaken, the Yamaguchi and Sumiyoshi are fierce enemies. I have a radical idea, but at this point, radical is what we need. Do you think you can put me in touch with the Yamaguchi?"

"Why would you want that?"

"Because the enemy of my enemy is my friend."

37

"Are you nuts?" Tamura asked as she stared at Gray.

"I imagine your boss said something similar when you told him you sent me undercover with the Sumiyoshi."

"That was different. We had control of the situation. I can't guarantee your safety with the Yamaguchi."

"All I'm asking for is a meeting with them. They lost a lot of men to those assault rifles. I bet a dollar they're still fuming over it and debating how to retaliate. We have a mutual interest in stopping weapons trafficking. It's a radical idea, but you see the opportunity in it. I can see it in your eyes."

"Okay, even if I were to entertain this idea. How would it work?"

"I approach them as Special Agent Gray and you as Inspector Tamura. We're on the up and up right from the beginning, making this all about the Sumiyoshi. We are not interested in anything they do, nor will we inquire. I want to spend time with them to learn how a traditional Yakuza organization operates. You have to admit, there's only so much one can learn from the outside. And that includes you. Talking to them might help me understand the problems within the Sumiyoshi. I know it's a long way around to figuring out who the real trafficker is. But if we do that, it's a win-win for the Yamaguchi and the TMPD."

"I don't know, Sterling. This is huge."

"I know, but the payoff is huge. First, we need to see if there is interest. Do you have access to them?"

"I do. They already know who I am and my position in the TMPD."

"That's good. Convince them that this is all about the Sumiyoshi. If they say no, we're right back to where we were. But if they say yes, we get to peek behind door number two and all it offers. See if you can set up a meeting."

"And if they say no to a meeting?"

"We put our efforts into finding Iwata, knowing he might not be our guy."

"I should warn you, the Yamaguchi are nothing like the Sumiyoshi. We'll need to mind our manners and choose our words wisely."

"Secure the meeting, and you can coach me then."

While Tamura made phone calls, Gray looked at Iwata's social media. He wasn't one hundred percent sure about his new theory. Of course, Iwata was involved, but what they needed to do was not make the same mistake the TMPD initially made. They needed to capture the mastermind of the operation.

An hour later, Tamura ended a call and spun around in her chair to face Gray. She had a smile on her face. "You were right, Sterling. The Yamaguchi is still very bitter about losing their men."

"They're open to a meeting?" Gray asked as he sat up on the bed.

"They are. They want to meet today."

"Where are they located?"

"Their headquarters is in Kobe, but I haven't run any of this by my boss. Of course, the answer would be no, and it would open up a can of worms. So if we go, there's no protection for us. I was told that you and I are to come alone and unarmed."

"What about the men loyal to you? Do you think they can tag along in the background?"

"Kobe is deep inside Yamaguchi territory. The odds of them sniffing out my men are high."

Gray ran a hand through his hair. "I'd be lying if I didn't say I'm a little uncomfortable."

"Same here. We can still back out."

"That's not going to happen. I just wish we had a fail-safe."

"Our fail-safe is showing respect and being polite."

"It's just a meeting, right? They must have hundreds of meetings with people they do business with."

"I'm sure they do, but those people aren't law enforcement."

Gray scooted across the edge of the bed, so he was closer to Tamura. "Are you cool with doing this? Be honest with me."

"I have the same concerns as you, but like you said, this is just a meeting. They will either say yes or no after hearing our proposal." Tamura glanced at her watch. "If we want to be on time for this meeting, we should leave now."

38

The Nozomi is Japan's fastest bullet train, reaching speeds of 186 mph. The trip from Tokyo to Kobe would take two and a half hours.

"This is the fastest train we have," Tamura said as they walked down the aisle.

"So we'll be whipping by buildings all the way."

"It won't reach top speeds until we clear the city limits. It's gradual. You won't notice that we're moving at a speed that could pancake us in an instant. These are our seats." Tamura pointed at a pair of oversized leather chairs.

"Roomy. It's like business class on a plane."

"It's because I got us first-class tickets."

Tamura and Gray settled into their seats.

"Do they feed us meals?" Gray asked.

"They'll serve a light snack. The trip isn't that long."

Ten minutes later, right on the dot, the train pulled out of the station. When Gray had finished his gourmet light snack and beverage, speakers announced their arrival in Kobe.

"Have they sent you the meeting location yet?" Gray asked as he and Tamura filed off the train. She'd been told they'd be given the next steps to take once they were in Kobe.

"Hang on. I just got a text message. It says a black SUV is waiting outside for us. It looks like we're getting the door-to-door treatment."

"Is that good or bad?"

"I'm not sure."

They quickly spotted the SUV parked next to the curb outside the station. A man wearing a black suit and dark sunglasses was standing next to it.

"I'm Inspector Tamura, and this is Special Agent Gray," Tamura said.

The man opened the door to the back seat and motioned for Gray and Tamura to enter. Once all three of them were in the vehicle, it drove off.

"Is the headquarters in an office building or something?" Gray asked Tamura quietly.

"I'm not exactly sure. I've never done this before."

The first thing Gray noticed about Kobe was that it was a port city much smaller than Tokyo. Secondly, there were mountains, and they were driving straight toward them.

"I'm guessing we're visiting someone's home."

Once outside the city and on the road leading up a mountain, the SUV pulled over to the side. The man in the passenger seat passed black hoods to them.

"He wants us to put them on," Tamura said.

Once they had the hoods secured over their heads, they started driving again. From there on, it was a quiet ride on a winding road with what felt like many switchbacks. They probably traveled for an hour before slowing and turning onto a gravel road. They were told they could remove the hoods when the car came to a stop.

Gray climbed out of the car. Two other men, who had appeared out of nowhere, immediately searched him and Tamura. They confiscated their phones, watches, Gray's wallet, and Tamura's purse. The men left with their belongings without uttering a single word.

"Don't worry, we'll get our stuff back later," Tamura said.

Up ahead was a concrete wall with a solid steel gate. Other than that, it was woods as far as he could see. They were escorted through the entrance gate and met by three men dressed similarly. Behind them was a garden with fine gravel neatly raked in artistic patterns. There were large and medium-sized boulders and small trees strategically placed throughout the place. A pathway made out of flat stone blocks led the way forward.

About fifty yards back was a traditional home complete with wooden framework and a gabled roof that ended in curved points. A veranda wrapped around the house.

"Nice place," Gray said as they followed two men to the home. "Will we be meeting with the godfather himself?"

"He's called the oyabun, and I highly doubt we'll meet with him. We'll meet with the wakagashira or shateigashira, the first or second lieutenants."

One of the men opened a sliding door and motioned for Gray and Tamura to enter the genkan, a sunken space where shoes are removed before entering the rest of the home.

The flooring in the home was covered in tatami mats, which gave off a subtle scent reminiscent of cut straw. Papered sliding doors separated the rooms. The whole place had a calming vibe. They were escorted to a room that had a low rectangular table. There were eight Japanese-style chairs, no legs or armrests, just the chair back, surrounding the table.

The two men who led the way remained by the door. Tamura and Gray sat next to each other on one side of the table. A few minutes later, another sliding door opened, and in walked seven men. Two men stood guard at that entrance, another two stood behind the table near the wall, and the other three, the oldest of the group, took seats at the table.

The man in the middle looked directly at Tamura and spoke a few words in Japanese. She answered in her language.

"For the sake of Special Agent Gray, we will speak in English," he said. "I am Masaru Ito. This is Noriaki Shimada." He motioned to his left. "And this is Shota Fukuzawa. Welcome."

Gray and Tamura bowed their heads and said thank you. Both sides simply looked at each other for a few moments until Tamura nudged Gray.

"Again, thank you very much for inviting us here. We believe what we have to share will be of interest to you. But before I start, I would like to reiterate that we are not here to investigate the Yamaguchi. We are not interested in your business dealings or any internal matters. We are here because we have a common interest: the Sumiyoshi."

Gray quickly recapped the current situation between the TMPD and the Sumiyoshi and what happened earlier with the turf war between the Yamaguchi and the Sumiyoshi.

"We believe the Sumiyoshi is responsible for trafficking high-caliber assault weapons into the country. Left unchecked, this can and will pose a grave danger to everyone in Japan. That includes your organization. You were able to see firsthand the destruction they are capable of. And I'm sure by now you've had time to process this and see where this type of power can lead. Inspector Tamura and I are tasked with identifying the mastermind of the trafficking operation so we can shut it down. Stopping the flow of weapons is our goal."

"Why are you sharing the directives of the TMPD with us?" Ito asked. "I fail to see how this can interest us."

"Because we need your help. As you know, the Sumiyoshi is organized differently from the Yamaguchi. They don't follow the same hierarchy of power. In fact, power in the organization is given to the men in charge of each federation. They are free to make many decisions without needing the leadership's permission. Because of this, it is much more difficult to pinpoint the mastermind. He is not the oyabun or the wakagashira. The dynamics inside the organization are off. I can't pinpoint what it is because I lack the knowledge to understand the inner workings of organizations like yours."

Gray looked across the table and saw nothing but emptiness in their eyes. They weren't buying his pitch. Gray focused his gaze on Ito.

"Ito-sama, my expertise is profiling. I strive to understand people and how they think and operate. By doing this, I can identify suspects based on personality traits, habits, beliefs, and so forth. I believe understanding how a traditionally structured organization like the Yamaguchi operates could provide me the insight I need to connect all the dots."

The three men looked at each other, unsure of what to say or believe.

"Look, the simple fact is the Sumiyoshi is on the verge of changing the dynamics of the Yakuza inside the country. This war the Sumiyoshi is having with the government will eventually spread to the other syndicates. Whether you want to believe it or not, sooner or later, the Yamaguchi will be drawn into this war. This is not a battle that your men can win. Your manpower is not enough to stand up to their unlimited firepower."

One of the men standing behind the three elderly men cleared his throat.

"Ito-sama, may I speak?" he asked.

Ito nodded.

"Special Agent Gray. I am Chihiro Tanaka. You come here telling us we must listen to you or we will face the wrath of the Sumiyoshi. The Yamaguchi is the most powerful syndicate in the world. We have always been the most powerful and will continue to be. How dare you come into our home and tell us otherwise. You said you know very little about organizations like ours, yet you can somehow depict the future and tell us it doesn't look bright for us."

"Tanaka–san, with all due respect, I am not trying to tell you what to do. What I want is to work together. By doing so, we can keep the Sumiyoshi in check."

"And if we don't, we are doomed?"

"I'll point back to your war with them a few weeks ago. You lost five hundred men. They lost a fraction of that. You can stick your head in the sand like an ostrich and pretend that didn't happen or believe it was an anomaly, but I'm here to tell you that it wasn't," Gray said, with his voice rising. "Look, I have no vested interest in what happens to the Yamaguchi. I don't care if you continue to be the largest syndicate in the world. I don't care if you go down in flames. It makes absolutely no difference to me. Because I'm here to catch a trafficker, not bow down to the Yamaguchi. I—"

"How dare you speak to me that way!" Tanaka shot back. "Who do you think you are?"

"You already know who I am."

Tamura grabbed hold of a heated Gray by his arm. "Calm down," she said in a steady voice.

"Yes, listen to your female boss," Tanaka chided.

At that point, Ito raised a hand. "Chihiro."

"Special Agent Gray. Inspector Tamura. Thank you for coming here and sharing your ideas. I ask you to wait while we consider your proposal."

Gray and Tamura were quickly escorted out of the room.

"Mariko, I'm sorry," Gray said as they walked down a hall. "I don't know what happened in there. I just . . ."

"I understand. It can be frustrating talking to someone who isn't open-minded."

"Exactly, but still, I shouldn't have lost my cool. I probably blew it for us."

"Until we hear their answer, let's not jump to conclusions."

39

Gray and Tamura were taken to a room and told to remain there until a decision was made. The windowless room had a low-level table, chairs, and nothing more. On the table were a teakettle, cups, and bottled water. A few minutes later, two women entered the room, placed two bamboo bento boxes on the table, and left.

"They're feeding us. So it can't be all that bad," Tamura said as she lifted the cover off one. "Come and eat. It's disrespectful to refuse food."

"I still can't believe I lost my temper back there," Gray said as he ate. "It's unlike me. I don't know what happened."

"You're frustrated. I'm frustrated. We know what we need to do, but we, unfortunately, need to involve others. And they don't see things as clearly as we do."

"I don't know how you manage to deal with this every day with your bosses."

"It's not easy. I've often thought of leaving the force, but I get a win every so often, and I decide to stay." Tamura leaned across the table. "Also, be careful of what you say. The room is most likely listening."

"What do you think? It was difficult to read their faces back there."

"I think we have a fifty-fifty chance. And that's good. That means they're actually having a conversation and debating our proposal. The worst would have been us being escorted back to the car."

"When you put it that way, I can see we're in the best position possible."

After eating, Gray and Tamura sat quietly, lost in their thoughts for the next hour. Suddenly the door opened, and in walked Tanaka, breathing slightly hard. The look on Tanaka's face told Gray he was still heated from their earlier exchange.

Tanaka's gaze settled on Gray. "Special Agent Gray, do you think Inspector Tamura can protect you? Do you think the TMPD can protect you? Is that why you disrespected me in front of my brothers?"

Gray sat up straight. "I apologize, Tanaka-san. I should have kept control of my emotions. I meant no disrespect."

"I have contacts at Interpol. They know nothing of you coming down here. That tells me you two are not here on official business."

"Interpol doesn't know everything," Tamura said. "I can assure you Special Agent Gray is very much a part of this investigation, which is very official."

"Silence!" Tanaka shot Tamura a nasty look.

"Does anyone know you are here in Kobe, locked away in the room, in a home high up in the mountains? You know how easy it would be for you to disappear?" Tanaka looked at Tamura. "That question applies to both of you."

Gray cleared his throat. "With all due respect. I am very much aware of the dangers of coming here. It didn't stop me. I'm an FBI agent. Situations like this are not uncommon in my line of work. With that said, I am not in favor of losing my life. I'm here because I believe with the Yamaguchi's help, we can catch the trafficker. It's a win-win situation. That is my goal. Nothing else about the Yamaguchi or their dealings is of concern to Inspector Tamura or to me. Prosecuting members of the Yamaguchi is the furthest thing from our minds."

A sinister smile appeared on Tanaka's face. "If it were up to me, I would have already severed both your heads."

Tanaka spun around and walked out of the room. The guards outside the room escorted Gray and Tamura back to the meeting room. The same men were waiting in the room, all in the same positions. Gray and Tamura took a seat at the table.

"We have made a decision," Ito said. "It did not come easily. Chihiro Tanaka made a very strong case to dismiss your proposal. Special Agent Gray, we understand that you have already been ordered to leave Japan. But here you are, supposedly working on an investigation that has not been sanctioned by Interpol or the TMPD."

"Ito-sama, if I may explain that situation," Tamura said.

"There is nothing more to explain. We have made our decision." Ito concentrated his gaze on Gray. "You are the best at what you do . . . am I correct?"

"Yes. That is what I've been told," Gray said.

"Well, then, Special Agent Gray, we are willing to see what you are capable of. Your proposal has been accepted."

Gray let out a breath of relief. "Thank you very much."

"There are rules that must be followed," Ito said.

Two men walked over to Tamura and ordered her to stand up.

"Breaking any of these rules will end our agreement."

The men then promptly escorted Tamura out of the room.

"First rule is only you will be allowed to remain here. Inspector Tamura will not be allowed to remain in Kobe and will be escorted back to Tokyo immediately. The second rule is that you will stay at our chosen location. The third rule is you will have a chaperone with you twenty-four hours a day. Do not try to separate yourself from him. If you are in agreement, I need an answer right now. Yes or no?"

"Yes."

40

As the Yamaguchi filed out of the meeting room, another man entered, one Gray hadn't seen before. He looked thirty to thirty-five, wore wire-frame glasses, and had a pleasant smile.

"My name is Daichi Yoshida." He extended his hand. "I will be your chaperone during your stay with us."

Gray shook Yoshida's hand. "It's nice to meet you. Will I be staying here?"

"No. I will take you to another residence owned by one of our members. He has graciously allowed you to be his guest there. If you would follow me, we can be on our way."

A car with a driver was waiting for Gray and Yoshida outside the gate. They both climbed into the back seat.

"I must ask you to put this on," Yoshida said as he handed Gray a black hood. "I hope you understand."

"Of course."

The car began to move as soon as Gray slipped the hood over his head.

"I thought we could take this time to go over what we are allowed to discuss," Yoshida said. "As it pertains to the Yamaguchi, I've been given permission to share information about our past, the founders, the organization's rise, our hierarchy, and the rules we abide by. You can ask me any question, but it doesn't mean I will answer."

"I understand. I'm excited to hear more."

"Now for the rules regarding your stay. You will not be allowed to leave the residence unless I'm in attendance. I will approve or deny all requests regarding an outing. Are we clear?"

"Very much."

Once they were off the mountain and back in the city limits, Gray was allowed to remove his hood.

"Are you from Kobe?" Gray asked.

"I'm from Osaka, not far from here. Have you been there?"

"No, my time in Japan has been spent in Tokyo. Do you mind if I ask how many years you've been a part of the Yamaguchi?"

"Eleven years."

"Eleven? I assumed most recruits are under the age of twenty-two when they join. You look between thirty and thirty-five. So a bit older when you got involved."

"Your intuitions are spot on. I am thirty-five and was much older than the average new recruit."

"So you finished university, I assume. What persuaded you to join?"

"I thought the prospect of becoming a salaryman for life was depressing. Being locked into one company, showing the ultimate loyalty . . . I didn't think it was for me."

"Forgive me if I come across as naïve, but what is the difference between being a salaryman and being a member of the Yamaguchi? Aren't you still locked into one organization for life? And if you were to leave, I assume reintegration into society would be difficult."

"It is true in that regard, but in this organization, I do have more freedom. To answer your question, I can leave if I want to. The reason men did not leave in the past is because of what you said. Acceptance back into society can be difficult. It's easier now. In fact, a lot of members have jobs or businesses outside of the organization. Believe it or not, our objective is to blend with society. We do not want people to fear us. Most of our dealings will never affect them anyway. What we want is a cohesive relationship with the people of Japan."

"That's interesting. So is that the freedom you speak of? The ability to have this other side of you that has nothing to do with the Yamaguchi?"

"That's correct. A salaryman is a company man and nothing more. That is his entire worth, his reason for existing. It becomes his identity."

"So, are you allowed to tell me about the Yoshida outside of the Yamaguchi?"

"Of course, Daichi Yoshida is a classically trained guitarist who has performed worldwide."

"You're kidding me, right?"

"It's true." Yoshida shrugged. "The guitar is a passion of mine. It has been since I was seven. Sometimes I perform by myself. Sometimes I'm part of a quartet. I have, on occasion, performed with a chamber orchestra."

"That's amazing. Do you have any plans to pursue it further?"

"I'm happy with what I'm doing now."

"Is this balance of an outside life and the organization unique to the Yamaguchi?" Gray asked because he saw this with the Sumiyoshi, too.

"It was at first, but the other syndicates have also pushed members to do the same. But it's not for the reasons you think. This is not about a work-life balance. This is about showing us in a better light."

"A legal light."

"You could say that."

Gray saw the difference. With the Yamaguchi, the separation was strategic. For the Sumiyoshi, it was a personality trait of the younger members.

The car stopped in front of a walled compound. The gate opened, and they drove through. It was a spacious property resembling a tea garden. A large house with traditional Japanese architecture could be seen.

"Whose home is this?"

"Ito owns this house," Yoshida said. "He stays here occasionally when he's in the city. I've never known him to lend his home out to a stranger. You must have left a positive impression on him."

"That's surprising to hear. Were you in the room when they were debating?"

"It doesn't matter how the decision was made. You're here now."

The car stopped in front of the home, and they climbed out of the vehicle.

"Are you hungry?" Yoshida asked.

"I could eat."

"Very well. We'll have lunch in the garden."

Right away, Gray noted that the house had the same minimalist decor inside as the one on the mountain.

"Will it just be you and me staying here?" Gray asked as he followed Yoshida down a hallway.

"Yes. This is your room," Yoshida said as he walked into a bedroom. "I know you didn't plan on staying here. But you'll find all the necessary toiletries in the bathroom." Yoshida gave Gray a once-over. "I will have some additional clothing brought to you. I'll come and get you when lunch is ready."

The bedroom was basic: a bed, a dresser, and a desk with a chair. No TV, laptop, or phone. Gray was completely cut off from the outside. Was that part of the plan?

A pair of sliding doors opened to a small empty closet. At least the room had a window with a view of the backyard. The attached bathroom was much larger than he'd anticipated. It had an open bathing area with a showerhead and a stool for sitting. There was also a soaking tub. Gray took a moment to freshen up. A little later, there was a knock on the door. It was Yoshida.

Lunch was served on the veranda at the back of the house. It was a simple bento lunch.

"Have you formulated any questions yet?" Yoshida asked.

"I am curious to know what Yamaguchi's thoughts are on the war between the Sumiyoshi and the government and what, if anything, you were thinking of doing."

"What is happening between them has nothing to do with us. At the moment, we're watching to see how it plays out."

"That makes sense. Right now, the war could weaken the Sumiyoshi, which works in the Yamaguchi's favor. But I still think it'll take a turn for the worse if it drags on."

"I agree, but I don't think the Sumiyoshi can win this war, even with all their weapons. The government is too powerful. They haven't even involved the Japan Self-Defense Forces yet."

"If it got to that point, I have to think it would be a dark time for the country, but I also believe the government will do whatever is necessary to come out on top. They have no choice but to do that."

"That is why we're comfortable sitting and watching. There's no need to involve ourselves prematurely."

"What would trigger Yamaguchi's involvement?"

"That's a good question. I don't know."

"I'm guessing signs of the Sumiyoshi winning, or worse, the government striking a peace deal with the Sumiyoshi. That could involve the government targeting the other syndicates."

Yoshida didn't respond and continued to eat.

"One thing that surprises me is that there wasn't any retaliation after losing all those men," Gray took a sip of his miso soup. "With the Sumiyoshi distracted, wouldn't this be a perfect opportunity to flank them?"

"That decision can only be made by the leadership. For now, they are in a holding pattern."

"Or in shock. I'm guessing the Yamaguchi has never faced a loss like that."

Yoshida smiled. "You're very astute. I imagine that's why you work in Behavioral Analysis."

"Something like that."

"After lunch, I thought I would take time to provide an overview of the Yamaguchi's history and how our organization works. After that, you'll have free time to do what you want. I am very interested to see what comes from your thinking and how it can help us. I will tell you now that it is to your advantage and safety that you make it worth our time. That's my motivational speech for the day."

41

Most of the history lesson that Yoshida gave Gray was familiar ground. Not much had changed in the way the Yakuza operated over the years. Yoshida did, however, show Gray his irezumi—body tattoos. But other than that, Gray found the information useless for his needs. He didn't think Yoshida was holding back information. He just didn't know what Gray was looking for. Not even Gray knew the answer to that. He would have to find some way to guide Yoshida.

After dinner, Gray spent the rest of the evening in his bedroom working. He tried to come up with more pointed questions or even topics of conversation that might open up new thinking. But it was difficult because he wasn't sure what he was searching for. He needed to keep talking with Yoshida and hope they'd crack an angle.

For one or two moments, Gray thought he had made a mistake coming to Kobe. But he quickly shook off those thoughts. He had to believe something would come out of it. He was staying in the home of the second-most powerful Yamaguchi. That had to produce something worthwhile.

Not having Tamura around didn't help either. She'd proven herself to be a great sounding board. Sitting alone in his bedroom wasn't the ideal environment. It made him feel sluggish. Yoshida had provided him with a pair of pajamas. He called them jinbei. They were made up of a top that looked like a short-sleeve kimono and matching shorts. Comfortable loungewear is what Yoshida labeled it.

Later that night, Gray felt a growl in his stomach and decided to leave his bedroom in search of the kitchen. The rules given to him said nothing about staying in his room. They were to not leave the premises. Yoshida never bothered to give Gray a tour of the house, so he decided to do it himself.

It was a little after eleven when Gray stepped into the hall. All the lights in the house were off except a few lamps. Gray didn't even know where Yoshida's bedroom was. He knew the way out the back of the house and the front of the house. He wasn't sure if the place had an alarm and if opening either door would trigger it. Gray continued down the hall, past closed sliding doors. He didn't hear anything as he walked past them.

He eventually found himself in the kitchen. He opened the fridge and saw that it was stocked with various beverages. He grabbed a bottle of unsweetened green tea and chugged half the bottle. He opened a few containers, found one holding dumplings, and popped it into the microwave. While he waited for it to heat up, he looked through the cabinets and found one stocked with instant ramen. Gray noted a hot water heater was already filled with hot water.

With his steaming hot dumplings and a bowl of ramen, Gray took a seat at the island in the center of the kitchen and began eating. It felt surreal because nothing about the place screamed Yakuza. It felt and looked like your average home—he was eating leftovers from the fridge. It didn't get any more normal than that.

Gray slurped the noodles into his mouth. They weren't as good as Tamura-san's homemade noodles, but they were good.

"I see you found the kitchen."

Gray looked up and saw Yoshida standing in the doorway. He was also wearing a jinbei.

"I like to eat late at night, too," he said as he opened the freezer and took out a container of ice cream. He put one scoop into a bowl and took a seat opposite Gray.

"What flavor is that?" Gray asked.

"Matcha green tea," Yoshida said. "Help yourself."

"I'm good with the dumplings and ramen. Do you live here? I ask because of the leftovers in the fridge."

"I have been staying here for the last three days. My place needed some repairs."

"I see I'm not the only one who is liked by Ito."

Yoshida ate a spoonful of ice cream. "Have you any progress to report?"

"I don't, but I am giving it much thought. How much time do I have?"

"Not much."

Yoshida finished his ice cream and placed his bowl into the dishwasher. "Good night."

"Same to you."

42

The following morning Gray woke with the rising sun. He hadn't slept well. Nightmares about being unable to access any information kept him tossing and turning. He knew he was at a disadvantage without any access to the internet. One doesn't realize how dependent they are on the World Wide Web until they have it stripped from them. Trying to recall Iwata's social media instead of just looking through it wasn't helpful at all.

You know what, I'll just tell Yoshida that to do my job, I need access to the internet. It's in everyone's best interest that I'm successful.

Gray lay in bed for another hour before forcing himself to shower. After, he dressed in the jeans and a polo shirt provided by Yoshida and made his way to the kitchen. He found Yoshida already fixing himself a coffee using the pour-over method.

"Can I make one for you?" he asked.

"Only if it's no trouble."

"None at all."

A few minutes later, Yoshida placed a cup of coffee in front of Gray. "Mmm, this is delicious. What kind of coffee is it?"

"It's called sumiyaki coffee. Instead of using hot air, these beans are roasted using charcoal. It gives it a much fuller, smoky flavor."

"Yes, that would be the way to describe it."

"Did you sleep well last night?"

"To be honest, I didn't. My mind wouldn't shut off from work. I do have a request. Is there any way I can get access to the internet?"

"I'm afraid that's not possible. You could easily upload messages and photos about your stay here, and that can't happen."

"Would it help if I said I wouldn't?"

"No."

"I hate to admit it, but I had no idea how reliant I was on the internet."

"Anything you need to know about the Yamaguchi, you can ask me. You'll receive information from the source rather than a third party."

"I realize that, but sometimes I'm looking for context. For instance, I find it interesting to look through social media belonging to the members of the Sumiyoshi."

"Tell me what you're looking for, and I'll fulfill your query."

"Eh, it doesn't quite work that way. I don't know exactly what I'm looking for, but just looking can trigger a thought. Does that make sense?"

Yoshida nodded. "The answer is still no. You've received an invitation today from Katsuhito Serizawa, the oyabun."

"The head of the Yamaguchi wants to meet me?"

"He would like you to join him in his personal onsen."

"That sounds like a big deal."

"It is. You must be on your best behavior. Disrespect him, and there will be nothing anyone can do to spare your life."

"That's comforting to know."

"You can ask questions, so I would use that valuable time wisely. Please be ready to leave in two hours."

Upon their departure, Gray was ordered to wear the hood, as he expected.

"The house where my meeting with Yamaguchi was held, is that where the oyabun lives?"

"No."

"Is he in Kobe or outside of Kobe?"

Yoshida didn't answer.

"Okay, I get it. No more questions about where we're heading."

They drove for what felt like thirty to forty-five minutes. Gray hadn't seen his watch since his initial meeting with the Yamaguchi.

When Gray was finally allowed to remove the hood, they were already inside a walled compound. Ahead was a large mansion with western architecture. The home's second floor could easily give a view over the wall. He wondered if he would only be allowed on the ground level of the property. The second thing Gray noticed was the high number of Yamaguchi men positioned inconspicuously throughout the grounds. A quick count already had him at fifteen before he was ushered into the house.

No tour, of course, once he was inside. He was led down a hall that bypassed most of the house and asked to step into a small changing room.

"Please remove all your clothing. I'll be waiting outside." Yoshida said as he closed the door.

Gray started stripping off his clothes.

"I don't see a robe or swimming trunks," Gray called out.

Yoshida opened the door and handed Gray a small face towel. "Clothing is not allowed in an onsen. You may use this towel to wipe your face, but do not let it touch the water. Please follow me. There are four bathing areas in the onsen; each pool of water has a different mineral composition. Please follow the oyabun's lead when he changes from one pool to another."

"Got it."

They entered an open shower area. There were wooden footstools placed in front of faucets and handheld showerheads. Each area had a small shelf lined with liquid soap and shampoo. There was also a bucket made out of bamboo next to each stool.

"Please scrub your entire body and wash your hair. You must cleanse your body of all the dirt collected on the way here."

Gray took a seat and did what Yoshida asked.

"The oyabun is already inside the onsen waiting for you. Please bow upon seeing him and sit in the pool of water opposite him, not next to him."

"How shall I address him?" Gray asked as he poured a bucket of water over his head. "Is there a title I should use? What do you call him?"

"You are not a member of the Yamaguchi, so you would not address him in the same manner as I. If required, you may refer to him as Serizawa-sama."

After Gray finished scrubbing his body and rinsing off, Yoshida led him outside the house to an area resembling a cross between a grotto and a Japanese garden. Smooth boulders separated the four pools of water. Flat rocks formed individual seats inside the pools. Some were large enough to swim across; some were small enough that no more than four people could fit comfortably. Two of the pools had clear water, and Gray could see the bottom was covered in smooth pebbles. The water in the other two pools had a milky consistency.

Serizawa was sitting in the pool closest to them and watched as they approached. No smile, no acknowledgment, just hard staring.

Yoshida bowed, "Oyassan, may I introduce Special Agent Gray."

Gray bowed but followed Yoshida's earlier instructions and said nothing. Serizawa motioned for Gray to enter the pool. At that point, Yoshida promptly turned and left them. Gray took a seat on a flat rock opposite Serizawa and placed his towel on a rock. The warm waters were soothing. Tiny bubbles rose to the surface and tingled against his skin.

Serizawa looked to be in his early sixties. He was in excellent shape and had a full-body tattoo. He still hadn't cracked a smile since Gray entered the onsen.

"Special Agent Gray, have you been to an onsen before?" he asked gruffly.

"I have not. Your invitation made my first visit possible."

"The water in this pool is carbonated. The bubbles have a relaxing effect on the body."

"I felt that immediately. This setting is very calm and peaceful."

"I like to come to the onsen daily. It keeps me young and filled with energy." Serizawa held up a balled fist.

"I don't doubt that one bit."

"I am seventy-five years old."

"Seventy-five? You look sixty to me, maybe even a little younger."

"It's because of my diet and the onsen," Serizawa said proudly.

"I hope these waters can do the same for me."

"You are the first gaijin to visit my onsen."

Gray bowed slightly. "I am very honored to be your guest on this rare occasion. Yoshida-san had told me not many people have been allowed inside here or your home."

"This is true, but he has been here many times. He wants to preserve his youth."

"Oh, really?"

"He didn't tell you, did he?"

"Uh, tell me what?"

"He is my mago . . . my grandson."

"No, he did not mention that."

That explains why he chose the Yamaguchi over other pursuits.

"He doesn't like people to know. He fears they will think he is favored. But it's not true. I don't give him any special treatment."

Serizawa stood, climbed out of the pool, and walked to the next pool. Gray followed his lead and, again, sat opposite him. These waters were much hotter than the first pool and didn't have carbonation. Gray settled into the soaking water.

"Why did you come to Kobe to meet with us? Did no one inform you of the dangers?" Serizawa asked.

"They did, but I believed we would both get something out of working together."

Serizawa nodded. "I once allowed a journalist to interview me. He said the story would be a win-win situation. It wasn't."

"I'm sorry to hear that, but I intend to ensure both parties benefit."

"You seem sincere in your efforts. I don't believe this journalist understood that word, so I taught him what it meant."

"Did he learn his lesson?"

"I believe so. I had him cut into one thousand individual pieces and then had those pieces laid out orderly, so I could personally make certain the count was accurate."

"I can assure you I'm here to do my job as an FBI profiler. My role is to help the TMPD catch the weapons trafficker. Nothing more. In fact, I have no jurisdiction here. I'm not even allowed to carry a weapon."

"You are risking your life for a government that isn't yours. I admire your loyalty and dedication to your job."

"It's my job to fight the bad. I don't discriminate when I'm working."

"The younger generation is different. They only look out for their own interests."

Gray shrugged. "Times change."

"We have young recruits, and the ones who fight tradition don't last long. Their mindset is better suited for an organization like the Sumiyoshi. There they can do whatever they wish."

"But isn't that freedom what allowed the Sumiyoshi to arm all their men with assault rifles?"

"You believe they are bringing the weapons into the country?"

"I think it's someone in the Sumiyoshi, but as you know, they are a fractured organization. There is no one set chain of command. And the men are free to make their own decisions. It doesn't work that way in your organization."

"Our way is what made us the largest syndicate in the world. We have operations in every major city."

"I don't doubt that for one minute, but the Sumiyoshi have broken new ground by arming themselves in a way no one has seen before. Those moves do not come from continuing with what worked in the past. It comes from new thinking."

"Both ways have their pros and cons. The Sumiyoshi is four thousand strong. Finding that person won't be easy, but when you do, please let us know how they brought the weapons into the country."

"Surely you and your brightest men have given this some thought."

"We have, but we aren't sure how they are doing it."

"I'd like to ask about your relationship with Yoshida-san if it's okay with you?"

Serizawa nodded.

"You mentioned that he is your grandson. Is he the child of your son or your daughter?"

"My son."

"Was he also a member of the Yamaguchi?"

"He was until he passed away from cancer. Daichi was a little boy at that time. Why do you ask?"

"My curiosity. You also said that you don't show him any special treatment."

"I would lose the respect of my men if they believe that to be true, so I'm harder on him."

"I can see how that could happen. One last question: if he were your daughter's son, would he still have joined the Yamaguchi?"

"I have a daughter, and she would have forbidden it. Your questions are strange, Special Agent Gray. I thought you would ask more pointed questions regarding our organization's operations."

"Sometimes a person has to go out of their way to find the answers they seek."

"Let's hope this detour helps you find the trafficker, or sadly, this will all have been a waste of time."

43

Gray spent another hour or so chitchatting with Serizawa about everything and anything. He believed Serizawa when he said the Yamaguchi didn't know who was responsible for bringing in the weapons or how it was being done. Serizawa had mentioned that they would have already killed the man responsible if they knew who he was. That would have stopped the inflow of weapons but not revealed how it was done. It was important to Gray that they find that out.

On the drive back to Ito's home, Yoshida did his best to find out what Gray and Serizawa had discussed. Serizawa did mention that Yoshida would pry and that it was up to Gray what he revealed. Gray did his best to give Yoshida an answer that sounded like an answer but was nothing more than an empty response.

Back at the house, Yoshida was keen to continue their conversation, but Gray politely declined, telling him all that soaking had made him tired, and he needed a nap.

"We'll talk later, over dinner, if that's alright with you," Gray said.

"Of course. Dinner will be at seven."

"Sounds great."

Of course, Gray had no intention of divulging anything at dinner, at least not until he picked through the conversation himself. Only then would he throw Yoshida a bone. Maybe.

Once back in his room, Gray took the opportunity to rehash everything he'd discussed with Serizawa. The man hadn't revealed anything that answered any of the many questions Gray had percolating in his head. Then again, Gray admittedly didn't ask any pointed questions. His gut told him that was a dead end and a dangerous one to pursue. And anyway, he was much more interested in how the oyabun of the Yamaguchi thought.

He found Serizawa to be normal for the most part if you put aside the whole bit about chopping up a person. The topic that interested Gray the most was his relationship with Yoshida. It felt normal, like what you would expect from any business where the family worked together, yet Gray sensed tension. His question on whether Yoshida would have joined the Yamaguchi if he were the son of Serizawa's daughter was interesting. Had that been true, Yoshida might have been touring the world as a famous classical guitarist. Gray wondered if Serizawa sensed regret from Yoshida? Did he secretly despise Yoshida, considering he didn't want to be there? Was there a similar dynamic playing out in the Sumiyoshi with Iwata?

Gray kicked around the other questions he had to figure out if he could see them in a different light. Still, the most baffling of them was why the Sumiyoshi had so many weapons in that warehouse if they had no intention of selling them.

And what about the other partners involved? Surely Iwata wasn't flying to the weapons manufacturer in Russia and buying the arms wholesale. And the partners that Iwata was in business with, what advantage did they have trading with just the Sumiyoshi? An arms dealer goes where the money is. Why only sell to the Sumiyoshi when they could also sell to the other syndicates? The demand had to be there. Why not fill it and reap the rewards?

Gray scratched his head. He found himself with an armload of questions and a handful of possible answers. It was a confusing place to be in. Especially since he convinced the Yamaguchi that talking to them could lead to answers. So far, no smoking gun had materialized.

It was coming up on seven, and Gray decided to take a shower to wake himself up and out of the funk that all his rehashing had put him in. As he stood under the warm water, his back pelted by the bursts of water from the massage setting on the showerhead, his mind wandered and found its way to the Chinese general Sun Tzu.

One quote that Gray recalled for no specific reason except that it had simply popped into his head came from Sun Tzu's book *The Art of War*: "The whole secret lies in confusing the enemy so that he cannot fathom our real intent."

There was no doubt in his mind that he was confused. So were Tamura and her people at the TMPD and the oyabun of the Yamaguchi. Was it all intentional?

Confuse the enemy, and they won't know your real plan.

Could Iwata be that smart? Was it all smoke and mirrors? And if that really was the case, what was Iwata up to?

Dinner with Yoshida was uneventful. He continued to pry, and Gray did his best to deflect. Gray did, however, broach the subject of internet access again, explaining that it would be helpful.

"I don't understand why you want to surf the internet. If it's that helpful, why make the case to come here and learn from us?"

"It's not a case of one or the other. It's a combination of both."

Yoshida chewed his food slowly for a moment while he thought. "I'll take it under consideration."

"I appreciate it. I, uh . . . never mind."

"What?"

"Why didn't you tell me Serizawa-sama was your grandfather?"

"I didn't see the relevance. How does knowing that help you find a trafficker?"

"You have to understand it usually isn't one piece of information that leads to an answer. Most often, it's a series of answers and tidbits of information that provide a direction for me to dive into. Profiling is not a cut-and-dried process."

"Why did my grandfather reveal our relationship?"

"I don't know. I didn't ask because I was unaware. But he did say you were not a huge fan of people knowing this."

"I'm not. It can cause problems."

"I can understand that, but surely everyone in the Yamaguchi is aware of it."

"You'd be surprised at the number of people I've managed to keep this from."

"How is your relationship with Serizawa-sama?"

"What do you mean?"

"Do you get along? Are you close?"

Yoshida eyed Gray for a moment.

"Did he say something about that?"

"Nothing in particular. I'm just making conversation here."

"When I'm involved in Yamaguchi business, our interactions are always professional and respectful."

"And when you're at a family function, is it different?"

"We rarely interact outside of the organization."

"He mentioned your father was also a member of the Yamaguchi but passed when you were a young boy. I believe he said it was cancer."

"Yes, that's partly true. He died when I was young, but when I was older, I discovered that cancer wasn't the cause. My father was gunned down."

Gray popped his eyebrows.

"I never learned the exact reason, but I always thought it was to protect me."

"So Serizawa is unaware that you know the truth."

Yoshida nodded.

"Did you learn the truth about your father's death before or after you joined the Yamaguchi? And did it affect your decision to join?"

"I had always thought that I would join the Yamaguchi when I was old enough. Of course, my father still wanted me to attend university and pursue a career in business."

"Why didn't you?"

"I did, but during my first year of university, I learned the truth."

"So, was joining the Yamaguchi about revenge? Did you want to go after the person responsible?"

Yoshida nodded. "And no, I haven't gotten my revenge."

Shortly after that revelation, Yoshida wasn't as talkative. So once Gray finished his meal, he excused himself and returned to his room. They'd stumbled across a sore spot in Yoshida's life, which made the situation awkward. The last thing Gray wanted was to turn Yoshida against him.

Later that night, Gray was abruptly woken. It took a few seconds for him to comprehend that he was repeatedly being punched in the face. Gray fought back, but he had multiple attackers striking him, and he quickly lost consciousness.

The next thing Gray remembered was waking up to bright lights and having to squint until his eyes adjusted. Standing over him was a man wearing a helmet with a metal grill covering his face. It had a ninja-like aesthetic to it. Leather armor covered his shoulders, arms, and chest, and he held a wooden sword in his hand. Gray looked around the room. It had soft mats covering the flooring.

Am I in a dojo?

"Get up!" the man shouted.

Gray didn't recognize his voice and what little of the eyes he could see through the metal slits wasn't enough for him to determine who this person was. He jabbed the tip of the sword hard into Gray's ribcage, causing him to wince from the pain as he curled into a ball.

"Get up, Gray!"

Now that sounds familiar. It's definitely not Yoshida.

The man thrust his sword into Gray's back, causing him to cry in more pain.

"You are so pathetic. You lie there like a little child."

I know that voice. "Chihiro Tanaka. So nice of you to stop by," Gray managed.

Two other men yanked Gray to his feet, and one of them placed a wooden sword in his hand.

"What do you want?" Gray asked.

Tanaka didn't bother to answer and lashed out at Gray with his sword, striking him in the side. Crippling pain rocketed throughout his midsection, nearly sending Gray to the ground, but he managed to stay upright. Tanaka struck Gray with a stinging blow to his outer thigh, causing his leg to buckle. Gray dropped to the mat in agony.

"For an FBI agent, you're not so tough."

Tanaka began to whale on Gray with his sword, targeting all parts of his body. Gray did his best to try and deflect the blows with his sword, but it was hopeless. Tanaka stood over him and could easily hit undefended areas. Each strike with the sword exploded in a piercing pain that Gray had never experienced in his life.

Is this it? Is this how I go out?

44

Throbbing pain greeted Gray when he opened his eyes. It felt like he'd been put into an industrial-sized washing machine with large rocks and then set on a high speed. His entire body ached.

I might not be dead, but that was the worst beating I've ever gotten.

Gray was lying on his bed. He tried moving, but his body quickly rejected his efforts. He glanced at the clock that hung on the wall. It was a little after eight in the morning.

I wonder if Yoshida knows that Tanaka beat me within an inch of my life? Was Yoshida involved? We did end the night on an awkward note. It's possible.

There was a soft knock on Gray's door. A second later, it opened, and in walked two women. One pushed a wheelchair. The women said nothing and avoided eye contact. The covers were pulled off of Gray, and they slowly helped him to sit up, causing him to grunt in agony.

The pain was indescribable, but he figured they were there to help. So he did his best to move into the wheelchair. It took a few minutes, and Gray broke a sweat but eventually reached the chair. He looked down at his naked body, and it was unrecognizable. Dark bruising covered him except for his lower forearms and hands.

The women wheeled Gray to a room he had not been in. This one had a large tub and what looked like a massage table but lower to the floor. Off to the side was a soaking tub filled with milky water. The women helped Gray to lie back on the table. They gently slathered some sort of herbal mixture onto Gray's body. It had a medicinal smell and was cool to the touch like it had been refrigerated. Almost instantaneously, the mixture provided relief from the pain. The women continued until they covered his entire body. They then put cucumber slices on each eye and laid a damp towel that smelled minty over his face.

Gray must have dozed off because he woke to one of the women gently rocking his arm while whispering into his ear. He didn't understand her but knew she wanted him to wake up. The women helped Gray into a sitting position and then to a standing position. One of them pointed to the tub. Step by step, he made his way there, leaning on the women for support. Climbing into the tub wasn't easy, but Gray slid down into a sitting position once inside. The bath upped the ante if he thought the herbal wrap was soothing.

One of the women handed Gray a cup and motioned for him to drink. He did as instructed and immediately coughed. The liquid had a bitter taste, and the burn told him there was alcohol in it. She pushed the cup back to his lips. Gray held his breath and drank the rest as quickly as possible.

After his bath, the women helped Gray out of the tub and gently towel-dried him before laying him back down on the table. They placed their hands on him and lightly glided their hands across his body. Gray didn't know who these women were, but they were highly skilled in pain management, treatment, and recovery.

Of course, it wasn't lost on Gray how absurd the situation was. Why beat him within an inch of his life and then send these women to help him recover? A lot of effort was being put into his recovery when he could have been left alone. Maybe the healing was Yoshida's doing, and he had no part in the beating. It was a little hard to believe that Yoshida wasn't aware. He was Gray's handler.

Was this beating ordered, or did Tanaka do it on the sly?

After his therapeutic massage, the women returned Gray to his room. They left a canteen filled with more of that horrible-tasting drink, instructing Gray to drink one cup every three hours.

When Yoshida came to his room, Gray had been sleeping on and off for about an hour.

"How are you feeling?" he asked.

"About as good as anyone can after getting a beating with a wooden sword."

"It was an unfortunate incident."

"Is that what you're calling it, an incident? Were you aware that this was going to happen? Tell me the truth."

"I wasn't, at least not until Tanaka arrived."

"And you let him do as he pleased, just like that?"

"Who am I to interrupt? Tanaka had permission to do what he did."

"So the beating was sanctioned? Did I say something offensive to Serizawa-sama that I was unaware of?"

"Tanaka had not stopped complaining about you since your arrival. To appease him, Ito gave him the okay."

Gray let out a defeated breath. "Well, I'm glad I could play the role of a punching bag."

"The treatment you are receiving will help to expedite your recovery."

"Those two women are good. I'll admit that. I'll just have to cover up my bruises until they disappear."

Yoshida removed his phone from his pocket and turned on his front-facing camera. "Take a look at your face. There is no damage. The same goes for your hands and forearms. Tanaka purposely left those places alone so that you could walk around without anyone knowing about your injuries. Of course, it doesn't work if you limp."

"Am I supposed to be thankful for that bit of consideration?"

"That is up to you."

"Any chance Tanaka will come back for a repeat performance?"

"It's done. Are you hungry? I can have food brought to your room."

"I don't really have an appetite."

Yoshida turned to walk out of the room but stopped. "You should eat something. I'll send a bowl of cut fruit."

45

By the time dinner rolled around, Gray was feeling much better. His headache was gone, and his body no longer hurt like before. As much as he disliked that herbal tincture the women left for him, he drank it every three hours. He welcomed anything that sped up his recovery process.

The wheelchair had been left in his bedroom, so Gray climbed out of bed and put some clothes on. He was slightly out of breath from the effort but eventually made it into the chair and wheeled himself out into the hall and to the kitchen. There, he bumped into Yoshida.

"You're mobile. That's a good sign. Dinner is ready. I thought it would be easier if we ate in the dining room."

Up until that point, they had always eaten at the island in the kitchen. Gray didn't even know there was a dining room.

"Follow me," Yoshida said.

The table had already been set with food when they got there.

"I was just about to come get you when you rolled into the kitchen."

"Do you cook all of this food?"

"No, there is someone here that prepares it."

"There are other people in the house? I honestly thought it was just you and me."

"You aren't supposed to notice them, but a staff is here to handle the cooking and cleaning."

Yoshida moved a chair out of the way so that Gray could maneuver his wheelchair into place. At each place setting, there were multiple dishes filled with different types of food: rice, pickled vegetables, miso soup, different types of sashimi, grilled fish, skewers of meats, dumplings, fried noodles, and even sushi. There were also a couple of bottles of sake.

"This looks incredible."

"I thought you should have a meal with traditional Japanese dishes. Please, enjoy."

The sight and smell of the food triggered Gray's appetite, and he dug in like he hadn't eaten in days.

"I hope this food gives you the energy to continue your work. I should tell you that Ito is expecting an update soon."

"An update? He just gave Tanaka permission to beat the crap out of me. Did he not think that might slow me down?"

"He doesn't care. However, I did step in on your behalf and tell him what you had told me about profiling. That it's a process that takes time."

"I appreciate that. Because that's exactly how it works."

"Today I watched a movie: *The Silence of the Lambs*. The agent in the film was a profiler."

"Yes, the most popular one of them all."

"It actually helped me to better understand the process. It's much like work a detective would do to solve a crime. You must piece together information."

"That's correct. Sometimes it's painting a picture of who the suspect might be, and sometimes it's trying to simply answer a question that can often be as vague as 'why?'"

Yoshida's eyebrows crinkled. "What do you mean?"

"Well, figuring out the motivation can lead to a person who might be responsible for the crimes. So I have to find the answer to this why question."

"And what is the why question you are struggling with?"

Until then, Gray hadn't provided any real information to Yoshida. He'd preferred to hold his cards close and bide his time. But seeing that the leadership was getting antsy, he opened up a bit.

"The why, in this case, is determining who the real enemy is. There's a Sun Tzu quote: 'The secret lies in confusing the enemy so that he cannot fathom our real intent.'"

"Yes, I'm familiar with that quote. So you think what is happening here is to confuse people?"

"I think it's a strong possibility."

"Well, the enemy is everyone who is against the Sumiyoshi?"

"Let's assume what you say is true. The enemy of the Sumiyoshi is the TMPD, your organization, and the other syndicates. There's truth to that. But let me ask you a question: what is it you think the Sumiyoshi is interested in right now?"

"In our case, it's to take over our territory," Yoshida said. "I think it's the same for the other syndicates. As for the TMPD, it's to demonstrate control. To show that they are the ones who hold it."

"Now, what if I told you that none of that was their objective, but only what they wanted you to think. What would you have to say to that?"

Yoshida shrugged. "Impossible."

"Wait a minute. Give it a chance."

Yoshida thought about what Gray said for a few moments. "If what you're saying is true, then everyone is thinking the wrong thing. And if that's the case, what are they after?" A smile formed on Yoshida's face. "So that is the why question you're trying to answer."

"I think they have a different plan that has nothing to do with the Yamaguchi, the TMPD, or the Japanese government. I haven't figured it out, but I plan to."

Yoshida used his chopsticks to dip a piece of tuna belly sushi into a soy sauce and mustard mixture before popping it into his mouth. "I hope you're right about this theory you have. It won't fare well for you if you're wrong."

46

Gray wasn't in a great mood after dinner. The seriousness of Yoshida's words had really set in, and he knew he'd have to come up with something that satisfied the Yamaguchi.

But therein was the problem.

Gray was reasonably confident he could cobble together something they would buy into, but would it help him catch the trafficker? Did it matter at that point? Maybe all Gray needed was to satisfy the Yamaguchi so he could leave with his life. Once back in Tokyo, he could get back to work.

But all that did was defeat the purpose of approaching the Yamaguchi in the first place. He had managed to embed himself within the organization. How many people could claim that? This was a profiler's dream assignment. Heck, it would be a dream assignment for many professions. Was Gray really considering squandering this opportunity? Gray didn't need to make any hard or fast decisions. He had better use of his time.

Gray took a seat at the desk and began writing down pressing questions he had about the trafficking.

- Why did the Sumiyoshi stock so many weapons?

- Why were these weapons not sold to syndicates the Sumiyoshi was friendly with?
- Was their goal to use the weapons to take control of more territory?
- Was something stopping them from being more aggressive?
- Was retaliation the real reason they assassinated the director of the TMPD?

These questions were valid and worth pursuing, but were the answers necessary? Gray's thoughts reverted to Sun Tzu's quote. Were these questions there to distract and confuse the enemy? Gray wrote down a list of enemies of the Sumiyoshi.

- Japanese government
- Law enforcement
- Other Yakuza syndicates

Were they all equal enemies, or could there be a primary one? Gray crossed out the other Yakuza syndicates. Gray never got the impression the Sumiyoshi was afraid or worried about them, especially the Yamaguchi.

The government directed the National Police Agency, overseeing the police departments representing each prefecture, including the TMPD. But they weren't really on the front lines. Gray crossed them off the list.

That left the TMPD. Tamura and her people had not been able to determine how guns were coming into the country. She said she had exhausted any and all leads before Gray was brought in to help. Tamura was also struggling internally with her superiors. He also realized that even with Tamura's progressive thinking, she was still utilizing policing methods from the old ways. Whether they realized it or not, their internal beefs were the problem.

Could Iwata have predicted that? Could he have known the TMPD was capable of hindering itself? It was certainly plausible, except Gray never got the impression when he hung out with Iwata that he was that smart. But someone else could have figured this out and brought it to Iwata.

This brought Gray to his final hurdle: Iwata's trafficking partners. Was Iwata's involvement a significant part of the operation or a minor part? Gray and Tamura had always assumed it was significant. But what if they were wrong about that?

Gray pondered that last question. *What if we're wrong? What if everything I've just written down doesn't matter, what if it was all part of this confusion to bog down law enforcement?*

Okay, Gray, let's continue down this pathway. You were wrong. Tamura was wrong. Everyone working on this investigation was wrong. Even what the Yamaguchi thought was wrong.

But the weapons in the warehouse? Iwata took me there to brag. Of course he's involved.

Gray pushed the voices out of his head and stepped away from the desk. He was falling back into a trap by revisiting them. They were there to confuse him. He didn't need to answer them all.

Maybe every question isn't meant to confuse. Perhaps one is truthful.

If Gray had to pick one, it would be the one about the weapons in the warehouse. Why stock so many weapons? It made no sense. Unless . . . a smile formed on Gray's face.

Damn you, Iwata, you almost had me there. You crafty son of a bitch. No one in their right mind would keep so many weapons in an unsecured location unless it was temporary. Those weapons are not inventory for the Sumiyoshi. Those weapons were in transit. Iwata, you're not trafficking weapons into Japan. You're trafficking weapons through Japan.

A warm feeling spread throughout Gray's body, the one he always got when he knew he'd turned a corner. Gray had come across an angle no one had considered, and it seemed to put all those other questions to bed.

Relax Gray. Give it the overnight test. See how you feel in the morning. If you still have the same giddy feeling then, go for it.

47

Gray didn't need to wait until morning to know he had crossed over into fertile ground. It was untapped and waiting for him to trounce around in it. All night he continued to think about this new theory: the Sumiyoshi was trafficking weapons through Japan, not into Japan.

He tossed and turned in his bed as he tried to poke holes in his theory. It was so wild, so out there. Surely it was crap. But the more he thought about it, the more he began to believe he'd cracked it. He needed input. He needed to hear from someone who wasn't in love with the idea like he was. He needed Tamura.

There was one problem. She was in Tokyo, and he could not get in touch with her.

As soon as the clock struck six, Gray crawled out of bed, showered, dressed, and made his way to the kitchen. He figured Yoshida would be there at any minute. It wasn't until he was halfway down the hall that he realized he didn't consider using the wheelchair, nor did he recall feeling the pain while showering or dressing. He was so hyped up on adrenaline that he couldn't even recall seeing the bruising on his body.

The kitchen was empty, so Gray fixed himself a cup of coffee the same way he had seen Yoshida do it. He was sitting at the island halfway through his first cup when Yoshida showed up, pulling him from his thoughts.

"An early riser today," Yoshida said.

"I had one of those nights where my mind wouldn't shut off. As soon as it neared sunrise, I got out of bed."

Yoshida began fixing himself a cup of coffee.

"I have a request to make. I would like permission to talk to Inspector Tamura."

Yoshida looked over his shoulder. "You want to do a video call?"

"I might have stumbled onto something, and I need to work through these thoughts with someone who's already a proven sounding board. That's Tamura. I want her to come to Kobe, to the house."

"What is it you think you stumbled on?"

"You'll know after Tamura and I have had a chance to work through it. I'm being serious right now. If you say no, that's your prerogative. But know that denying this request hurts the Yamaguchi as well. You don't have access to assault rifles. The Sumiyoshi does. You need me to be successful. Tamura can be held to the same rules as I am. That's not a problem, but I need her here."

Yoshida took a seat on the island. "You seem to be healing well."

"I am. I don't think I need the wheelchair."

"You will receive another treatment later this morning. It's necessary."

"Okay. What about my request?"

"Why don't you want to tell me your idea?"

"It's too early, and the last thing I want to do is start crowdsourcing this with people I haven't worked with. That's you, my friend."

"What makes you so sure she's willing to come and bow to the same rules as you?"

"Because she wants to catch this trafficker more than anyone."

Yoshida placed his cell phone on the island. "Make a call to her on speakerphone right now. If she answers, the answer is yes. But if she doesn't, the answer is no, and you will not make this request again. Do you understand?"

Gray nodded and dialed the number, and they both waited for Tamura to pick up. In Gray's experience with Tamura, she rarely answered her phone. But he was hoping this was the one time she did.

One ring.

Two rings.

Three rings.

Come on, Mariko, answer the phone.

Four rings.

Five rings.

Yoshida cleared his throat.

Six rings.

Seven rings.

"She's a heavy sleeper. She mentioned that once," Gray lied.

Eight rings.

Nine rings.

A groggy voice answered. "Hello?"

Gray snatched the phone off of the island. "Mariko, it's Sterling."

"Sterling? Where are you? Are you back in Tokyo?" She asked, her voice much clearer as her senses sharpened.

"I'm still in Kobe, but I need you down here. I think I turned the corner."

"What is it?"

"It's better if you come. When can you make it here?"

"I need to take care of something quick at headquarters, but I'll catch the next train after that. Will you be meeting me?"

Gray looked over at Yoshida. "I believe it'll be the same procedure as the last time." Yoshida nodded. "Expect instructions once you get to Kobe."

"Okay."

"Great. I'll see you soon."

Gray disconnected the call. "So you'll take care of the arrangements?"

"I will."

"Will Tanaka be a problem? Because if he gets involved, he'll be the person to blame if our efforts fail."

"I'll make sure you and Inspector Tamura are left alone."

The same two women arrived a little after nine to give Gray another round of treatment. They insisted that the wheelchair be used to transport him, even though he showed them that he could walk. They weren't impressed. At least this time he could wear a robe instead of being wheeled around naked. The treatment felt even better the second time, and Gray had completely lost track of time and forgot that Tamura was on her way. When the two women returned Gray to his bedroom, he found Tamura waiting for him.

"Sterling, what happened to you?" She came over to him and pulled his robe open.

"Chihiro Tanaka is what happened."

Gray thanked the two women, and as soon as they were clear of the room, Gray told Tamura about Tanaka's visit in the middle of the night.

"I can't believe it. I'm so sorry. And you had no way to notify me."

"I'm fine now. Those two women are treating my injuries. You should have seen me yesterday. Really, I'll be okay. I just got my butt kicked, that's all."

"Is this why you asked me to come here?"

"No, this has nothing to do with it. Give me a minute to change into some clothes."

After Gray dressed, he led Tamura out the back of the house for a walk in the gardens. Gray wasn't sure if his room had listening devices in it or not. The park would provide some level of privacy. Yoshida joined them, keeping fifty steps behind them.

"I'm dying to know what you have to tell me," Tamura said quietly. "Start with the meat of it. You can fill me in on the backstory after."

"Alright. I don't think the Sumiyoshi is trafficking weapons into Japan. They are trafficking weapons through the country."

Tamura stopped dead in her tracks. "Through the country, as in on to another destination?"

"Yes."

"That would mean they're not a major player in the trafficking. Someone else is spearheading this."

Gray smiled. "I knew you'd see it immediately. The Sumiyoshi facilitates the process, providing protection as the weapons move through the country."

"This is unbelievable." Tamura shifted her weight to one foot as she rested her hands on her hips.

"I know. Trust me, I spent the better half of the night trying to poke holes in it. I wasn't able to."

"This is why they had so many weapons stashed in that warehouse."

"Exactly. I'm betting those weapons are only there for a couple of days, a week tops. It's a stop in the route. Which also explains the unsecured location."

"It also answers why the Sumiyoshi didn't try to profit off the weapons. They're not their weapons to sell."

"That's what I'm thinking. The arrangement could be that the Sumiyoshi provide safe passage, and in return, they can arm themselves, possibly for free or minimal costs."

"I feel like there needs to be an exchange of money. The Sumiyoshi isn't that generous," Tamura said.

"They could receive a percentage of the final sale on the weapons."

"That could work. Gray, this theory opens up so many doors. How did you find your way here?" Tamura asked.

"All the information I'd been collecting fell into place. I think what triggered it was my conversation with the oyabun of the Yamaguchi."

"Wait, you actually got to meet Katsuhito Serizawa?"

"Yeah, we spent a couple of hours in his private onsen. Just him and me."

"I don't believe it."

"I'm not kidding. He made the offer out of the blue."

Gray quickly filled Tamura in on how Yoshida and Serizawa were related.

"So Yoshida's real surname is Serizawa?"

"Yup, he changed it to hide his identity. But there's definitely some other dynamic going on there. Relationship issues within a criminal organization usually aren't explored. I'm wondering if that could be an issue with the Sumiyoshi."

"Why would that matter to us?"

"Well, if my theory is right, then Iwata isn't our guy. But he's connected to the person we want."

"Yeah, and?"

"Why would he screw that up by taking me to that warehouse?" Gray asked. "I think there's something else driving his actions and figuring that out might help us pinpoint the real trafficker."

"It's worth a shot. Any thoughts on what our next step should be?"

"We should determine if any of the surrounding countries have experienced increased gun violence or trafficking of illegal weapons. This theory has some solid footing if we can determine a pattern."

"Right, let's get started."

"That's a problem." Gray let out a defeated breath. "I'm completely cut off from the outside world here." Gray looked back over his shoulder at Yoshida. "It's completely counterintuitive to what I need to accomplish, but my handler, the Yamaguchi, won't have it any other way. They're paranoid that I'll pass along secrets about the organization."

"You could be doing that right now."

"I know."

"It's this type of thinking that hurts them," Tamura said. "One person thinks something, and if he's in charge, everyone follows it without question."

"You'll need to head back to Tokyo and work on this alone. I can't help. You think you can handle it?"

"Yeah, it won't be a problem, but let me ask you, do you need to stay here longer? Seems like we got what we need. Yeah, I know we're back to square one if it doesn't pan out. But if that happens, is there more to mine here?"

"Good question, hard to answer. I don't know, but sticking around for a bit longer won't hurt."

"Okay. I'll hit up all my contacts and see what comes in. I don't know how long it will take to gather this data. It could be a couple of hours. It could be a couple of days."

"I understand. Just do what you need to do. I'll be fine here."

"Are you being pressured for answers?" Tamura asked. "I know we were warned about withholding information."

"There's been some pressure. I've given Yoshida a little to satisfy his curiosity, but eventually, we need to give him something substantial."

"You have reservations about telling them about this?"

"No, but I've seen enough of how the Yamaguchi operate and think. Bringing them in too early could screw it up. They might take over or worse, react and try something stupid with the Sumiyoshi."

"Okay, we'll keep this between us until we have a foolproof way to spoon-feed it to them."

48

Tamura stayed for a quick lunch. The story they gave Yoshida was that Tamura and Gray were still debating the issue, but she needed time to think about it.

After she left, Gray and Yoshida were sitting on the veranda enjoying tea.

"How was your visit with Inspector Tamura?"

"It was good to see her again and receive an update on what the TMPD is doing back in Tokyo."

"And?"

"All of their attention is focused on squashing the Sumiyoshi. Someone's got to lose that war, right? What has the media been reporting? I'm sure you're following it."

"They're reporting essentially what you've just told me, that the TMPD is confident that they will restore order to the capital." Yoshida took a sip of his tea. "I know I don't need to remind you, but you are on a time limit here."

"Are your bosses pressuring you for an answer?"

"Let me put it this way. The longer it takes, the more they'll believe Tanaka was right. What has come out of your conversation with Inspector Tamura? And please don't tell me she needs to think about it."

Gray needed to give Yoshida something. "I think the Sumiyoshi are working with someone else. They have a partner."

"Of course they do. They don't manufacture weapons."

"I'm saying that the Sumiyoshi was hired to help the real trafficker."

"They have nothing to do with the trafficking?"

"I'm saying they're not the brains behind the operation. They play a much lesser role than what is perceived."

Yoshida took a moment to think about what Gray was saying. "So they provide protection for the trafficker?"

"That's a strong possibility."

"Is this what you conveyed to Inspector Tamura?"

"It is."

"And she's doing what now?"

"I want you to understand something. This is nothing more than a theory that we still need to prove. My first step was to see if I had enough meat on the theory to satisfy Tamura. And I did. She'll put feelers out to see if she can get some additional validation. Secondly, I can already see by your look and your questioning that you also believe there's something here. That's a good sign, but you must let me run through my process. I'm the profiler. Let me do my job."

Yoshida leaned back in his chair to further consider what he had learned. "You know, I do think there's something here. But it's a radical idea to suggest that the Sumiyoshi is nothing more than the hired help. This is not how our organizations work, whether it be the Yamaguchi or the Sumiyoshi."

"Your bosses will be confused by this?"

"I don't doubt this idea you propose will give them headaches."

"Why are you not confused by it? Why are you so accepting right now?"

"Believe it or not, I do not share the same thinking as the leadership of the Yamaguchi or most of its members. I am much more open."

"Like the Sumiyoshi."

"That's one way to put it."

"So you believe me?"

"I'm not entirely convinced, but you are the profiler, and I want to see where this goes."

Gray leaned forward and clasped his hands together. "If you recall that Sun Tzu quote about confusing the enemy, you'll see that the Sumiyoshi is doing exactly that."

49

The women who'd been treating Gray showed up for the third day in a row, and he happily welcomed them with a smile. The treatment they'd been giving him had done wonders for his body. His mobility was nearly at one hundred percent, the pain had mostly vanished except for a bit of stiffness in the morning, and the bruising had lightened significantly. That didn't mean he'd forgotten about Tanaka's beating. He still wanted to punch the guy in the face. Gray wasn't afraid of him. In fact, he viewed him as a bully who only picked fights he knew he could win. Expecting Gray to be skilled in kendo was a perfect example. Tanaka was like a professional boxer who picked a fight with someone who had never stepped foot into the ring. But Gray shook off any thoughts he had of Tanaka by the second day after his beating. He had better things to spend his time thinking about.

On his way to the treatment room, Yoshida informed Gray that Tamura would arrive soon. To say he was eager to see her was an understatement. It was much sooner than he'd expected. Did that mean it was bad news? Did she strike out quickly with her contacts? Was there not enough data to support weapons trafficking into the surrounding countries? Or was this a bigger undertaking than he'd imagined, and this would take months to figure out?

After his treatment, Gray took a walk in the gardens behind the house to focus. Yoshida opted to remain on the veranda and not shadow him.

Tamura showed up thirty minutes later. Gray was at the far end of the garden near a pond filled with colorful carp. He watched her as she walked over to him. She had a great poker face, as he still couldn't tell if she was delivering bad or good news.

"How are you doing?" Tamura took a seat on the bench Gray was sitting on.

"Oh, you know, just passing the time in the backyard of a person who is the second-in-command for the Yamaguchi syndicate. Tell me you have good news."

"Is Yoshida eyeing us?" Tamura asked as she kept her gaze on Gray.

"Like a ravenous hawk."

"Okay, control your emotions, so we keep him guessing."

"Got it."

A tiny smile formed on Tamura's face. "It's good news."

"Where?"

"The Golden Triangle—illegal arms trading has exploded in that area. It used to be known as a hot spot for drug trafficking. It still is, but the weapons have made a huge difference."

The Golden Triangle was located at the confluence of the Mekong and Ruak Rivers, where the borders of Myanmar, Thailand, and Laos meet. In the 1950s, the area had become a hot spot for opium trafficking. Almost all the world's heroin, originating in Afghanistan, passed through the triangle.

"I have a contact working in Thai Border Control, and he responded so quickly it wasn't even funny. He said there's been a steady rise in illegal weapon seizures in the area over the last year. And it's not just Thailand. He's heard it from people he knows in Laos. He said it's unlike anything they've seen."

"Do they know where the weapons are coming from?"

"Initially, they thought the weapons were coming into the country either from Myanmar or China, but they haven't found any evidence to support that. Plus, China denies that the weapons are crossing over their borders."

"Does he believe them?"

Tamura nodded. "For the most part, because the weapons they're seizing are all Russian."

"The weapons the Sumiyoshi are armed with are Russian. The Kalashnikov MA is the assault rifle they've been using."

"That rifle and other Russian-made arms are what my contact says they've been confiscating."

Gray shook his head in disbelief. "I can't believe it. I was fifty-fifty that this theory had legs, but . . ."

"I know. Same here, but we've got traction. That's not all I learned."

"Hold that thought. Yoshida's walking over here."

"Any progress?" Yoshida asked as he approached.

"We're just getting started," Gray said.

"Of course. Lunch is ready. Please come into the house."

Gray and Tamura followed Yoshida inside and to the dining room, where the table was set. There were several different dishes, just like the dinner Gray'd had the night before with Yoshida.

"It looks great and smells delicious," Gray said.

"This looks wonderful," Tamura said as she took a seat. "Did you prepare this?" she asked, even though she knew Yoshida had been watching her and Gray.

"I can't take the credit. A staff member is responsible."

"Staff?" Tamura looked around. "I thought it was just Sterling and you in the house."

"That's what I thought as well," Gray said. "They're very good at staying out of sight."

"When do you think you'll be able to share information with me?" Yoshida asked.

"Tamura only just got here. I know your bosses are eager for an update, and I imagine they're pressing you, but give us some time. I want to make sure the information I turn over to you is right. The last thing I want is for you to relay some half-baked theory to your bosses. I hope you understand."

"Is there a time limit on how long I'm allowed to stay today?" Tamura asked.

"Not necessarily. Do you think you'll need the entire day?"

"I'm not sure, but if I do, I'm hoping that won't be a problem."

"It shouldn't be."

During the rest of lunch, Gray kept the conversation light and away from topics that would allow Yoshida to start prying. He brought up Yoshida's side gig: playing classical guitar.

"He's toured worldwide," Gray said to Tamura.

"No way. That's amazing."

"Sterling is giving me a compliment that is much too big. I'm not a famous guitarist. A lot of the time, I'm filling in for someone. I was once allowed to solo when playing with a chamber orchestra in Vienna."

"That sounds pretty famous to me," Gray said.

"When is your next performance?" Tamura asked. "I would love to hear you play. Wait, do you have a guitar here? Please tell me you do."

A grin appeared on Yoshida's cheeks, burning red from embarrassment. "I have to admit, I do have one. Playing helps me relax."

"Will you play something for us after we finish eating?"

"That's a great idea," Gray said.

"I'm not sure," Yoshida started.

"We won't take no for an answer. Quid pro quo," Gray said.

After lunch, Yoshida, Gray, and Tamura moved to the veranda, where he played his guitar for them. He'd only been playing for fifteen minutes when his cell phone interrupted their mini-concert.

"I'm sorry, I must take this call," he said. "I'll be back."

When he was safely out of earshot, Tamura turned to Gray.

"He's an interesting character, isn't he?"

Gray nodded. "Watching him play, even for that short amount of time, it's pretty obvious to me that he would have much rather pursued being a professional guitarist than join the Yamaguchi."

"I wonder if he was forced to join?"

"Yoshida told me his reason was revenge. His father was a member and was gunned down. Would he have still joined had that not happened? Most likely not."

A few seconds later, Yoshida returned. "I apologize for the interruption." He picked up his guitar and took a seat. "Shall we continue?"

50

Yoshida played for a solid forty minutes. And even though Gray was eager to return to work, he didn't have the heart to interrupt Yoshida. He seemed like an entirely different person. His guarded personality faded as he became lost in the moment.

After the performance, Gray and Tamura continued their conversation in the garden. They took a seat on the bench near the pond. It was late afternoon, so the midday sun was no longer a factor.

"We left off talking about how the weapons being confiscated in the Golden Triangle were Russian-made," Gray said. "You were about to tell me something else when Yoshida interrupted us."

"That's right. Gun violence has risen. And not just among gang members. Civilians are getting their hands on guns. A few months ago, a study in Thailand reported that civilians in the country have possession of an estimated 10.3 million guns. Registered guns account for 6 million. The remaining 4 million were illegally obtained."

"Are you serious?"

"Yes. In the past two years, Thailand has seen two mass shootings, the latest being at a daycare center involving thirty-eight victims, of whom twenty-four were children. Gun violence has exploded among civilians."

"Did he mention who the manufacturer of the weapons is?"

"He said a mix of Chinese, American, European, and now Russian guns are showing up."

"And now Russian . . . that means the weapons passing through Japan end up in Southeast Asia. Any news if other countries in the region have experienced the same?"

"I knew you would ask me that. My Thai contact turned me on to someone working for the Ministry of National Defense in Vietnam. He's confirmed that weapons seizures are up, and the number of illegal arms floating around the country has risen drastically. Gun violence in their country has also skyrocketed. There used to be a time when the only people who possessed guns were the military and police. He said now they're finding more civilians are arming themselves illegally. He confirmed that Russian-made guns have been confiscated. I'm waiting to hear back from a contact I have in Cambodia."

"So the way I see this, Southeast Asia had primarily seen their supply of weapons coming from China, Europe, and America, but now it looks like the Russians want a piece of the action."

"Russia has always had a lock on selling weapons to the Middle East, and China has always been a huge supplier of weapons to Southeast Asia," Tamura said. "The expanse of their country pretty much blocks Russia from having access. Unless they find another way, like, say, through my country."

"The whole secret lies in confusing the enemy so that he cannot fathom our real intent. That's what Sun Tzu said." Gray winked at Tamura.

"Sun Tzu also said in the midst of chaos, there is opportunity. Our trafficker has definitely created chaos in my country. We know why the weapons are in Japan and where they're heading. We still don't know how they're being brought in and who's behind it."

"All in good time. I feel positive we'll figure it out."

Tamura drew a deep breath and looked around the garden. "As beautiful as this place is, it lacks the tools we need to do our jobs effectively. One thing we—"

"Hold up. Yoshida's on his way over here."

"Inspector Tamura, your time is up."

"Oh, so soon?"

"It's almost five o'clock."

All of Tamura's possessions had been taken upon arrival, including her watch. Neither Tamura nor Gray had any idea of the time.

"The day flew by fast, didn't it?" Gray said. "And we were just starting to make some progress. Asking her to leave now would hamper our efforts. That's bad for everyone."

"How much more time do you need?" Yoshida asked.

Tamura looked over at Gray. "I, uh, I'm not sure."

"Look," Gray said. "We're not answering a survey of questions here. It's impossible to gauge how much time is needed. I suggest you allow Inspector Tamura to spend the night. That way, we can continue working around the clock. Please don't cut short our time right now." Gray turned to Tamura. "Are you okay with that?"

"I think it's a great idea. The longer we keep working together, the more progress we'll make."

Yoshida took a few moments to think about their proposal before answering. "The same rules that apply to Special Agent Gray will also apply to you, Inspector Tamura."

"I'm fine with that. I think one night here will be plenty of time."

51

With an okay secured from Yoshida, Gray and Tamura continued their discussion up to and through dinner, which they'd politely declined. Gray told Yoshida they'd rather work and could eat instant noodles later.

Both had bought into the idea that the weapons were simply passing through Japan and the Sumiyoshi were facilitators. The fact that Russian weapons were suddenly finding their way into Southeast Asia while illegal arms and gun violence were on the rise seemed more than a coincidence. They had no hard evidence, but they didn't need it. As far as they were concerned, they were on a path that provided answers.

The weather was mild so working in the garden wasn't a bother. There was accent lighting throughout the park, so it wasn't completely dark. Tamura stood and stretched her arms above her head.

"How about a break, partner?" she said.

"Sure. Are you hungry?"

"Not really, but I am curious about the house. Have you seen all of it?"

"I haven't. I've only been in my bedroom, the kitchen, the dining room, and the room where I receive my treatments."

"Come on, let's go be nosy."

They headed into the house and made a detour to the kitchen, where Gray grabbed a bag of rice crackers and continued. They found their way into a large sitting room with comfy leather chairs. They plopped down into them.

"Oh, this feels wonderful," Tamura said. "I could pass out here and be just fine."

"Hey, no sleeping. We still have work to do. Here, have some rice crackers. They're spicy, so there's a little heat."

Tamura grabbed a handful and then walked over to a couple of wooden cabinets. She opened one, and it was lined with wooden boxes.

"I found Ito's stash," she said.

"What's in those boxes?"

"Bottles of whisky, and it's not the cheap stuff." She looked back at Gray. "You think he'd mind if we opened one?"

"I don't get the impression he spends much time here."

Tamura grabbed a box, along with two rocks glasses, and returned to her chair. "This is arguably the best—and probably the most expensive—Japanese whisky one can buy. The first edition of Suntory's Yamazaki is a fifty-year-old single malt."

"That's a long time to wait to sample the goods. I'm assuming that's not something you can get off the shelf at a liquor store."

"Probably bought it at an auction or was gifted it by some other rich guy."

"Are you serious? Tell me that's not a million-dollar bottle."

"I'm guessing between two or three hundred thousand."

"Maybe you should pick another bottle."

Tamura cracked the seal on the cap. "Too late now. And anyway these guys are so loaded, Ito has probably forgotten he has these bottles."

She poured a bit into both glasses and then handed one to Gray.

"Here's to progress," she said as she clinked Gray's glass. "That's interesting," she said after a sip. "I didn't think it would be that intense. A little on the spicy side, but really smooth."

"I agree. It also has a sweetness to it. The aroma reminds me of sandalwood."

"Look at you, doling out reviewer notes." Tamura chuckled.

"I am not a big whisky drinker, but I could drink this all night."

"How did you last with Iwata? That's all they drink."

"I just powered through. I liked that we were drinking a bottle of Irish whiskey at one point. So it wasn't that bad."

"That's impossible."

"What is?"

"Drinking Irish whiskey. The Yakuza only drink Japanese whisky."

"Well, maybe the younger generation is departing from just Japanese whisky."

"Nah, not that. First, I know I'm partial, but Japanese whisky is better than Irish whiskey."

"That's a matter of taste."

"Almost every Japanese man is obsessed with whisky, Japanese whisky primarily. It's the unofficial national beverage."

"I can't argue with that. I like those highballs."

"Suntory is a powerhouse. When they introduced the fifty-year-old Yamazaki to America, it exploded."

"I hear you, but I promise you, we were drinking off a bottle of Irish whiskey. I remember seeing that amber-gold-colored liquid in that squatty bottle. It was the '18 reserve. I know I had a lot to drink, but I remember that bottle."

"Well, maybe it was just you drinking off it. It probably belonged to another gaijin in the bar."

"Nope, Iwata drank from it, and so did Mizuno. I remember Iwata filling our glasses. And I want to say I was the only gaijin in that bar. I could be wrong; part of my time was a blur."

"I'm guessing this was in the Golden Gai. Do you remember the name of the bar?"

"Couldn't tell you, but I remember seeing a mural of a green samurai on the wall."

"A green samurai? What? Like the Hulk?"

"No, it just had a lot of green in it. There were other colors, black was used for the outline of the samurai, but that shamrock green stood out to me."

"That's an interesting choice. Most samurais are filled in red, white, silver, and dark blue. Sometimes there's green, but I've never seen it as the dominant color."

"I take it you're not familiar with a bar with a mural of a green samurai?"

"There are so many bars in that area. A lot of them are hidden. You know, the entrance will be like a wall of kegs that you have to slide to the side. Very speakeasy."

"It might have been one of them."

"It's still bizarre because drinking Japanese whisky is not only a Yakuza thing. It's a Japanese thing as well. Are you sure there weren't other gaijin in that bar? It would help me wrap my head around this anomaly. You know, maybe that person left the bottle behind or something."

Gray took a sip of his whisky as he thought about Tamura's question. "Maybe. Wait a minute." He snapped his fingers. "Now that I think about it. There was another gaijin at that bar."

Tamura gave her thigh a slap. "I bet it's his bottle. He's sharing it, and Iwata took advantage."

"It could be, but he wasn't sitting with or near us. He was standing in the entranceway. I passed him as we were leaving. Really he could have just been peeking inside. I wasn't paying enough attention to determine if he was coming or going. But I definitely would have known if he was sitting with us. He had bright red hair."

"Then it's his bottle. I'm positive," Tamura said before pouring them another healthy serving.

Gray and Tamura's conversation never did return to the investigation. After a few more glasses of whisky, they decided to call it a night.

Gray woke to use the bathroom. When he returned to bed, bits of his conversation with Tamura popped into his head. It was the tangent they went off on regarding Japanese whisky and how it's all Japanese people drink.

I know I wasn't that drunk. We were drinking Jameson. I saw Iwata pour it into our glasses. We cheered. I watched him drink it. Maybe it was that gaijin's bottle, and he did sit with us or leave his bottle for us. I was drinking a lot. But I'm pretty sure it was a Sumiyoshi bar. When I first entered the bar, all heads turned to look at me. And they weren't smiling. It wasn't until Iwata came up behind me that everyone looked away. So if he was drinking there, he had to have been invited.

Gray drifted off back to sleep in mid-thought and slept soundly until morning. But as soon as he opened his eyes, that red-haired guy popped back into his head. Gray got out of bed and put on a robe. Tamura was in the bedroom next door. He slipped quietly into the hall and knocked on her door.

"Tamura?" he whispered.

He knocked once more. This time the door cracked open, and Tamura was looking up at him. Her hair was a mess, and she was wearing a robe.

"What's wrong? Is everything okay?"

"Get dressed quickly. I have something to tell you. We'll head outside, okay?"

She nodded, and Gray left.

About thirty minutes later, they were both in the garden sipping coffee.

"What's on your mind? I'm guessing you had some revelation."

"Sort of, but I'm not sure if it's anything. Remember when we talked about Japanese whisky and how that's all the Yakuza drink?"

"Yeah . . ."

"And then I said Iwata and I were drinking Irish whiskey?"

"I remember all of this. Get to the point."

Gray began a count on his hand. "The Sumiyoshi is just facilitating the trafficking of weapons through Japan. Iwata is involved with the operation. We were both drinking from a bottle of Jameson. There was another gaijin in that Sumiyoshi bar."

"You think that person might be connected to the trafficking?"

"We've already established that the trafficker is a foreigner who has somehow hired the Sumiyoshi. This guy was in a Sumiyoshi bar. He had to be invited. This might be our guy."

"We need to find him."

"And quickly before the trafficking operation is pulled from the country."

"There's only one problem I can think of," Tamura said. "You're still a wanted man in Tokyo. It's not safe for you to be walking around. Everything we're doing right now isn't sanctioned by the TMPD. I can't guarantee your safety."

"I'm not asking you to. But I think I know some people who might be able to help protect me."

"Who?"

"Our new friends, the Yamaguchi."

52

When Yoshida showed up in the kitchen for his morning coffee, Gray and Tamura headed back inside. If they wanted the Yamaguchi to provide protection, they would definitely need Yoshida.

"Good morning," Tamura said as she entered the kitchen.

"Why are you up so early?" Yoshida asked.

"Back to work," Gray said. "We want to share with you if you have a moment."

Yoshida motioned to the island, and they all took a seat. "I'm eager to hear what you have to report," he said.

"I'm giving you an overview of what we're thinking. You can ask questions if you want to drill down deeper. As you know, we don't think the Sumiyoshi are responsible for trafficking weapons into Japan. They are the hired help. We believe the weapons are being trafficked through the country. Southeast Asia is the final destination."

"The number of weapons being trafficked through the Golden Triangle has exploded over the last year," Tamura said. "My contacts tell me that more and more of the weapons they're confiscating are Russian-made."

"It makes complete sense. The Russians or someone working with the Russians are bringing the weapons through Japan to get to Southeast Asia," Gray said. "We believe the Sumiyoshi are providing safe passage.

In return, they receive weapons and most likely a commission off the deal."

"So what does this all mean for us?" Yoshida asked.

"Well, we now know we're looking for a foreigner, not someone inside the Sumiyoshi. Remember, we need to catch the brain of the operation. There is nothing more for me to gain from being here. I need to return to Tokyo so we can continue our investigation."

"There are a lot of gaijin in Tokyo. How will you narrow it down?"

"We have a lead. I might have bumped into the person."

A look of disbelief fell over Yoshida's face. "You bumped into the trafficker?"

"I know it sounds very far-fetched."

Gray explained how he met Sora Iwata and ended up partying with him.

"One night, we were in a Sumiyoshi-only bar, and that's where I saw this other gaijin. A member of the Sumiyoshi had to have given him the okay to come inside."

"Maybe he's just another person like you, there to have a good time."

"It's possible, but we need to run down this lead. We can't do it from Kobe. You do understand that, right?"

"So you want to leave?"

"I do, but I still need the Yamaguchi's help. Iwata wants me dead. He already tried to kill me before I came to Kobe. He believes I was the one who tipped off the TMPD about the warehouse full of weapons."

"And did you?"

"He did," Tamura said. "But it wasn't so we could raid the place. My plan was to watch the place. But my bosses had other plans and raided the warehouse without telling me."

"I want to ask the Yamaguchi for protection in Tokyo."

"Are you serious? Tokyo isn't our territory. Why can't the TMPD protect you?"

"Because what we're doing isn't officially sanctioned by the TMPD," Tamura said. "My boss knows what we're doing here, but he's not putting his butt on the line. If it works, he'll take credit. I'm sure you know what I'm talking about."

"I do. But what you're asking isn't a small favor. First of all, you ratted out the Sumiyoshi. You could do the same for us. Ito will see it this way."

"And that's why I need you to vouch for me," Gray said. "You know everything we're doing is to catch the trafficker. We're not interested in the Yamaguchi."

"Tokyo isn't our territory," Yoshida said. "Men we send there will also be in danger."

"I realize that, but that's the risk. Look, nothing we do will be without risk. This is the business we're both in, but if we catch the trafficker, it's a win for us and a win for the Yamaguchi."

"Sterling's right," Tamura said. "What the Yamaguchi do after that is their business. All we want is to catch the trafficker and stop the flow of weapons into Japan."

For the next two hours, they continued discussing the plan. Yoshida asked more questions, and Gray and Tamura did their best to fill him in. Gray no longer felt like he needed to hold his cards. He laid them all out for Yoshida to see. They required the Yamaguchi's help and Yoshida was the only person who could convince Ito of it.

"Although I fully understand the situation and what you're proposing is the best way forward, I can't guarantee the answer will be favorable," Yoshida said.

"We understand," Tamura said. "If Ito declines to send men, we'll still move forward, but our efforts will be hampered."

"Look at everything we've done so far," Gray said. "This is incredible progress."

"I need no more convincing. I'm on your side and will do my best to make the case. Inspector Tamura, you must realize that I will be fighting the same battle you fight with your superiors. Their thinking is outdated. So is that of my grandfather and many of the leaders inside the Yamaguchi. If you'll excuse me, I need to make a few calls if this meeting is to take place today."

Tamura turned to Gray once Yoshida was out of sight. "That actually went better than I had anticipated. I thought there would be more pushback."

"Yoshida is different. Honestly, I don't think he wants to be here. You saw him yesterday. He'd much rather be playing guitar for an audience."

"Do you think he has the fight to make a convincing case?"

"That's a good question. We need to hope he does if we're left out of the meeting."

For the next hour or so, Gray and Tamura spent their time on the veranda honing their pitch. They still weren't sure they would be allowed to personally make their case, but they wanted to be ready if it came to that.

"Good news," Yoshida said when he appeared on the veranda. "Ito is willing to meet today. The bad news is you will not be allowed to speak. I will have to do all of the talking."

"But we'll be in the room, right?" Gray asked.

"You will be there, but I don't think you will be in the room. He is aware of why I'm requesting the meeting. That's a good sign. It means he's willing to hear an explanation of why you want him to provide a security detail for you. I do have a few more questions that I'm anticipating might come up in the meeting."

"Ask away," Gray said.

"Inspector Tamura, you mentioned earlier that your visit here is unsanctioned by the TMPD. How much, if any, of your most recent discovery do they know?"

"Nothing yet," Tamura said.

"And do you plan on briefing your boss?"

"That's not a decision I've made yet. Like you said earlier, my bosses can be difficult. It might make more sense to hold on to this information until a good enough reason presents itself."

Yoshida looked at Gray. "You agree with this strategy?"

"I do. Tamura understands the thinking and the politics inside the TMPD."

"Are you expecting help with your investigation from Yamaguchi men or just protection?"

"Protection," Gray said. "If we get into a gunfight, I expect them to shoot back. They will be armed, right? I think that's a necessity."

"I just wanted to be clear on expectations. That's all the questions I have for now."

"In your experience, how do decisions like this go?" Gray asked.

"In my experience, I've never had or heard of a meeting about something like this."

"So we continue to break new ground with the Yamaguchi. Can't deny we're not making a lasting impression."

"What time is the meeting?" Tamura asked.

"We will leave in one hour. Please be ready to go by then."

53

Yoshida remained tight-lipped about the meeting location and had Gray and Tamura wear hoods during the drive. When Gray removed his hood, he saw they were at the home where the first meeting occurred.

"No surprise here," he whispered to Tamura. "I don't know why Yoshida was so secretive about it."

"Maybe he's following protocol."

As expected, Gray and Tamura were led to the same holding room they'd been kept in during their first visit. Yoshida had parted ways with them as soon as they entered the home. All they could do was sit tight and wait.

"I wonder how long this will take?" Tamura said.

"I think the shorter the meeting, the greater the odds Ito doesn't rule in our favor. How long was the last meeting? An hour?"

"I think that sounds about right."

"I wonder if Tanaka is in that meeting?" Tamura asked. "He's definitely not some ordinary foot soldier."

"I'm sure he's in that meeting. That guy can't stand me. He's probably making the case right now to cut me loose."

"I hope not, literally. You think Yoshida can hold his own against him?"

"Yoshida might be on the quiet side, but from what I can tell, he doesn't get shaken easily. I have faith in him."

Since Gray and Tamura still had no personal effects on them, they had to guess when an hour had passed. They felt good about the timing. It meant there was a lot of debate.

Tamura stood and stretched, which triggered Gray to yawn and Tamura to follow.

"It feels like it's been an hour and a half at a minimum," she said.

Just then, the door opened, and in walked Yoshida. "Your presence has been requested."

"Has a decision been made?" Gray asked as he got up off the floor.

"Please, follow me quickly."

Sitting at the table inside the meeting room were the same three leaders of the Yamaguchi: Ito, Shimada, and Fukuzawa. Standing behind them was Tanaka.

"Welcome, Special Agent Gray and Inspector Tamura. I apologize for the long wait. We are ready to inform you of our decision. Please have a seat."

Gray and Tamura took a seat at the table.

"Both of you know that most of Tokyo is controlled by the Sumiyoshi. There are a few neutral pockets and areas where we have a presence, but make no mistake, that is Sumiyoshi territory. Special Agent Gray, do you understand that if one of our men were to be seen in their territory, it would surely invite an attack?"

"I am aware of that," Gray said.

"Then you should understand how serious this request is. You want protection from us, yet we must also look out for ourselves. Finding a gaijin with red hair might seem easy to you, but there are still over thirteen million people living in Tokyo. Timing had to be considered as to whether you could meet your objective reasonably. May I ask you what you think is a reasonable time?"

"That question is difficult to answer," Gray said. "If I say a couple of days and you agree, I put myself in an impossible position. If I say a couple of weeks, that may be too long for you, and the answer is no. I fully understand the commitment and danger to your men and the organization. A

Yamaguchi presence could trigger a war with the Sumiyoshi. But if you haven't already considered this, the Sumiyoshi is now distracted. Their men, thinking, and resources are all focused on the TMPD and the government. If there was ever a time that favored what I'm suggesting, it would be now."

The three men looked at one another as if they wanted further discussion. From what Gray could tell, Tanaka seemed to be the only one not buying into his moving speech. Tanaka glared at Gray as if he only wanted to jump across the table and attack him.

"I appreciate your honest answer, but you did not answer the question," Ito said.

"That's because it's an impossible question to answer."

"We agree with your assessment regarding the Sumiyoshi. They are distracted at the moment. And we have not forgotten what our real purpose is here. Stop the trafficking of weapons. Your request for protection is granted."

Gray smiled as he clapped. "That's wonderful."

"Chihiro Tanaka and his men will be responsible for your security detail. His responsibility is to keep you alive, not to help with your investigation. He does not report to either of you. You have one week. Good luck."

Without another word, Ito and the other men stood and exited the room. Gray looked across the table at Tanaka, and for the first time, he had a grin on his face.

We're screwed.

54

Yoshida ushered Gray and Tamura out of the room and straight to the car. Once their hoods were secured over their head, they began the drive back to Ito's home.

During the drive back, all Gray could think of was that he was being set up. This would be the perfect opportunity for Tanaka to put a bullet into his skull, and even Tamura's, if needed. He thought briefly about questioning Yoshida, but assumed that he would not give Gray an honest answer if that were the truth. Yoshida might not entirely like being a member of the Yamaguchi, but his loyalties were without question.

Once they were back at the house, Yoshida informed them that Tanaka and his men would arrive in two hours and they would leave Kobe at that time.

"Are there any questions you have for me?" Yoshida asked.

"Not at the moment," Gray said. "But I'd like to take the opportunity to thank you for your hospitality while I was here. I enjoyed your company."

"The feeling is mutual. I know you are worried about Tanaka, but you should also know his orders are to protect you. He will face the consequences if he fails."

"Tanaka and I don't exactly get along. So coming from you, that does make me feel better. Is there a reason why they put Tanaka in charge? Surely Ito is aware of his disdain for me."

"Tanaka and his men are trustworthy and very good at what they do. Even I have total confidence that he will do his job to the best of his ability. Please, help yourself to anything in the kitchen before you leave."

Yoshida walked away as he made a call. Gray and Tamura headed to the kitchen.

"What's your take on all of this?" Gray asked.

"There's no bowing out now," Tamura said. "Tanaka has been assigned to us for the next week. Whether we need him or not, we're stuck with him for seven days. As for whether or not he'll see this as an opportunity for collateral damage, that shouldn't happen. Tanaka must obey his orders."

"Did you see the creepy grin on his face back at the meeting? Forgive me if I'm not trusting of the guy."

"Let's not jump to the worst-case scenario. Tanaka might surprise us and be an asset. In the meantime, we'll just keep a close eye on him. If it makes you feel better, I can probably get you a weapon, but if you use it and are caught . . ."

"I know. I'm screwed. Forget it; Tanaka doesn't scare me."

Tanaka and his men showed up in three black SUVs. They didn't bother to come inside. Instead, they sat in their vehicles and waited. Yoshida walked Gray and Tamura outside.

"Wait here."

Yoshida had a short conversation with Tanaka.

"He wants both of you to ride in the second vehicle. He intends to drive to a hotel that the Yamaguchi secretly manage in the Shibuya district. Both of you will stay there. It'll be easier for him to watch over you. Will that work?"

"I'm fine with it," Gray said.

"Same here," Tamura said. "But he knows we'll need to go out. We're not staying in the room."

"He's aware. I think he'll be more comfortable staying there because it's familiar ground, but once you're there, you can coordinate specifics."

"I get the impression Tanaka is offering protection at the hotel," Gray said.

"Yes, that's the case. It's dangerous for them to walk around with you. It'll have to do."

"It's fine," Tamura said. "Are they armed?"

"Yes."

"I'll need my service weapon. I can have it delivered to the hotel."

"That's fine."

Gray stuck his hand out. "Yoshida, it's been an interesting ride. Maybe we'll meet again."

"So long as it's not on official business."

Gray and Tamura climbed into the SUV, and they drove off. A driver and a man were sitting in the front of their vehicle. Two more men were sitting in the third row.

"If the other two cars are filled, that's a good number of men," Tamura said.

"How do you see this working?"

"I'm sure Tanaka will have an opinion, but it makes sense that they stay out of sight. We don't need a walking shield."

"I agree. So long as we can reach them on the phone and they can be wherever we are quick, it should work."

The drive to Tokyo took seven hours—it was nothing like riding the bullet train. The three SUVs stopped on a narrow road, and everyone got out. Gray looked around but didn't see any signage for a hotel.

"Must be a secret hotel."

"Most likely a love hotel, a discrete one like the one you stayed at earlier," Tamura said. "This will be helpful."

They followed Tanaka through an unmarked door. There was a small lobby with kiosks to check in. An elderly man appeared and had a short conversation with Tanaka.

"I think he's the manager here," Tamura said.

Tanaka spoke in Japanese to Tamura.

"He said we're all staying here. The manager will show us to our room."

The elderly man led Gray and Tamura to their room on the second floor. It didn't have an over-the-top theme like the last hotel Gray had stayed in. The walls were painted red with white and pink hearts. The bedcover was red with heart-shaped pillows and on the ceiling was a mural of a cupid to ensure there was lovemaking.

Gray peeked out the window and watched the three SUVs drive off.

"Are you sure Tanaka is staying here?"

"That's what he said."

"I have a feeling Tanaka will give us the bare minimum."

"I don't doubt that one bit." Tamura held out a bowl filled with heart-shaped candies. "Sweets for my sweetie."

"Ramen sounds better." Gray glanced at his watch. "It's eleven, so all the bars in the Golden Gai should be open. We should figure out how we'll find this bar without being seen by the Sumiyoshi."

"Let me make a quick phone call. I want to let my men know we're back." After she ended the call, she put her phone down. "I'm sending a couple of my guys to the Golden Gai tonight to see what they can find. If that doesn't work, we'll need another plan."

"What about bringing your boss into the fold? Any plans in that area?"

"I'm still on the fence. I haven't updated him on our most recent revelations because I worry they'll just screw things up as they did with the warehouse. I feel asking him for help right now isn't in our interest."

"We have Tanaka for seven days. I don't know if that's an advantage yet," Gray said.

"Let's see what my guys find out tonight. Any idea where in the Golden Gai this bar might be?" Tamura asked.

"I've been wracking my brains over this. Everything is a blur before I was in that bar and everything after is the same. It's so strange. All I have is the description I gave you of the inside."

"Keep thinking. You're bound to remember something."

About thirty minutes later, one of Tamura's men showed up outside the hotel. She talked briefly with him and returned to the room with her laptop and service weapon.

"They're all set."

"Great. Maybe they'll get lucky."

Gray and Tamura spent the next few hours fielding phone calls from her men. Every time they thought they had something, they would send a photo. They even started texting pictures of Sumiyoshi-owned bars and the lanes they were on, but so far, nothing was striking Gray as familiar.

"I hate to say it, Mariko, but we need to go there. It'll be our best bet at jogging my memory."

"I'm thinking the same thing. What are the odds of Tanaka agreeing to accompany us?"

Gray shrugged. "Can't hurt to ask."

"I think we need to sweeten the pot before we go to him."

"What do you mean?"

"It's dangerous for them to enter the Golden Gai. It's a stronghold for the Sumiyoshi. If we can lessen the risk, he's much more apt to agree."

"And how do you propose we do that?" Gray crinkled his brow.

"I think we bring my boss into this. If he can increase the number of raids around the Golden Gai, it'll create a distraction."

"Chaos. The Sumiyoshi will be focused on the TMPD."

"Exactly."

"You think you can convince him to do that?"

"It's worth a try."

55

The plan the following morning was for Gray to talk to Tanaka while Tamura headed into headquarters for a conversation with her boss. After saying goodbye to Tamura, Gray headed back inside the hotel. He had no idea which room Tanaka was staying in or if he was even in the hotel. Tanaka hadn't given them a way to contact him, and it hadn't dawned on Gray and Tamura until after the fact.

The elderly man from the night before was nowhere to be seen, but Gray wanted to hear back from Tamura before approaching Tanaka. Gray headed back up to the second floor and walked down the hall, listening. Tanaka had a very distinct voice, but Gray heard nothing. He walked to the third floor, which was the top floor. As he reached the end of the hall, one of the previous doors opened and one of Tanaka's men stepped out.

So they are staying here. That's good to know.

The man didn't see Gray and headed to a row of vending machines near the stairwell.

Another door opened and out walked another Yamaguchi. He, too, headed straight for the vending machine.

It looks like it's breakfast time.

Just then, the door right next to Gray opened quickly. Standing in the doorway was Tanaka.

"What are you doing here?" he asked gruffly.

"To be honest, I was trying to figure out if you were staying at the hotel. But now that I found you, we need to talk."

"About what?"

"I think we should have this conversation inside your room and not in the hallway."

Tanaka eyed Gray for a moment before stepping back and allowing Gray to enter his room.

"I wanted to wait until I heard back from Tamura before speaking with you, but since I have your attention..."

"What is this about?" Tanaka's face turned angrier.

"You know we're looking for a gaijin with red hair, right?"

Tanaka nodded.

Gray explained the situation and how having Tamura's men search didn't have great results.

"I need to go to the Golden Gai. I think it'll help me remember if I'm there."

"So go."

"That's the problem. The Sumiyoshi want me dead. I need you and your men to take out any Sumiyoshi that come after me. I know it's crazy because it will endanger you guys. I also realize the Golden Gai is—"

"Okay," Tanaka said.

It took Gray a beat to comprehend what had just happened. "Wait, did you just agree?"

"I don't like you, Special Agent Gray. But I hate the Sumiyoshi. If I can put a bullet in some of their heads, I will do it."

"Great. Tamura is at TMPD headquarters trying to convince her superiors to increase the raids on the Sumiyoshi around the Golden Gai. It'll distract them further. One more thing, drop the title. I don't need anyone knowing my profession."

"Okay, but tonight we go there even if Tamura is unsuccessful. I want to avenge my brothers."

Tamura had secured a meeting with her boss, Izumi. It was just the two of them in his office.

"I haven't heard anything since you and Agent Gray went to Kobe," Izumi said.

"I apologize, but there wasn't anything to report until now."

Tamura updated Izumi on Gray's theory on how the weapons are trafficked through Japan and not to Japan.

"You can't be serious?" Izumi said. "How can he know this?"

"I reached out to a bunch of contacts in Southeast Asia. They all report a huge rise in illegal guns entering their countries . . . the same Russian guns the Sumiyoshi are using. While we can't prove it, the data makes a strong case. Surely you can see that."

Izumi nodded. "So, what is the plan now?"

"We're pretty sure a foreigner is running this operation. We have a lead —a redheaded individual."

"A person with red hair will stand out, but Tokyo is still a big city."

"That's where you can help. I have two requests. Make this person of interest official. If every officer at the TMPD is aware of this, we should be able to locate him."

"What is your second one?"

"Increase the raids on the Sumiyoshi near the Golden Gai."

"Why?"

"Gray recalls seeing this individual in a bar with a distinct mural inside. Some of my men searched for it last night, but they came up empty. It's almost like a hidden bar. Gray might recall where this bar is if he goes into the Golden Gai."

"That's insane. Is he looking to get killed? We can't guarantee his safety in there."

"I realize that, but we can help by distracting the Sumiyoshi even more. And we have bodyguards. A few Yamaguchi men accompanied us for that sole purpose. The Yamaguchi is also interested in stopping the flow of weapons into the country."

"Now you're running an operation with the Yamaguchi. This goes beyond anything we discussed previously."

"You can continue to deny knowing any of this. That's not changing. If things go sideways, you can cast us as rogue agents."

"If something happens to him, worse, if he ends up dead, I can't have his blood on my hands."

"We feel pretty good about our chances. I don't want anything to happen to him, either. And plus, Gray has to go along with this as well. It's not like I'm forcing him."

"Are you telling me he's not worried?"

"There's a concern, but if he honestly felt like it was too dangerous, he would bow out. Let's not forget he is a trained FBI agent. He *can* handle himself."

Izumi shook his head as he let out a slow breath.

"We can even arm him with a—"

"Not another word," Izumi said. "I don't want to know the details. Go do what you need to do."

56

Everyone was set to go at nine o'clock in the evening. Rather than drive to the Golden Gai, Tanaka wanted to head there on foot. He believed it was safer, even though they'd be out in the open. Tanaka had ten men with him, and they were all armed; that made a group of thirteen people—not exactly covert. Still, Tanaka argued it was the best way. Also, he'd told Gray and Tamura that they could go alone if they didn't like his plan. To make matters worse, Tanaka wanted to cover most of the distance via the metro.

"Are you sure that's a good idea?" Tamura asked.

"You worry too much," Tanaka said. "It's a five-minute ride."

The group left the hotel with Tanaka leading the way down a semi-lit street. It was impossible *not* to notice them, especially since the Yamaguchi loved their black suits. Eventually, they popped onto a road filled with eateries, convenience stores, and various retail shops. Even though no one seemed to be paying them any attention, Gray struggled with the number of people outside when there were active gunfights between the police and the Sumiyoshi.

"I know the Sumiyoshi has gained a following, but you'd think because of what's happening, people would stay indoors," Gray said.

"Tokyo is one of the most populated cities in the world," Tamura said. "It's impossible to keep people cooped up," Tamura said. "Plus, most people see this as a police–Yakuza problem. If anything, I bet many of them are hoping for something interesting to happen so they can post to their social media."

"Everyone is chasing fame, even the Yakuza."

The group continued down a busy road and passed by a burned-out koban that had been roped off. Tanaka turned into a narrow walkway that took them right under a large shopping center. When they popped back up to ground level, Tanaka stopped.

"The entrance to the metro is around that corner." He pointed ahead.

"This isn't as bad as I thought it would be," Gray said to Tamura as they continued.

"Yeah, so far, so good."

They rounded the corner and ran smack into Tanaka, who had stopped abruptly. Up ahead, they saw a tactical unit from TMPD converging on the entrance of the metro. The group quickly moved back around the corner.

"We have to go to the next entrance," Tanaka said. "It's not far."

A second later, gunfire erupted. Gray looked around the corner and saw the Sumiyoshi firing on the TMPD tactical unit.

Tanaka yanked Gray by his arm. "Come on, we need to go."

The group darted across the road, keeping their heads low, eventually making their way to a huge intersection where five streets converged. Tanaka stopped the group right near a building. The entrance to the metro was on the other side of the intersection. Next to it was a koban, but there were no police officers in it. Tanaka watched for a few more seconds before moving the group toward the metro entrance.

Getting on the train was seamless. One of Tanaka's men knew the security guards, so the group could pass without being checked by handheld metal detectors. They entered a car that was crowded, but not to the point where people were pressed against each other. Gray and Tamura slipped between a few people, so they weren't standing next to Tanaka and his men.

"It's just five minutes," Gray said.

"Crap," Tamura said under her breath. "Don't make it obvious when you look, but there are Sumiyoshi near the front of the car."

Gray was taller than everyone on the train, so all he did was turn his head slightly. He saw a group of men, five of them. They were young and dressed in fashionable clothing.

"How can you be sure?" he asked.

"I know one of them. My best guess is that they're heading to the Golden Gai."

"Great."

"Let's hope Tanaka doesn't sniff them out."

No sooner had Tamura uttered those words than a gun went off, and people in the car started screaming. Tanaka had his gun out and was firing at the group of Sumiyoshi. Gray and Tamura followed everyone else and hit the floor.

People were screaming and scrambling to escape the firefight as the Sumiyoshi returned fire, sending bullets flying over their heads. Gray looked back over his shoulder as he crawled away and watched Tanaka run up to a Sumiyoshi and shoot him point blank. Blood spattered the window behind him as he fell back against the seats. Tanaka had shown absolutely no hesitation for his own safety. He wanted that man dead.

Within seconds the barrage of gunshots ended, and all five Sumiyoshi men were lying on the ground, motionless. Tanaka and his men had wiped them out just as the train pulled into the station.

Tanaka walked over to Gray and Tamura. "Get up. We need to keep moving."

57

Iwata and Mizuno had been laying low for the last couple of days. Things between the Sumiyoshi and the TMPD had escalated beyond what Iwata could have imagined. The TMPD had the men and the firepower needed to suppress the Sumiyoshi. Many of their men were either being killed or taken into custody. It was evident to the leadership that if this battle continued, they'd lose. The leadership had now begun to focus on de-escalating the war. Iwata had heard that his uncle contemplated negotiating a truce with the government. If they were successful, his uncle's attention, and that of the other leaders, would eventually turn back to the root cause of everything. And Iwata was still the most likely suspect.

"We're screwed," Mizuno said out loud.

"We're only screwed if Gray is still in Japan."

"But if the TMPD comes out and says that they had help from the FBI, everyone is going to suspect us because everyone already thinks we had something to do with it."

"There's no proof unless someone outs Gray or he comes forward and speaks. And anyway, we're not the only ones who party with gaijin."

As Iwata spoke, even he had a hard time believing his words. The only chance they had guaranteeing they lived through this was to hope Gray hadn't left Japan, find him, and kill him.

Mizuno answered his phone. "What? When?" After a few seconds, Mizuno turned to Iwata. "There's been a shoot-out between Sumiyoshi and Yamaguchi in the metro."

"Yamaguchi? What are they doing here?" Iwata asked.

Mizuno spoke a little more with the person on the other end of the phone. "The Yamaguchi got out at the Shinjuku stop. There was a gaijin with them."

"Was it Gray?"

"Mizuno shrugged. "They don't know. They just said a gaijin was with them. A tall one."

"It's got to be him. They're probably going to the Golden Gai."

"But why would he go there with the Yamaguchi? They know we own that entire area."

"I don't know. Get the men ready. We'll find out ourselves if this is Gray."

"I still don't get it," Gray said as they walked along a crowded street. Loads of young people were out for a fun night, many on their way to the Golden Gai.

"Young people think they're invincible," Tamura said. "Plus, the TMPD is too busy with the Sumiyoshi to enforce a curfew. Really, the only way they can manage that is if they bring in the Ground Self-Defense Force. And involving the military in anything is very political. Actually, what concerns me at the moment is you."

"What am I doing?"

"It's not what you're doing. It's your height. You look like Gulliver walking around Lilliput. Maybe you should crouch a little and blend with us locals. It'll only get worse when we enter the Golden Gai. We have to assume it'll be crawling with Sumiyoshi."

"Only Iwata and his men know who I am. So long as they're not here, we should be okay. And wouldn't most of the Sumiyoshi be caught up in their fight with TMPD?"

"We'll find out soon."

"You know Tanaka and his men already have targets on their back, and that shoot-out back at the metro didn't help matters. They're probably more wanted now than I am. They'll be doing us no favors if they come into the Golden Gai."

"You're right."

Gray and Tamura had a quick conversation about the situation with Tanaka, and at first, he disagreed. Gray could tell from the look in Tanaka's eyes that he wanted to take out more Sumiyoshi. He'd gotten a taste of it earlier.

"If we can't do what we need to do, which is to search those bars without distraction, this will all be a waste of time," Tamura said to Tanaka.

"Stay outside the Golden Gai and keep watch," Gray said. "If we run into trouble, we'll call for you."

Tanaka finally nodded. "I'll position my men around the perimeter. Don't die in there, Gray. I still have a beef with you."

As they neared the Golden Gai, Gray and Tamura parted ways with him.

"I feel like we're finally on the same side with Tanaka if you ignore that last comment of his," Gray said.

"Do you remember if you entered the Golden Gai from the front or rear?"

"From the front."

Tamura hooked her arm around Gray's. "We're boyfriend and girl-friend. Do your best to make it look real, okay?"

"No problem."

58

The Golden Gai was already bouncing with people looking for a good time despite the situation in Japan. Lanterns hung above the tiny lanes, lighting the way as people decided where to start drinking. Some smaller bars, which simply had a bar top with four or five stools on the lane, were already filled.

"It definitely wasn't any of these walk-up bars," Gray said. "And that's all there is on this lane. Let's try a different one."

The bars in the narrow pathways between the lanes were even smaller. Some didn't even have seats. One just stood next to a countertop. There was one bar that had indoor seating. Gray peeked inside, saw the vampire theme, and quickly shook his head.

The following lane had a mixture of walk-up bars and bars with indoor seating. One by one, they made their way past the places, looking inside the ones with indoor seating. But nothing was jogging Gray's memory.

"Does this lane even look or feel familiar?" Tamura asked.

"Not really. Is there an area where the Sumiyoshi bars congregate?"

"Not really. In fact, that's one right there. The one with the Charlie Chaplin theme."

"I never would have guessed."

"What about landmarks? Do you recall seeing anything unusual? You know, something like that?" Tamura pointed to a red telephone box.

"You know, now that you said that, I recall this image of two cartoon pigs holding chopsticks."

"I know that sign. It's promoting an all-you-can-eat buffet."

Tamura led the way through the maze of lanes until they stood in front of a small billboard with two pigs holding chopsticks.

"This is it. I can't believe we found it."

Gray spun around to face the bar opposite it and headed inside. A few seconds later, he reappeared, shaking his head.

"We'll just check all the bars on this lane. One of them has to have a mural of the green samurai."

They began searching the bars right next to the billboard, but so far, none of them contained the mural.

"Any luck?" Gray asked as he came out of a bar at the same time Tamura exited another.

"No. But let's keep moving south. We can always loop back and cover the ones north of the billboard."

Tamura grabbed Gray by his arm as they were about to split and tackle two more bars.

"Up ahead . . . Sumiyoshi."

"I see them."

Three men were standing outside of a bar. One of them looked in Gray and Tamura's direction. Tamura hooked her arm around Gray's and playfully led him into the nearest bar, which specialized in chūhai. The bar was decorated with pastel colors, and posters of women dressed in school uniforms hung on the walls.

"This place looks interesting," Gray said. "Do they sell soda here?"

"Kind of. Those drinks are called chūhai. It's a mixture of fruit juice, shochu, and sparkling water. It's delicious."

"There must be thirty different flavors to choose from."

"Yeah, it's a popular drink. This bar also specializes in something else."

Tamura sat Gray down in a chair so that his back faced the door. She straddled him and threw her hair over his head to hide his buzz cut.

"What's happening?"

"Those Sumiyoshi men are coming toward us. If they come inside, I'm no longer your girlfriend. You're now my customer."

"Got it."

"Crap. They're standing at the entrance."

Tamura started to sway her hips to the music.

"One of them decided to do a walk-through of the place. I have no idea if this will work, so be ready to act." Tamura accentuated her movements. "This might deter him from bothering us."

It didn't, because he stopped and started talking to Tamura in Japanese. Gray could see the man's shoes as he stood next to their table, but that was it.

Tamura turned her head to speak to the man, leaving her long hair covering Gray's head and face.

As the two continued talking, Gray ran through several scenarios. None of the three Sumiyoshi were big men. He was confident he could take them on. But Gray had to assume they were armed. He could stand up quickly while swinging an uppercut that would knock out the guy talking to Tamura. But then what? Tamura would have to draw her weapon and fire at the two in the doorway, assuming they were still standing in front of the doorway and she had a clear shot.

The man placed his hand on Gray's shoulder. It felt like he wanted a look. Tamura started talking faster and knocked the man's hand away, but he placed it back on Gray's shoulder and gripped harder. Both of them began to speak faster and the level of the voices rose.

This is it. Get ready.

Gray's thigh muscles tightened as he tensed up. He was ready to explode off the chair.

I'm knocking him into next week if he doesn't leave in five seconds.

Suddenly the Sumiyoshi released his grip and removed his hand. A few more words from Tamura, and the man walked away.

Tamura turned her head to face Gray again. "That was close."

"What did you tell him?"

"I kept telling him my mother was sick and that I was working and needed the money from my customer."

"Are they gone?"

"Yeah, they left." She got off of Gray. "That was close."

"I think I might need a weapon," Gray said.

"I'm sure Tanaka has one he can give you, but just know what will happen if you get caught with it, or worse if you have to use it. My government will deny any involvement and prosecute you."

"They'll deny involvement anyway. I am more concerned for my life."

"You're right. I'd arm myself if I were you. Come on, let's keep moving."

59

Iwata and Mizuno slipped past a TMPD patrol and quickly made their way into the Golden Gai. They stuck to the smaller lanes that housed the bars that weren't that popular. They headed into a small alley and stopped in front of a narrow doorway. Iwata knocked, and a few minutes later, the door opened, and they entered. The space inside was a little bigger than a standard bedroom. In the corner was a tiny bar with a bartender behind it. Two other men were sitting at a table drinking whisky. Iwata and Mizuno took a seat, and the man behind the bar brought them a bottle of whisky with two glasses.

"Why did we come in here?" Mizuno asked as he filled each glass with whisky.

"I need a drink to take the edge off. Where are the rest of the men?"

"Some are on the way. Some are already at the bar."

"And the gaijin?"

"He's at the bar, but he's restless. Do you think Gray knows about him?"

"Probably. Why else would he have come back here?"

"I don't understand how he figured it out. Even your uncle doesn't know anything about our partner."

"I should have never taken him to the warehouse. That's the reason for everything getting screwed up."

"How could we have known he was an FBI agent? Huh? We're not psychic. We need to move him to another location." Mizuno lifted his glass. "He's not safe here anymore."

"If Gray knows what he looks like, then we need to change his looks."

"Yeah, he needs to wear a hat."

"No, we need to shave his head." Iwata downed the rest of his whisky. "Send a message to the men. Let them know we're coming."

Mizuno did what Iwata asked and then quickly finished off one more pour. The two moved slowly, eyes peeled for Gray or TMPD. Iwata stopped at the mouth of the alleyway and looked both ways down the lane before heading right. They moved quickly until they reached a bar that didn't have the typical signage that the others had. No hanging lanterns or lights were next to it, and no cute women enticed men to enter.

Mizuno pulled open the door, and they headed inside. The bar didn't have an over-the-top theme. If anything, it resembled a typical dive bar. Japanese rock music blared from the speakers, and old-school rock and roll memorabilia hung in various places. And painted on the rear wall was a mural of a samurai. It looked totally out of place next to the framed photos of Elvis and Jimmy Hendrix. It was a recent addition, something the gaijin had requested.

Iwata scanned the room quickly, recognizing the men inside. They were Sumiyoshi, but not part of his crew. They walked to the rear of the place and into a narrow hallway that housed the bathrooms. Mizuno walked up to the end of the hallway, pushed on the wall, and opened it, revealing a hidden space with a spiral staircase.

At the top of the stairs, they were met by one of Iwata's men, standing guard outside a door.

"What's he doing?" Iwata asked. "Drinking?"

The man nodded and stepped away from the door. Iwata and Mizuno headed inside.

"Jesus, Mary, and Joseph, it's bleedin' crazy outside, isn't it?" the redheaded man said in a thick Irish accent.

He was watching a rugby game on a laptop while drinking from a bottle of Jameson.

"I keep seeing reports about the police sorting you guys out. Is everything okay?"

"It will be after we give you a haircut," Iwata said.

"What the hell for?"

"We need to take some precautions. It'll grow back."

"But my hair gives me my dashing good looks. It's what always makes me, Manus Murphy, the man of the hour."

Tamura led Gray into another bar. At first look, Gray thought it was a bar for couples until he realized it was a hostess bar.

"Why'd we come in here?" he asked.

"These women usually have a pretty good pulse on what's happening. Having a quick chat with one of them might be worth it."

Tamura looked around for a hostess who wasn't occupied with a customer. She spotted a woman exiting the bathroom and going to sit by herself on a sofa. She immediately started looking at her phone.

"Excuse me, can I buy you a drink?" Tamura said as she and Gray sat next to her.

The woman put her phone away. "Are you guys a couple?"

"Does it matter?"

"No."

A few minutes later, the woman returned with a bottle of whisky, mixers, and glassware. She started mixing drinks for the table.

"It's not common for couples to come here," the hostess said.

"We're not your typical couple."

The hostess held up her glass. "Here's to new beginnings."

Tamura placed her glass down on the table after taking a sip. "We're looking for someone, and I'm hoping you can help us."

"You're talking to the wrong person. I don't help the police." She looked at Gray. "Even handsome ones."

"That's too bad," Gray said as he placed a bunch of yen on the table. "I was hoping we'd have a lovely conversation."

The hostess got up and sat next to Gray. "What do you want to talk about?"

"The last time I was here, I visited a bar with a samurai painted on the wall. Know anything about it?"

"A lot of bars have pictures of samurais."

"This wasn't a picture. Someone had hand-painted a mural on the wall. It was a green samurai. Does that sound familiar?"

"Maybe." The woman gave Gray a flirtatious smile. "My memory comes and goes."

Gray removed more money from his wallet and tucked it into the hostess's cleavage.

"I remember now. There's a bar not far from here with a green samurai on the wall, but I don't think you have visited it before. Not just anyone can enter, especially a gaijin like you. The Sumiyoshi own it. The name is Black Hell."

"We'll have to take our chances," Gray said.

Gray and Tamura thanked the woman, paid their bill, and left.

"You think it's smart to head over there?" Gray asked.

"No, we're better off having a tactical team hit that bar. Let me call it in."

60

Tamura's boss got on board right away with the request, and an hour later, a tactical team raided the bar. Gray and Tamura observed from a safe distance, near the entrance to a small alleyway that connected two lanes. They eagerly waited for a redheaded man to be escorted out of the bar, but so far, no one who matched that description had appeared.

"If I could look at that mural, we'll know for sure if we hit the right place," Gray said.

"We should be okay to go inside. I'm just waiting for word."

A few minutes later, Tamura's phone rang.

"They found a hidden room," she said after ending the call. "Let's go have a look."

As soon as Gray entered the bar, he recognized the mural on the wall. "That's it." He walked up to it for a closer look. "Definitely the one I remember."

"Inspector Tamura, the room is back here," an officer said.

Tamura and Gray followed the officer down a hall.

"It looks like a normal wall, except if you press on it, it opens, revealing a stairway," the officer said. "I need to warn you that the team needs to hit another location. They'll be leaving shortly."

"Got it," she said.

They followed the officer up the stairs and into the small room above the bar.

"Did you find anything?" Tamura asked.

"Nothing of interest, but there were people in here. There's an open bottle of alcohol, a couple of used glasses, and a bunch of food containers. We'll collect it and see if we can pick up any DNA from it."

Gray walked over to the bottle of Jameson. "Irish whiskey. I have a feeling our guy was here. He's also a smoker." Gray pointed at an ashtray filled with cigarette butts.

"Iwata must be on to us," Tamura said.

Gray bent down and ran a hand across the floor. "Hey, come look at this." He held up his hand and short, red hair covered the tips of his fingers. "Looks like they shaved his head."

Tamura turned to an officer. "Pull the security footage from the cameras surrounding the Golden Gai. Look for any bald foreigners leaving the place tonight."

Iwata, Mizuno, and Murphy quickly escaped from the bar and into a waiting car. Murphy removed the ball cap he wore and ran a hand over his freshly shaved head.

"I can't believe my lovely hair is gone. Did you really need to take it all, mate?"

"It'll grow back," Iwata said. "We can't risk someone finding you. This operation is too valuable."

"They'll never crack how I'm doing it. Your people need to fix this problem with the police. That's screwing things up."

"If they catch you, the operation goes down."

"It's your job to protect me. So I say, get better at it."

Iwata's phone rang, and he answered. "They did? Are you sure? Kill him, now!"

"What is it?" Mizuno asked.

"Gray was seen entering the bar, and the assault team just left. I sent him a nice surprise."

"Who are you killing?" Murphy asked.

"Never mind."

———————

"There's not much more to see here," Tamura said. "We shouldn't overstay our welcome in a bar owned by the Sumiyoshi, especially since the tactical team has already left."

"Yeah, you're right. Let's rendezvous with Tanaka and head back to the hotel."

On the way down the stairs, Tamura sent a message to Tanaka, letting him know they were done and wanted to know where they should meet.

"I want to get a photo of that mural," Gray said as he walked over to it. He snapped a picture with his phone.

"Hey, stand next to it. I'll take a picture of you with it," Tamura offered.

Gray folded his arms across his chest as he backed up against the wall.

"Yeah, that looks good. When we catch this guy, this will make a nice souvenir."

Tamura walked over to a lone officer who stood next to the bar. "Are you the only one here?"

"Yeah, aside from the techs upstairs, everyone else moved to another location. I'll be heading over there as soon they finish upstairs. Are you guys leaving?"

"Yeah, we're finished."

"Do you need me to escort you anywhere?"

"No, I think we'll be fine. But I appreciate the offer."

"Let me just check and make sure everything is okay outside," the officer said as he hurried ahead and peeked outside.

A second later, a bullet struck him in the head.

61

"Get back!" Tamura shouted as she drew her gun and returned fire.

Gray ducked behind a booth while Tamura kept her gun trained on the doorway. She moved back behind a table and flipped it over for cover. A second later, a Sumiyoshi appeared and she fired, dropping him instantly. A barrage of firepower tore up the entrance to the bar, sending splintered wood and shards of glass flying everywhere.

Two men were dead in the doorway, and an assault rifle lay next to the Sumiyoshi. Gray moved up closer to them. It was the closest he could get to the doorway without being exposed to fire.

"Sterling, don't do it," Tamura shouted. "It's too risky."

"There could be ten of them armed with assault rifles. No way we can hold them off with just your handgun."

"I've already called for backup. Plus, that weapon is outside of the bar. It's too risky."

"What about the officer?"

"I think he's unarmed."

The longer they waited, the chances of grabbing that assault rifle diminished. The gunfire came from the right side of the bar, so that's where the Sumiyoshi was approaching. Gray dropped to his belly and slithered forward to the door until he was right up against the doorframe. He looked at the officer's waist. Tamura was right. He was unarmed. Gray grabbed the officer's hat and flung it out of the bar.

Rapid gunfire erupted. Gray reached out, snatched the assault rifle, and quickly shuffled back toward safety. He hurried back to where Tamura was, flipped another table over, and took cover.

Gray looked over at Tamura. "Now we have a fighting chance."

Gray popped the magazine out of the gun and took a look.

"How much is in there?" Tamura asked.

"I might have to downgrade that 'fighting chance' to 'wishful thinking.' I got half a mag. Let's make our shots count," Gray said as he took aim and readied his finger on the trigger. Tamura did the same.

Gray saw shadows on the pavement growing larger. They were closing in when, suddenly, it looked like they stopped. A moment later, the Sumiyoshi began shooting inside the bar through the windows. Gray and Tamura both ducked as bullets struck the tables they were behind.

Gray peeked from the side of the table. The front windows and the curtains were destroyed entirely, giving him a view outside at the head of a Sumiyoshi. He took aim and fired once, striking the man in the forehead. Another Sumiyoshi stepped into the doorway, spraying the place. Tamura put two bullets into his chest.

Gray continued to fire out the window, but he knew he was closer to an empty mag each time he pulled the trigger. From the corner of his eye, he could already see Tamura reloading a fresh mag. The Sumiyoshi continued to fire into the bar as if they had an unlimited ammo supply, which they probably did.

Suddenly the firing grew louder and much more rapid, as if more Sumiyoshi had joined the fight. Gray pulled the trigger and fired his last round.

"I'm out!"

"Me too!" Tamura yelled back.

"Who are they firing at?" Gray said as he looked up. "None of the rounds are coming into the bar."

The rapid gunfire outside lessened and eventually came to a halt. They could hear the crackling sound of broken glass being stepped on.

"Agent Gray, are you still alive?" a voice called out.

Gray peered above the table and saw Tanaka in the doorway.

Gray and Tamura let out a breath of relief as they stood up.

"I never thought I'd say this, but boy am I glad to see you," Gray said. "Where did you get those guns?" Gray pointed at the Uzi in Tanaka's hand.

"I kept it in my backpack," he said. "We have to get out of here. Reinforcements might come."

"Are we heading back to the hotel on foot?" Tamura asked as she scavenged an assault rifle and ammo from a dead Sumiyoshi. Gray took some ammo.

"We don't have a choice. It's not safe here for us."

The group ran down a lane that led them out of the Golden Gai. Just as they popped out onto a larger road, two cars came skidding to a stop. A bunch of Sumiyoshi jumped out of the vehicles and fired on Gray and the others.

Gray grabbed Tamura in his arms and rushed her back into the lane while Tanaka and his men returned fire. Two of Tanaka's men were shot dead instantly. Gray watched Tanaka throw something. A few seconds later, a grenade went off, and one of the cars erupted into flames.

"Tanaka and his men are better armed than I thought they would be," Gray said. "But this is getting out of control."

"If we stick around, we'll end up dead," Tamura said. "I say we cut loose from Tanaka."

"No arguments from me."

Tamura led the way back into the lane.

"We can exit on the east side of the Golden Gai and flag a taxi. It'll be safer than being out on the streets."

Gray looked over his shoulder and saw Tanaka launch another grenade.

62

Ever since Iwata had taken Murphy to a small hotel not far from the Golden Gai, the Irishman hadn't stopped bitching about his hair and everything else.

"What the hell are we doing here?" Murphy asked as he climbed out of the car. "Don't you have a place?"

"It's too risky to go there. It could be raided at any moment," Iwata said. "We know the owner of this hotel. We'll be fine here for a day while I figure things out."

The group headed into the building and settled into a couple of rooms.

Mizuno ended his call. "Yamaguchi showed up. Gray got away."

"Dammit!"

"We lost men at the bar and a couple more just outside the Golden Gai. The rest of the men are on their way here."

"How many?"

Mizuno shrugged. "Maybe ten, maybe more. I can't be sure."

"Who's this Gray fella you keep popping off about?" Murphy asked.

"Never mind about him," Iwata said. "He's our problem."

Murphy rested his hands on his waist. "Look, mates. Whatever problem you have with the police or this Gray guy, you feckers better deal with it."

"Maybe we can put a hold on the weapons," Iwata said. "At least until it calms down a bit."

Murphy shook his head. "Our agreement ain't changing. I need to keep things moving. You need to fix this problem."

"It's not that simple."

"I don't care. A lot of work has gone into perfecting this operation. I'm not losing it because you can't handle things on your end. I've handed you guys the deal of a lifetime. You're getting guns at a discount and a piece of the action."

"You've moved thousands of weapons through Japan without any problem," Iwata said. "Why are you worried?"

"Because I need to keep moving the product. I can't have any holdups. There's another shipment coming in next week. I ain't stopping it."

Murphy walked over to the minibar in the room and started poking around. "And if you think I won't pull the deal, try me."

"Things keep getting more screwed up," Mizuno said as he and Iwata huddled on the other side of the room. "If Murphy pulls out, we're screwed. Your uncle totally thinks we're running the show. If he finds out we aren't the ones in charge. . ."

"I know, we'll be dead for lying about the operation, dead for bringing an outsider into our business, and dead for showing an FBI agent our warehouse full of weapons."

"We can't babysit this guy and hunt for Gray."

"We don't have a choice. We need to keep Murphy safe. This deal with him can't fall apart. He'll just take it to one of the other syndicates."

"Hey, when you two tools stop making out in the corner, can you get me a bottle of Jameson?" Murphy called out. "This crap here won't cut it."

Gray and Tamura couldn't flag down a taxi, so they kept moving on the streets. That part of town was quiet, and not many people were out. Still, sporadic gunfire could be heard in the distance.

"What's the plan?" Gray asked. "We can't stay on the streets for very long."

"I'm not sure." Tamura checked her phone. "Tanaka still hasn't answered my text message."

"It doesn't mean he's dead."

"I know, but it doesn't look good."

"I think we should go to another hotel, just in case Tanaka or one of his men is compromised."

Gray and Tamura found a love hotel buried in the dead end of a small lane and checked in.

"I never thought I'd spend so much time in love hotels without making love," Gray said. "It's more like a roommate hotel for me."

"Tough life, right?" Tamura took a seat on the bed and kicked her shoes off. "That feels good."

Gray popped the mag out of his rifle to double-check the magazine. He did the same with Tamura's gun.

"We're good on ammo," he said. "You still got your service weapon?"

"Yeah," she placed her hip holster on the bed. "But it's empty."

Tamura made some calls to see if their suspect had popped up in the CCTV footage. So far, there was nothing. Tamura made a request that the TMPD hit all known locations associated with Iwata.

"We're doing a better job than the department," Gray said. "And we're doing it with very little support."

"They'll be less helpful now that we're looking for a bald man. I'm afraid it's up to us."

"If I were Iwata, I wouldn't take this guy to any place I own. I'd go some-place unexpected."

"You know, this investigation could start dragging on," Tamura said. "Assuming Tanaka and his men are out of the equation, there's still a great deal of danger surrounding you. I hate to say it, but maybe you should reconsider staying here."

"You saying I should leave?"

"I'm saying think about your options. You've done the job you were brought here to do. Being shot at by Sumiyoshi isn't really part of the deal."

"I know, but we've come so far. I need to see this through."

"I'm happy to have you as my partner, but it's your call."

"This is all Kita's fault. He jinxed it from the very beginning."

Tamura laughed.

"He's probably soaking up the sun with a mai tai in each hand and not a worry in the world."

"I'm sure that's pretty close to it."

"Any chance Iwata might have headed outside of Tokyo?"

"Maybe, but my gut tells me he's sticking around here. It's familiar ground, and he has backup here if he needs it. Technically, we're still in the Shinjuku district, which is one of their strongholds."

"You think he's here? His guys just had a huge shoot-out with the Yamaguchi."

Tamura shrugged. "Iwata favors this district the most. I wouldn't put it past him to stay put. You know the saying, hide in plain sight."

"In light of everything that just happened, I'm feeling hungry," Gray said. "I'll get us some snacks from the vending machines down the hall."

"Get me something with curry."

"Will do."

He left the room and headed toward the vending machines. There were four of them. One specialized in different types of ramen, another focused on chips and candies, and another served up different entrees like curry katsu, fried rice, and even hamburgers. The last held beer, sake, fruit juice, and colas.

Gray bent over to get a better look at the photos for each option. There were a lot of interesting choices, but because he couldn't read Japanese, he had to compare pictures to tell the difference between each bowl.

"These machines are deadly," someone said as he walked up to the vending machine next to Gray. "I love the broiled eel with rice."

"Yeah, and the food tastes pretty good," Gray said without looking at the stranger talking to him.

"Beer in a vending machine. Brilliant."

It finally dawned on Gray that the person beside him spoke English. He glanced up and saw a white guy wearing a ball cap.

"The ramen is good," he said as he stared at his vending machine. "I've never had a bad dose myself."

"How long have you been in Japan?" Gray asked.

The man finally looked over at Gray. "I travel back and forth a lot for business. I'm an importer/exporter. What about yourself?"

"I'm a real estate developer. I'm new to the market here," Gray said.

"We have two of the most nebulous jobs to exist, right?"

"As long as it keeps me coming back. The women are something else here." Gray said as he straightened up. The stranger was the same height as him, but thinner.

"Beauties, aren't they?"

"I see we have the same plans tonight," Gray motioned to their surroundings.

"I wish it was like that for me, but it's not." The man fed money into the machine, and a beer bottle came out. "You can't miss the broiled eel. Give it a lash."

"I might do that."

The man turned and began walking away.

"Excuse me, just one more thing," Gray said.

"Yeah, what is it mate?" The man stopped and looked over his shoulder.

Gray struck him square in the face with a fast right, dropping him to the carpeted floor. The man looked up at Gray, clearly dazed. Before he could open his mouth to speak, Gray hit him once more, knocking him out.

63

Tamura heard the knock on the door and popped off the bed to let Gray in, only it wasn't just him outside. An unconscious man was lying on the floor next to him.

"Hold the door open so I can drag him inside," Gray said.

"Who is this?" she asked as she stepped to the side.

"Close the door. We need something to bind his hands before he wakes up." Gray disconnected the cord from the telephone. "This should hold him."

"Wait." Tamura reached under her leather jacket and produced a pair of handcuffs. "Who is this person, and why am I cuffing him?"

Gray looked up at Tamura. "There's a chance I might be wrong, but I think this is our guy. Look at his eyelashes; they're red." He removed the cap. "He's bald, speaks with an Irish accent, and claims he's an importer/exporter. It doesn't get any more suspect than that."

"This is unbelievable," Tamura said. "What are the odds?"

"You said earlier Iwata wouldn't stray from his comfort zone. We're not that far from the Golden Gai. Look, if this isn't our guy, we'll apologize and send him on his way. But if he is . . ."

"Iwata's in this hotel, and he'll be looking for him in a few minutes."

"Right, we need to get out of here. Have you been able to reach Tanaka?"

"Not yet. I still have no idea if he's alive or dead. But I need to call this into headquarters. We need help."

"We can't wait here for them to mobilize."

Just then, the man began to stir. Gray grabbed his rifle and pressed it against the man's chest.

"Who the hell are you?" he mumbled.

"Sorry about smacking you earlier, but we need to question you," Gray said.

"I ain't telling you shit."

Gray pressed the barrel of the gun harder. "I got no problem pulling this trigger, but if you answer my questions, you might just get out of this situation breathing."

The man stared at Gray for a moment or so before a look of realization appeared on his face. "You're Gray, aren't you?"

"I have no idea what you're talking about."

The man glanced at Tamura. "The look on her face tells me I'm right. Everything makes sense now."

"What makes sense?"

"Why I had my head shaved and why I'm on the run."

"What's your name?"

"You're not Japanese, you have an American accent, but you're chasing someone in Japan. Are you FBI?"

"Do you know Sora Iwata?" Tamura asked.

Murphy looked over at Tamura. "Are you his detective sidekick?"

Gray slapped the man hard across the face before punching him in the stomach, causing him to curl up in a ball.

"I know who you are. You're working with Sora Iwata and the Sumiyoshi," Gray said. "And you're right. I am an FBI agent. And my partner is an inspector with the TMPD. That means you're burned."

"He's right," Tamura said. "You'll become enemy number one to them. They'll hunt you down and kill you regardless of whatever deal you have in place. That's how the Yakuza work. Right now, we're your best friends and your only hope of staying alive."

"You're lying. They need me."

"Believe what you want, but I know how they think and operate."

Gray leaned in. "You think they're indebted to you because you gave them weapons? Iwata and Mizuno are wondering right now if they should whack you and cut their losses. In a few minutes, they'll come looking for you. When they see you with us, they'll know you're flapping your lips."

"I ain't told you anything!"

"That's not what we'll say." Gray smiled. "You cut a deal with us to save your ass."

"Iwata's uncle is one of the top leaders in the organization," Tamura said. "If Iwata doesn't take you out, his uncle will. And he'll search the world until he has your head, literally. You can't hide from them." Tamura looked at her watch. "Time is running out."

"She's right. You're screwed. Your only option now is to cooperate with us. What room is Iwata in?"

"He's on the floor above this one."

"How many men are with him?"

"I don't know, maybe ten or twelve."

"I hate to keep referring to you as the redheaded guy. Give me a name," Tamura said.

"Manus Murphy. What kind of deal can you cut me?"

"We want to know everything about the trafficking operation, how it's done, who's involved, what Iwata's role is . . . everything. Help us with that, and you'll stay alive."

"Iwata's role? He has no role. He works for me as muscle," Murphy said. "That's it. In exchange, they get weapons at below cost and a small percentage of the sale."

Gray lifted Murphy to his feet. "This is a good start, but we must get out of here. It doesn't take long to buy something from the vending machines."

The three left the room and headed downstairs. Just as they entered the lobby, they heard shouting upstairs.

"They know," Tamura said as she pushed the front door open.

They cleared the building and moved quickly away. Gray glanced back to the hotel and spotted Iwata watching them from a window.

64

While running down the street, Tamura was on the phone talking to her boss.

"I swear he's our guy, but we got the Sumiyoshi on our butts. We need backup now!"

"Tell me he's sending a team of people to us," Gray said as he dragged Murphy beside him.

"He's given us directions to an extraction point where a tactical team will meet us," she said after ending the call. "It's about twenty minutes by foot from here."

"Twenty minutes? Does this idiot understand we have the Sumiyoshi chasing us with assault rifles?"

"It's the best I can do. We need to get there."

Tamura's phone rang again.

"He better not be calling to cancel!" Gray shouted.

"It's Tanaka!" Tamura shouted. "Where are you? That's not far from us. We'll meet you there. One other thing, we have a gang of armed Sumiyoshi chasing us."

Tamura led the way to a small square where they met up with Tanaka, who was very much alive and still had six of his men with him.

"I can't tell you how excited I am to see you again," Gray said, slightly out of breath.

"This is the man you were looking for?" Tanaka asked as he eyed Murphy.

"He is," Gray said.

"We need to get to an extraction point where TMPD will have a team waiting for us," Tamura said. "Can you help us get there? They aren't there for you and can provide an escort out of Tokyo if you need it."

One of Tanaka's men pointed. Off in the distance, a pack of men could be seen running straight toward them.

"This way!" Tamura shouted and started running down the road. They didn't get far before bullets started flying past them from another direction.

"We're being flanked," Gray said.

"Go there," Tanaka said as he returned fire.

"But our extraction point is this way," Tamura said.

"You need to find another location," Tanaka said as more bullets streaked past the group.

"Hey, it's me. Stop shooting!" Murphy shouted. Bullets kicked up pieces of asphalt near him just as Gray pulled him out of the way.

"Keep standing around, and you'll end up dead."

Tamura started making calls as they ran.

"You see, what I said earlier is true. You're nothing to the Sumiyoshi," Gray said.

"They were shooting at you."

"You are dumber than I thought if you believe that crap. Now keep moving!"

"Who are these guys?" Murphy asked as he pointed at Tanaka.

"Yamaguchi."

"For crying out loud. No wonder the Sumiyoshi are shooting at us. I can't believe you're in bed with the Yamaguchi!"

"So you know them."

"I know all the syndicates here. Why are the Yamaguchi helping you?"

"They can't stand the Sumiyoshi, for starters. Second, the Sumiyoshi's firepower gives them an advantage. I always wondered why you didn't just sell the weapons to all of the syndicates in Japan. There's plenty of demand,

and it's a lot of money to leave on the table. But then I realized the Yakuza weren't your customers."

"Is that what you're feelin'?"

"It is. Japan isn't and never was the final destination for your weapons. Southeast Asia is the target."

"You've got a deadly imagination, my friend."

"Deny it all you want, but we're on to how your operation works."

"Then what do you need me for?"

Gray noticed Tamura putting her phone away.

"Do we have a new extraction point?" he asked.

"We do, but it's about the same distance. They have a tactical team in that area already." Tamura hurried to catch up with Tanaka.

More bullets slammed into the building near them as the group of Sumiyoshi closed in. Gray ducked and pushed Murphy to keep moving.

"If you don't pick up the pace, you'll end up like roadkill," he told Murphy.

"Easy for you to say. Uncuff me, and I'll run faster."

"Mariko, give me the keys to the cuffs."

A few seconds later Gray removed the cuffs. "Run, and I'll not only beat you but also cuff you so tight you'll cry with every step you take."

One of Tanaka's men went tumbling down to the sidewalk. He'd been shot in the leg. Gray grabbed the guy by the arm and helped him back up to his feet, only to see another bullet strike the man in the head. Gray dropped the dead man and continued to push Murphy forward.

Tanaka stopped and pitched a grenade at the group of Sumiyoshi. The grenade went off, taking a few men down and scattering the rest.

"Keep moving!" Tanaka said as he continued to fire.

Tamura ducked behind a vending machine and returned fire to help fend them off.

"Don't stop!" Tanaka shouted at her. "I'll cover you."

Tamura turned and started running as bullets struck the row of vending machines she'd used for cover.

Gray ran behind Murphy, continually pushing him forward. As luck would have it, Gray's foot caught the curb, and he went down, tumbling across the sidewalk. A sharp pain shot up from his ankle, but Gray bit the bullet and forced himself to his feet.

"Sterling!" Tamura yelled. "He's getting away."

Gray looked up just in time to see Murphy running across the street and disappearing into an alleyway.

That son of a bitch. Gray sucked up the pain and gave chase, but bullets ricocheting off the road forced him back into the doorway of a building.

"I'll cover you!" Tamura said. "Go!"

She started shooting, and Gray took off after Murphy.

65

Murphy was exiting at the other end when Gray made it into the alleyway. Gray picked up the pace and soon popped out onto the next street. Murphy had already crossed over to the other side of the road. Gray was quicker though. With every step he took, he closed the distance to Murphy.

Fifteen feet.

Ten feet.

Five feet.

Gray slammed Murphy's back with his shoulder, sending the man flying forward. Murphy hit the sidewalk hard and tumbled to a stop face-down. Gray dropped his knee into Murphy's back, pinning him down.

"You're killing me!" Murphy cried out in pain. "I can't breathe."

Gray removed his knee and flipped Murphy over. His face had taken the brunt of the impact. It was covered with scrapes, and he bled from his mouth and nose.

"Get up!" Gray said as he yanked on Murphy's arm. "You sure got a death wish, don't you?"

"Look at my choices. Get shot dead by the Sumiyoshi or locked up in a Japanese prison."

"You're still alive in prison."

Gray forced Murphy to walk up against the building to keep them out of view. He didn't think backtracking was the best way to go, not with the Sumiyoshi so close to them. He could still hear gunfire in the distance. Gray took his phone out to call Tamura.

"Dammit!"

"What's got your knickers in a twist?" Murphy asked.

"My phone's dead. Let me use your phone."

"It's back at the hotel. What about the extraction point? Didn't your partner mention something about that?"

"She did, but I don't know where it is. Iwata's men started shooting at us right then."

Gray and Murphy kept walking forward. Every couple of steps, Gray looked back over his shoulder.

"Give it a rest," Murphy said. "They're gone. It's just us, mate. Two foreigners caught up in a mess. What brought you all the way out here anyway? Doesn't your country have problems of its own?"

"I'm working for Interpol temporarily, so I help out on investigations worldwide."

"You're joking."

"It's true."

"So you got sent here to help with an investigation. How's that going?"

"Stop acting like you don't know what's happening here."

"So you're looking to be the big star that cracked the case?"

"All I want is to turn you over to the TMPD and hop on the next plane out of here."

Gray led Murphy into another alleyway and stopped about halfway inside.

"What are we doing?"

"I'm thinking."

"So what's the story?" Murphy said after a few moments of silence. "What gave me up?"

"All of this?" Gray motioned around him. "The fighting, the shoot-outs, us being chased . . . it all started with Iwata."

"What do you mean?"

"We ended up drinking together one night, totally coincidental, and he took a liking to me. The next thing I knew, we were talking about guns. One conversation led to another, and eventually, he took me to a warehouse full of weapons."

"That bleedin' idiot. So you're the one that tipped off the TMPD about the warehouse. No wonder he wants you dead. But how did you get to me? I want to know that."

"One thought led to another thought, and I figured it out . . . why Iwata would keep so much inventory in an unsecured place if they weren't selling it. The weapons were moving through the country to another destination," Gray said. "That's when I realized his partner in the operation would be the real brains, not Iwata. I saw you, but I didn't know at the time that you were connected. It was in the bar with the mural of the samurai."

"Iwata had that painted for me to celebrate our partnership. I've always loved the samurai."

"If it wasn't for that mural, I doubt we ever would have found you. Personally, I think Iwata would have whacked you anyway. With all the problems that grew out of that raid, Iwata needed to be sure he couldn't be tied to it."

"Kill you, and you can't talk. But me, I won't talk," Murphy said.

"It's the same," Gray said. "You're still a liability because you're a gaijin like me, and you were allowed a lot of access to the Sumiyoshi. The leadership thinks Iwata is running the entire show."

"That's a laugh. You know, Iwata isn't as smart as you think he is. He just saw an opportunity. He's a dope when it comes to the details and logistics."

"So, are you giving up?"

Murphy shrugged. "Can't see how I can continue anyway. It's banjaxed. Know what that means . . . beyond repair, mate."

"If I hadn't caught you, would you have shut down your operation?"

"I was already making plans to shut it down. But I had to keep Iwata thinking I was still committed. The war between the Sumiyoshi and the police was getting out of hand, and he was freaking out. I figured the bastard would turn a gun on me. But I'm also not looking to go to prison. The Sumiyoshi can get to me in there. If they lock me up, I'd be dead within a month. Cut me a deal, and I'll tell you how I moved the weapons. I know you haven't sorted that out."

"It's not up to me. You'll need to plead your case to my partner, but I'm sure something can be worked out. Come on, we need to double back just a little bit. I don't hear gunshots."

Gray grabbed Murphy by the arm and led him back out of the alleyway and straight into Iwata and Mizuno.

66

Tamura tried to run after Gray, but gunfire had her pinned down. As soon as Tanaka and his men could fend off Iwata's men, she hurried into the alley after Gray. She ran through it and popped out on the other side, but Gray and Murphy were nowhere to be seen.

Tanaka came up behind her. "Where are they?"

"I don't know, but we need to find them."

"They should be heading to the extraction point."

"I never had a chance to tell Gray where it was."

Tamura pulled out her phone and tried calling Gray, but there was no answer. She sent a text message for him to call her.

"We were heading east, so, hopefully, he would continue doing that. Let's head up this road."

"We don't know if he still has the red hair man," Tanaka said.

"I know, but we have to find him. I can't leave him out here."

"We're deep in Sumiyoshi territory. I can't guarantee his or your safety anymore."

"I understand."

"We need to spread out."

Tanaka sent some of his men to the next road over so that they could cover more ground.

Iwata had his handgun aimed at Gray and Murphy as he eyed the rifle in Gray's hand.

"Drop it, or I'll shoot you dead right now."

Gray bent down slowly and placed the rifle on the sidewalk.

"Kick it over here."

Gray did as he was told, and Mizuno picked up the rifle.

A smug look appeared on Iwata's face. "I must be lucky today," he said. "Running right into you, Jimmy. Or should I call you Special Agent Gray? Which name do you prefer?"

Gray didn't bother to answer him. Instead, he looked beyond the two men. Iwata's men were nowhere to be seen.

"What are we going to do with you two?" Iwata said as he sauntered around them. "So much trouble has been caused by your actions, Agent Gray. And you, Manus, I expected more loyalty from you."

"Loyalty? I don't work for you. Remember, this is my operation."

Iwata looked at the dried blood covering Murphy's face. "Yeah, it looks like you've got things under control."

Iwata and Mizuno both laughed.

"He still thinks he's in control," Mizuno said. "Did Agent Gray do that to your face?"

"I fell."

"You fell?" Mizuno burst out into more laughter.

"Yeah, and when you tell your bosses they no longer have access to the weapons, what then, huh? Kill me, and that's what will happen."

Mizuno grabbed Murphy by his arm and yanked him away from Gray.

"Do you really think you can revive his operation after all that's happened?" Gray asked. "The TMPD knows everything. Word will get out that Sora Iwata was the one who showed an FBI agent the Sumiyoshi's stash of illegal weapons, the catalyst to all of what's happening now. You're screwed either way."

"Not if you're dead." Iwata raised his gun and aimed it at Gray's face. "What's the saying . . . dead men tell no tales. Anything you want to cry about before I end you?" Iwata said.

"Watch your backs."

Bam!

The gun dropped from Iwata's hand, and he cradled it against his stomach as he cried out in pain. Mizuno turned around just as Tanaka slammed right into him, sending him flying through the air and crashing down onto the sidewalk.

A second later, gunfire erupted.

67

Tanaka's men appeared from the other end of the street, running toward them while firing. The rest of Iwata's men closed in from the opposite end, firing back. Everyone ducked for cover.

Gray jumped on top of Murphy and punched him until he stopped trying to crawl away.

"Sterling!" Tamura shouted as she crawled on her belly to him. "Are you okay?"

"I'm okay now. You guys got here in the nick of time." He grabbed the rifle lying next to an unconscious Mizuno. Iwata had already disappeared.

"We need to keep moving," Tamura said. "The extraction point isn't far from here. Tanaka, let's go."

Tanaka nodded and scrambled to his feet.

Gray yanked Murphy to his feet, and they followed Tamura with Tanaka and his men following, providing cover.

Bullets whizzed by them. Two of Tanaka's men were hit, sending them to the sidewalk. A shot caught Gray in his arm.

"You okay?" Tamura asked.

"Yeah, it's just a graze," Gray said as he grabbed his left bicep.

No sooner had Gray said that than Murphy took a tumble.

"I've been shot in my leg," he cried out.

Gray pulled Murphy back up, causing the man to yell even louder.

"Can you move?"

"I've been shot."

"And you'll be dead if you don't keep moving."

Murphy limped alongside Gray, unable to move faster.

Iwata's men were still shooting and closing the distance. Tanaka stopped and opened fire.

"Go!" he shouted.

It was Tanaka and a few other men against ten or more Sumiyoshi. Gray and Tamura both knew it was a suicide mission.

"Go, now!" Tanaka yelled once more. "I'll catch up."

Tamura and Gray helped Murphy to move.

"How much farther?" Gray asked.

"It's up ahead." Tamura was looking at a map on her phone. "The next right."

When they reached the location, Tamura paused briefly as she looked down the lane.

"What's wrong?" Gray asked.

"This doesn't feel right. Look, it's a dead end."

The lane didn't have an opening at the other end. It was just the back-side of another building with a closed door.

"Maybe we're supposed to go into that door," Gray said. "Check once more."

Tamura double-checked again. "This is the right location."

They headed inside and made their way to the door. Tamura tried to open it, but it was locked.

"Call your boss," Gray said. "We're running out of time."

"Gray!" A man shouted.

Gray spun around and saw Iwata standing at the front of the alleyway. He was limping and still had his right hand cradled against his stomach. Mizuno was missing, but he had three other men with him.

"Nowhere to run now," he said as they entered the alley.

Gray was still holding his rifle against the side of his thigh. Iwata couldn't see it from where he stood.

He spoke quietly out of the side of his mouth. "Mariko, as soon as I start shooting, I want you to pull Murphy down behind that trash receptacle."

"Are you crazy? They're all armed."

"There are only three of them. I would rather go down shooting than just stand here like a deer in headlights."

Iwata stopped at the halfway point. "You have caused enough trouble." He held an assault rifle in his left hand, but it was clear from how he held the gun that he didn't have much control over it.

Gray tightened his grip on the handle of his gun.

You're mine, Iwata.

Suddenly the alley was awash with bright lights from spotlights above. Gray looked up and saw a team of officers from the TMPD leaning over the rooftop's parapet. They opened fire on Iwata and his men, cutting them down in seconds.

Iwata's gun went off as a hail of bullets struck him. Gray jumped on top of Tamura and Murphy, forcing them to the ground as they narrowly missed being hit. Bullets chipped away at the building above their heads, raining bits of concrete down on them.

Gray kept everyone pinned against the pavement. When the shooting stopped, he looked over at Iwata and saw him lying in a crumpled mess beside his men.

"Everyone okay?" Gray asked as he looked over at Tamura and Murphy.

"I'm fine," Tamura said as she rolled away and stood.

Murphy only had the one gunshot wound to his leg, and Gray helped him to his feet.

"Were they using us as bait?" Gray asked while looking up.

"Would you be surprised if I said yes?"

"Nope."

68

Gray and Murphy were taken straight to the hospital for treatment. Gray's wound wasn't that bad and only required a few stitches. It would take a week or so to heal. While not life-threatening, Murphy would need an operation to remove his bullet.

Tamura remained at the scene and went in search of Tanaka. She found his body not far from the alley where they had been cornered. He and the rest of his men had been gunned down. They did, however, take down a good number of Sumiyoshi.

On the way back to the crime scene, she ran into her supervisor, Izumi. He was surrounded by a security detail of at least ten men. His movements were jerky, sweat had bubbled on his forehead, and he flinched at just about any noise. For someone who was surrounded by a team of armed men, he still acted like a scared little boy.

"Inspector Tamura, where's our trafficker?" he asked as he looked around.

"He's at the hospital with Gray."

"Was he shot? How bad is it?"

"A bullet grazed Gray's arm. He'll be fine."

"Not him, the suspect."

"The suspect is Manus Murphy. He was shot in the leg, but he'll survive."

"Are you sure this is the person responsible for the weapons?"

Ah, you're wondering if it's okay to relax and start taking credit.

"We've already learned a lot about him and his trafficking operation. I expect to learn more when I interview him. Those three bodies over there are members of the Sumiyoshi who were working with our suspect. As we believed, they did nothing more than provide safe passage for the weapons while in Japan."

Izumi nodded. "I look forward to seeing the full report. You and Agent Gray did an excellent job. But I had a feeling you would."

Yeah, right. Now that everything worked out, you'll be our biggest cheerleader.

Over the next couple of days, Tamura interviewed Murphy extensively. Gray sat in the viewing room and fed her questions as they came to mind. Murphy had agreed to cooperate. In exchange, Murphy was put into the government's witness protection program. He would still do time in an undisclosed location, but not a Japanese prison.

During Tamura's questioning, they learned that Murphy was the Russians' sole distributor for their weapons into Southeast Asia. Murphy and the Russians worked out a route that involved hiding the guns in shipments of slag, a stony waste matter produced from metal smelting, commonly used in cement production. Russia was the ninth largest exporter of slag in the world, and Japan imported 33.7 billion tons of slag, ore, and ash every year. The weapons were simply hidden in those shipments. It would be nearly impossible for authorities to catch that unless they knew to look for it.

Once the weapons entered Japan, Iwata and his men were responsible for the storage and transportation. Since Japan's largest export is motor vehicle parts, the weapons were hidden inside those shipments. The total time the weapons were in Japan was no more than a week before they were out and on their way to Southeast Asia.

In return, the Sumiyoshi got weapons below cost and took a percentage of the arms sales. This made it a no-brainer for the Sumiyoshi leadership to follow the plan. The only caveat was that Iwata had to take full responsibility and credit for devising the operations. The Sumiyoshi would never agree to Iwata partnering with an outsider to this degree. Murphy liked the deal because it removed him and his partner from any direct ties to the Yakuza. They acted like silent partners.

"If you hadn't caught me, I would have walked away freely," he'd told Tamura. "Iwata would have been left holding the bag."

Unfortunately for Murphy, he underestimated Iwata. The speedy success of the operation had turned Iwata into a rock star within the organization. He was deemed an out-of-the-box thinker by the leadership, especially his uncle. But along with that success came a swollen ego. That marked the beginning of the end of Murphy's near-flawless operation.

The war between the government and the Sumiyoshi wound down quickly once the TMPD touted that they'd caught the real person responsible for trafficking weapons into the country: a foreigner who had managed to hire the Sumiyoshi.

This revelation alone knocked the Sumiyoshi off their high horse. In the eyes of the other syndicates, they were laughed at because of how they'd been used. Even the public had turned on them. They weren't the brilliant and successful gangsters that the media had painted them to be. There was no end to the humiliation Iwata had brought upon the organization. And because he was dead, only one person could start repairing that damage: Iwata's uncle. But Matsumura killing himself was a small price to pay for the damage done.

For her efforts in the investigation, Tamura was given an award internally in a private ceremony. In public, Izumi continued to field interview after interview, allowing him to take credit for his department's success. Not once were Gray's efforts ever acknowledged in any of the press releases or interviews.

Gray had stuck around for an extra week to participate in Tamura's interviews with Murphy. He'd become captivated by Murphy's ability to plan a massive operation and manage all the moving parts involved. Testing revealed Murphy had an IQ of 185. He was like a savant when it came to smuggling.

During that time, Tamura allowed Gray to pick Murphy's brain to learn more about his personality and how the man's mind worked. During those conversations, Gray didn't see Murphy as a criminal, but as a fascinating subject.

"I'll admit, I shouldn't have caught you," Gray had told Murphy in one of their meetings. "Iwata was the weak link that made it happen."

"You think I'd be a free man if it weren't for him?"

"I do."

"I also wouldn't have gotten this operation off the ground if it weren't for him," Murphy had said.

"Iwata was his own worst enemy, the foil to his success. You were unfortunate enough to have gotten mixed up in that."

Gray would learn two months later that the Russians had figured out a way to get to Murphy while he was in witness protection. Even though Murphy had kept his mouth shut about their involvement, they still viewed him as a loose end that needed to be tied up.

When it was time for Gray to leave Japan, Tamura insisted on accompanying him to Narita International Airport. They'd even made a quick stop at her parents' home, so Gray could say goodbye to them. He promised her father he would continue to perfect his noodle-making skills.

Gray and Tamura were sitting at his gate, waiting for boarding to start.

"Hey, I meant to ask. Do you think there will be any blowback from the Yamaguchi because of what happened with Tanaka?" Gray asked.

"From what I hear, they're not happy, but they also know we did what we set out to do."

"I just want to go on the record and say that you're getting the short end of the stick here. You deserve so much more from this investigation, especially from Izumi."

"Thanks. I appreciate it, but it was a team effort. I couldn't have done it without you. Did you ever hear back from Kita?"

"I did. He thanked me and said he would write a positive report."

"That's all he said?"

"I wasn't really paying much attention. I was distracted. Kita's about two skin tones darker now."

An announcement came over the speakers instructing passengers to begin boarding the aircraft.

"Well, this is it." Gray gave Tamura a hug. "Good luck with everything here. Also, look me up if you ever find yourself in London."

"I will. Take care of that arm."

Gray boarded the plane and got settled into his seat. As with every assignment, he found himself contemplating how much of what had happened he should reveal in his report. He wasn't worried about Kita's report. That guy was clueless as to what had happened.

You know what, Sterling, just keep it on a need-to-know basis. It's worked well so far.

There was no covering up the war between the Japanese government and the Yakuza. It had made headlines back in the UK. From the moment Gray met up with Gaston and Pratt in the pub, Gaston had been bombarding him with questions about it.

"Mate, how do you run an investigation when everyone is shooting up the place, and you can't carry a weapon?" Gaston asked.

"Carefully," Gray said.

"Chi, you do understand that Sterling isn't out running and gunning around?" Pratt said before taking a sip from her pint. "He's a profiler working behind the scenes."

"He did more than that when he worked with me on that serial killer investigation. Ain't that right?" Gaston said.

"I do what's necessary in the field and from behind a desk."

Gray had decided not to mention being shot in the arm to Gaston and Pratt. It would only lead to more questions from them. And ultimately, it would put Pratt in an awkward situation at Interpol.

On the other hand, Gray had also considered it could be the final straw that got him sent back to the states for good. But as he looked across the table at his two friends, he questioned his real reason for wanting to return to America. What was he really returning to? Sure he had family there, but it's not like he had a wife and kids waiting on him. He could barely manage a girlfriend. His supervisor, Phillip Cooper, would only be able to ride him harder if they were in the same building. As it stood now, Cooper was hands-off. Did he really need to go back as soon as possible? He'd need to carve out time to visit his sister and his niece and nephew, but as far as moving around and trying to resume his old life, Gray wasn't so sure he had a resounding yes for that just yet. Life in London wasn't terrible. And to be honest, it felt better than back home.

"So listen," Gray said. "This Saturday, I'm inviting you guys over for dinner. While in Japan, I learned how to make ramen noodles by hand."

"That sounds lovely," Pratt said.

"Shall I bring some of my homemade cheese?" Gaston winked.

"Why not. Who doesn't love a smorgasbord?"

"Sounds delicious to me," Pratt said. "I'll bring sake."

"Great. It's settled." Gray lifted his glass. "Cheers, mates."

MURDER BOARD
A BOSTON CRIME THRILLER NOVEL

On the tough streets of Boston, justice requires a detective who isn't afraid to break the rules.

The crime sent shockwaves through the entire city.

But for Boston homicide detective Michael Kelly, the case hits particularly close to home.

Kelly was born and raised only a few blocks from where the girl's body was found. He still has friends living in the old neighborhood.

Some are cops.

Others run the Irish mob.

And when Kelly's investigation uncovers a shocking conspiracy, he realizes that he'll need to use all of his unique connections to solve the case.

Because Kelly is determined to bring the killer to justice.
Whatever the cost...

ABOUT THE AUTHORS

Brian Shea has spent most of his adult life in service to his country and local community. He honorably served as an officer in the U.S. Navy. In his civilian life, he reached the rank of Detective and accrued over eleven years of law enforcement experience between Texas and Connecticut. Somewhere in the mix he spent five years as a fifth-grade school teacher. Brian's myriad of life experience is woven into the tapestry of each character's design. He resides in New England and is blessed with an amazing wife and three beautiful daughters.

Ty Hutchinson is a USA Today best seller. Since 2013, Ty has been traveling nonstop worldwide, all while banging away on his laptop and cranking out international crime and action thrillers. Immersing himself in different cultures, especially the food, is a passion that often finds its way into his stories.

Sign up for the reader list at
severnriverbooks.com/series/sterling-gray-fbi-profiler

Printed in the United States
by Baker & Taylor Publisher Services